WITH ALL MY HEART

EMILIA FINN

beelieve

PUBLISHING, Pty Ltd.

With All My Heart

By: Emilia Finn

Copyright 2019. Emilia Finn

Publisher: Beelieve Publishing, Pty Ltd.

Editing: Brandi Bumstead

Cover design: The Hatters

www.emiliafinn.com

The best way to stay in touch is to subscribe to Emilia's newsletter: emiliafinn.com/signup

If you don't hear from her regularly, please check your junk/spam folder and set her emails to safe/not spam, that way, you won't miss new books, chances to win amazing prizes, or possible appearances in your area.

Kindle readers: follow Emilia on **Amazon** to be notified of new releases as they become available.

Bookbub readers: follow Emilia on **Bookbub** to be notified of new releases as they become available.

For Bry

ALSO BY EMILIA FINN

Winner Takes All

Checkmate

Stacked Deck - Rollin On Next Gen

Wildcard

Reshuffle

Game of Hearts

Full House

No Limits

Bluff

Seven Card Stud

Crazy Eights

Eleusis

Dynamite

Busted

Gilded Knights (Rosa Brothers)

Redeeming The Rose

Chasing Fire

Animal Instincts

Inamorata

The Fiera Princess

The Fiera Ruins

The Fiera Reign

Rollin On Novellas

(Do not read before finishing the Rollin On Series)

Begin Again – A Short Story

Written in the Stars – A Short Story

LOOKING TO CONNECT?

Website
Facebook
Newsletter
Email
The Crew

BEGIN AGAIN

THEN

"Hey, Bert." He leans in obnoxiously close until his engine grease and cheap coffee musk intoxicate me. With chocolate eyes and dark stubble that looks too old on his nineteen-year-old face, he rubs a square jaw along mine the way a spoiled house cat would rub his face on his owner. With muscles that are too grown when you compare them to all the other guys his age, thick hands that promise they know what they're doing, and fingers that make a girl who's definitely *not* crushing on this arrogant jerk tingle, I work to hold in my sigh.

He could take me back to his cave now, I wouldn't even mind.

I'm such a whore.

"You need to get off me, Kincaid."

"Nah." His deep voice is lazy. A drawl that promises of a sticky time between warm sheets and tangled legs. "Don't wanna." He flashes a savage grin. "I like being on you, Bert. But now we've gotta try it without clothes. It's more fun that way."

He pins me most days after school. He gives me no choice but to endure his unwanted – *but absolutely wanted* – advances. We both know this can't happen. We both know I'm unavailable to him and his jaw rubbing, finger tingling, leg humping shenanigans, and yet, his hand slides over my cotton shirt to an exposed navel. When his calloused fingers touch on bare skin, his pearly white teeth glint in the afternoon sun.

It's like he's the big bad wolf.

I'm his slutty Red.

I shouldn't want him. I should knee him in the balls and call my boyfriend to come beat his ass. I *should* be a little more offended that he thinks he can pin me between hard chest and hard car.

But that's not going to happen, because my boyfriend's my boyfriend only because my daddy said he had to be. But *this* arrogant man, this six and a half feet of too much muscle and a wicked smirk, this is the man I think about when Shane's smooth fingers stroke my belly. When Shane's hazel eyes look into mine. When Shane tries to talk me into bed.

I can't give it up to my boyfriend when I'm thinking about someone else.

That would *definitely* make me a slut.

I'm just half a slut. A pretend slut. A slut who thinks of one man while she's hanging out with another.

Bryan Kincaid is my sugar, but I'm a girl on a super strict diet.

Shane is lettuce.

Bryan Kincaid is a bakery full of cinnamon rolls with icing drizzled on top, and even if I wanted to go to that bakery, roll around in the sugar, lick the cinnamon dust from the windows, taste the icing...

No! That would be bad for me.

Super bad. Super, *super* bad.

Imagining a possible 'eat all the things and get super fat' future, also known as 'give into Bryan Kincaid and possibly have my world altered in a super scary way,' I step out from between him and his black Mustang and watch his face fall when his hand slides from my skin.

"Not today, Kincaid. You won't convince me to get fat today."

"Fat?" His chocolate eyes dance playfully, but switching moods in the single beat of my heart, he snaps fast hands out and snags my narrow hips. Yanking me against his hard body, a body hardened by martial arts training and too many hours spent screwing around with his best friend at Piper's Lane, the breath bursts from my lungs as our bodies collide. "Not fat, Bert. Perfect." His stubbled jaw goes to work on my neck.

This is wrong. So wrong I should give myself an uppercut. But like the universe likes to play tricks on me, it *feels* right.

"Your body's exactly right." He strokes a rough hand over my left hip. "Can't wait to take you for a ride." I *should* be offended. "Just let me know when you realize fuckface isn't man enough for you."

"Chantelle?"

Like Bryan Kincaid is suddenly made of electrical wire, I jump so fast the top of my head slams against his jaw until his teeth snap shut. Bryan lets out a grunt of pain, but when I spin and find Shane – my *boyfriend* – watching us curiously, Bryan's pain is forgotten as his hands pull me back against his chest and his hardened length rests again my backside.

Oh my gawd! His dick is hard. For me.

And Shane just tilts his head like a curious puppy.

"You have my number, Bert." Bryan's stubble tickles my ear. "I know you dial it late at night. I know you hang up before I answer."

The blood drains from my face.

"And I know you got my number, because I made sure you got it." He chuckles. "I *know* it's you, because I can *feel* you just on the other end. Aren't you curious about why we can feel each other, Bert? That's not normal. It's special." His fingers play with the soft flesh of my lower belly. "Are you in bed when you call? In a silky nightie, with silky smooth legs, and little panties you bought while thinking of me."

Yes.

I clear my throat and attempt to step forward, but his strong hands keep me close.

"Let me go, Kincaid."

"You know you wanna come for a ride with me. You know it. I know it. Fuck," he licks my ear, "even Shane Turdsky knows it. You see him there watching us? I have my cock inching into your ass, my hands on you, my lips on you, and that pussy just watches."

His strong hand squeezes my hip and almost has me convulsing.

"If you were my girl, any other guy looks at you for too long, he's a dead man. You better prepare yourself, babe, because once you're mine, you're *mine*." He bites my earlobe and sends sparks of electricity shooting straight down to my nunnery. "Turn around, get in my car. Let me show you how it's really done."

"No." My word is a whisper, a breathy whisper that's half yes and half *please make me!*

Shane's too-innocent eyes watch us curiously. Like everything I'm doing right now – Bryan holding me, and me *absolutely* leaning into it – is okay.

It's not okay!

I'm a whore.

I'm not sleeping with either of them, but I'm still a whore.

"Call my number tonight. I'll come to you."

Yes. "No."

"You'd rather I spent the night with a different girl, then?"

No! "Yes."

One more squeeze of my hips. One last punctuating grind of his groin into my ass. One more lave of my neck from base to ear that melts me into a whimpering mess of teenage hormones. "Okay." He pushes me forward until I stumble into Shane's chest. "Catch you 'round, Bert. Sleep well. I know you'll dream of me."

CHAPTER 1

BRYAN

I pull up to the dirt circuit five miles outside town, and smile at Geo's irritated glare. As soon as I cut the engine, Richard Marx's *'I'm gonna fuck all the girls'* voice cuts out and the roar of revving V8 engines replace it.

It's loud. It's dirty.

Its adrenaline fueled, and gets me almost as hot as Chantelle Robertson.

"You leave that girl alone!" As soon as I climb out of the car, he's on me. "I mean it, Bry. She said no!"

"Cool it, Geo." I slam the door on a laugh and meet him at the hood of the Mustang. "I know. No means no. Maybe means no. Yes means yes." I grin arrogantly. "I'll get the yes, then I'll show her the time of her life."

"Or!" He taps out a cigarette from the roughed-up packet in his breast pocket. "You could just leave her alone. She's too sweet for your cynical ass. Let her be happy with that wet noodle."

I snort. "Wet noodle. Limp dick. He's a fucking pussy, Geo. I was just eating her ear and he watched. He *watched!*"

Buzzcut on the back and sides, slightly longer on the top, Geo

Blair smiles his snake-eyes-dimpled smile and shakes his head. "What the fuck is the matter with him? It's like he's scared to touch a girl, like he's too scared to admit he's a poof, so he *wants* you to snatch her away. What kinda pussy just watches?"

"Not me." I accept a cigarette and snatch the matches when he's done. One cigarette. One time... per day. Smoking kills! "Once I get the yes, she'll have to adjust to the fact that, unlike Shane, I won't just stand by and watch another man piss on her leg."

Geo shakes his head as he leans back on the car I intend to race – in exactly twenty-seven minutes – with a grunt, and takes the weight off his recently healed broken leg.

I tap my scarred work boot to his. "You good?"

He nods thoughtfully and blows plumes of smoke into the darkening sky. "It's good. I'll be racing again soon. You ready?"

I look up as Kirby revs his rusty-orange Thunderbird. "For him? Yeah. He's a bigger pussy than Turdsky."

Tossing his half-smoked cigarette to the dirt and stomping out the ball of flame, he pushes off my car. "Maybe think of that pretty girl at the finish line. That'll get you there faster."

"Don't call her pretty!" I slam my fist into his chest. "You shouldn't know. You shouldn't be looking!"

He barks out a laugh. "A pretty girl's a pretty girl, Bry. There's no denying it. She ain't yours yet, and even if she does say yes–"

"*When*, asshole. When she says yes, not if."

He scoffs. "*When* she says yes, you can't stop the rest of us from looking." He skips away on a weak leg. "A guy's gonna look, Kincaid. He just can't touch."

"You don't get to look! You're my best friend. Where's the fuckin' respect?"

"Those yuppies, man." He shakes his head like a moron. "They ruined everything the minute they started handing over twenties for a meal."

"Kincaid!" The guys wave me toward the line. "Get your car ready. It's almost time."

Four hours later, I lay awake in the back seat of my soft-top Mustang 5.0, and stare up at the stars. As Bryan Adams hums through my speakers and out into the quiet street, I tap my boot against the door frame.

Victorious from my race, with a couple of twenties in my pocket to refill the tank of gas I used and buy a hot meal on the side, I count stars and wonder which ball of light sits directly above Nelly's rundown ranch six blocks away.

I want to take her out of there. Put her up in a pretty house.

Fuck her until we're crippled.

Right on cue, the pay phone rings and snuffs my victory from a moment ago. Winning a race is easy. I do it three, sometimes four nights a week. A couple times on weekends. A few times in a single day at the big race meets.

Racing is easy.

Getting her to make those calls, though. That's a special kinda victory.

Every night, she rings. Every night, she makes sure I'm the last thing on her mind before she sleeps.

If she'd just say yes, I could be the first thing on her mind when she woke, too.

Each night, she lets it ring three times, chickens out, hangs up, and pretends she's not crying out for me.

I act like I'm in charge. I let her think I'm suave as shit, cocky to a fault, arrogance personified, but I *need* her to come to me. To make it right – to take what's fundamentally mine, but on the surface, belongs to someone else – then she needs to come to me.

The phone rings once. Twice. Three times.

My heart pounds with exhilaration when I think tonight might be my night; when I think it'll ring a fourth time and make all my dreams come true, but just like every night, the shrilling turns silent and the cicadas remind me I'm a loser.

She's not ready for me yet.

Maybe tomorrow.

CHAPTER 2

CHANTELLE

I walk through the front door after school and stop at the sight of my dad leaning on the kitchen counter. In his work overalls, one shoulder strap hanging loose, grease on his back pockets, and too-long oily brown hair hanging in his eyes, he flicks through the mail and hums dangerously.

Electricity; *too fucking expensive.*

Grocery receipts; *we eat too much.*

Phone... my heart trips as he scans the bill.

I gamble every single night when I hide under the covers and twirl the stretched-to-capacity phone cord around my finger. The day Bryan Kincaid answers his phone is the day his number will show up on our bill. That's the day my dad takes his leather belt to the backs of my legs and reminds me who's in charge.

"Afternoon, Daddy."

"Pumpkin." He takes me in a rough side hug and drops a kiss on the top of my head. He's hugging, which means the bill's fine for today. "How was school?"

"It was good. Got an A in math."

"That's my girl." He smiles and shows off a set of coffee stained teeth and bright green eyes. "I'm proud of you. You're the smartest person I know, sweetheart."

Not so smart.

I still come back to this rundown house every day, even knowing he'll beat me if I speak out of turn or burn his dinner.

Not so smart.

I want to jump into Bryan Kincaid's hotted up car and go for a lap around Piper's Lane.

I don't know which makes me stupider.

"You still seeing that boy?"

"Yes, Daddy."

He nods and distractedly folds the phone bill. "Good. He's a good boy from a good family. You're a smart girl, Pumpkin. Stay smart."

"Yes, Daddy."

He smacks my backside and sends me moving toward the fridge. "What's for dinner?"

"Ah, I was going to do steak and potatoes. Is that okay?"

He flashes a smile anyone who didn't know better would swear is pure adoration for his angelic little girl. Mostly, it's *conditional* love. For as long as I'm a 'good girl', for as long as I make him happy, he adores me. But when I don't, even if unintentional, I lay in bed with brand new welts and the fear that tonight might be the night he ends it all.

My life is spent on eggshells that balance on a razor blade. Each slip results in fresh welts on the backs of my legs from the metal buckle of his belt, and the barrel of a Kingston .22 teasing the delicate skin of my temple.

"Perfect. I'll be in the living room watching the game."

"Okay." I pull the already marinating steak from the fridge. "I'll let you know when it's ready. It'll be about an hour." Just as he steps from the kitchen and into the living room, I pluck up the heart-pounding courage to make my move. "Um, Daddy?"

He turns back, but his mind is already engrossed in football. "Yuh?"

"I was wondering; you like Shane and his family. And I got an A in math..."

Already out of patience, his eyes narrow. "Spit it out, Pumpkin."

"I was wondering if I could call Shane a little later. Just to say hello."

A low rumble works at the back of his throat. Disapproval sends shards of glass skittering through my blood. "That costs money, Chantelle. I'm not a money tree."

"No, I know, Daddy. But I thought maybe I could do some extra chores to make up for it. I just wanna say hello. Tell him goodnight, that sort of stuff."

His eyes turn to feral slits. "He's keeping his hands to himself, right? I want you to marry that boy, Pumpkin. He's our ticket outta here, but he's not gonna buy the whole cow if you're giving up the milk for free."

"He's a perfect gentleman, Daddy."

"You better still be a virgin, young lady."

I can't believe he can say that without squirming. "Yes, sir, I am. I'm a good girl. Saving myself for marriage, just like you want me to."

"Does he pressure you?"

"No." I don't sigh out loud like I want to. "He's a gentleman."

Narrowed eyes, poor Shane's death planning itself in his mind, he nods once. God help us all if he ever found out about Bryan Kincaid marking me on a daily basis. "One call. Five minutes. Don't make me regret this decision."

Excitement bursts in my chest like fireworks on New Year's Eve. Lights flash, bells jingle, my heart soars with excitement... *on the inside*. On the outside, I simply nod. "Thank you, Daddy."

"And to make up for it, I want you to weed the yard this weekend."

"Okay. I promise." I turn away when my smile threatens to break free. Flicking on the stove and prepping the pots, I get busy making dinner. "I'll call you out in an hour for dinner."

"Bring it to me. I wanna watch the game."

I'm calling Bryan tonight. I'm going to speak to him. Daddy will only ever see that I made *a* call. He doesn't have to know what number I called. "Yes, sir."

Five and a half hours later, an hour later than the time I normally call, I slide into bed in my nightie, with freshly shaven legs, hair still damp from the shower, and a sneaky smile, I dial the number I got from Tammi St James. She got it from Geo Blair. Geo Blair is the boy she'd go down on in a dirty bathroom if he simply smiled at her.

Which I'm pretty sure he has.

I burrow deep under my covers, despite the fact it's a sticky May night and way hotter than it should be.

The phone rings once.

My heart thrums with exhilaration.

The phone rings twice.

My palms sweat, but that might not be nerves as much as it's hot as hell under the covers.

The phone rings a third time.

Laying on my side, I curl into a ball and touch my knees to my chest.

I'm entering brand new territory here.

The phone rings a fourth time.

"Bert?"

Silence. I can't speak past the lump of nerves that lodge in my throat.

"Please, God, tell me that's you, Bert. The phone rang a fourth time. Don't break my fucking heart."

"I meant to call Shane." I clear my throat nervously. "Wrong number."

He chuckles softly. The worry in his voice is instantly replaced with arrogance. "I don't even care that you lie to cover up the fact you want me. I don't judge you, Bert. Your boyfriend's a pussy. It doesn't count."

My heart pounds in my throat. "Shane's not *just* my boyfriend. I'm gonna marry him someday."

"Nah." Rumbling, his voice comes out deep and vibrates through my ear. "You won't marry him. Whatcha doin' right now, Bert? What changed your mind?"

"Didn't change my mind."

"Oh, right." He laughs obnoxiously. "I forgot, *wrong number*. Okay, just stick with 'whatcha doin'?"

"Lying in bed."

His laughter cuts off in an instant. "In your silky nightie?"

Satin. "Yes."

"You got panties on? They got my name on them?"

My pulse, no longer in my throat, beats elsewhere. Much, much lower. "I can't answer that, Bryan. I have a boyfriend."

"Mm." A low growl plays in the back of his throat. "Say my name again."

"Bryan."

"Good, now say it softer."

"Bryan."

"Now say '*fuck me, Bryan.*'"

"No!" Forgetting where I am, I stop breathing and wait for my daddy to come beat down my bedroom door.

"Bert?"

"Shh." The darkness surrounds me. The cicadas chirp outside my window. The sports channel still murmurs through the house. I left

Daddy asleep on the couch with the first quarter of an old game on repeat. "I can't be loud."

"I'm sorry." He whispers, too. "You're hiding out from your old man?"

"Yeah. He's asleep on the couch."

"You eighteen yet?"

My brows pull together in confusion. "Next week. Why?"

"Wanna run away with me?"

At least I don't shout a second time. "No. I'll have a ring on my finger before my cake's cut next Monday. A wedding to plan soon after that." And no more cinnamon rolls for me. "What are you doing right now?"

He clears his throat the way I did when I was lying. "Lying in bed. Touching my dick and thinking of you."

I frown. "Why are you always so crass? How am I supposed to pretend talking to you is okay and innocent when you insist on being so rude?"

"Because I've waited a long time for you. I'm not like Shane. I won't stand by and watch you slip through my fingers. It does me no harm to make sure you know what I'm thinking. But if you didn't know..." He lets out a gusty sigh. "Not letting you slip away."

Despite the fact I'm laying down, my shoulders still manage to droop. "I can't be with you. I'm promised to someone else. To a better family."

"Better than mine?"

"Truthfully?" I pause to consider his family, though there isn't much to think about. It's almost like he's here all alone.

I don't know who his folks are. I don't know if he has brothers and sisters. I don't know anything about him, except his name is Bryan Kincaid, he moved here three years ago with whatever he had in his Mustang, he bumped into me on my first day of sophomore year, and since then, he's been nibbling on my ears, talking dirty, and fueling my wet dreams. Not once has he cared that I had a boyfriend. "Yes."

"If you became my family, you'd up my image. Make my family name worth something again."

I laugh softly. "You proposing marriage, Bryan? Because I get the feeling you're more of a 'fuck 'em and run' kinda guy. My daddy will kill me if I toss Shane over for you."

"You care about money over passion?"

"No, I mean my daddy would *literally* kill me. I'm choosing life over death. I'm choosing to keep my brains in my head, rather than splattered over my bedroom wall."

Displeasure rumbles through the phone. "Come to me next week. On your birthday. I'll take care of the rest."

He thinks I'm a fool. "You wanna seduce me when I'm legal, you think that'll keep you outta jail for screwing a minor?"

He scoffs. "No, I just don't want you to jump when your daddy still has the power to yank you back. I'm choosing life for you too, Bert. I'm choosing a long and happy life for you... with me."

Knowing my five minutes are long over, knowing I'm racking up the bill and will cop a flogging when the mail comes in this time next month, I listen out for Daddy's deep snoring, and when I hear him clearly from the couch, I turn further into the mattress with a smile. "Bryan?"

"Mm?"

"Why do you call me Bert?"

Like my change of tone took him by surprise, he makes noises of hesitation. "Oh, um. I figured it was obvious. Your last name is Robertson. Robert. Bert." It's like I can hear his shrug. "Bert. No one else calls you that. I like having a name for you that no one else uses."

I like that he gave me a name that no one else uses.

"If you marry me, we can use Robert for our firstborn son. You know, so you don't lose your history."

I snort. "Jesus. I swear, you give me whiplash. Marriage. Babies. Running away together. This is our first ever real talk."

"I know. And it only took three years. I have the patience of a fucking saint, woman."

"That's a cool idea," I mumble thoughtfully. "Naming my first son Robert. There's a lot of history in that one name. Shitty history, but history nonetheless."

"He wouldn't even need a middle name," he replies equally as serious. "Robert is heavy enough for a little baby."

CHAPTER 3

BRYAN

"Robert is heavy enough for a little baby."

"Did you win your race tonight?"

I stop halfway outside the phone booth with a cigarette in one hand and the phone in the other. "Um…" I cough to clear the smoke. Every time I walk by her immediately after a smoke, she frowns disapprovingly. She doesn't like it. She doesn't like the smell. So I don't smoke during the day until after I've pinned her in the parking lot. "You know I race?"

She scoffs adorably. "Of course I know. Everyone knows."

"Well, I hope not everyone." I toss the almost finished cigarette to the ground and crush it beneath my boot. "It's illegal. Cops'll impound my car if *everyone* knows about it."

She snickers. "Okay, obviously not everyone. But *I* know. Almost everyone at school knows."

"You should come down and watch. I'll win for you." I win for her every time. Every dollar I make goes into amassing that fortune her daddy wants her to marry. It just sucks for me that fortune grows by only a couple hundred bucks a week. It's slow going, but I'm on my third year now.

I'm a racer.

I'm a fighter.

My whole life works in three-minute increments. Everything's fast as shit, life or death, winner or loser. Life zooms out ahead of me in one-hundred and eighty second increments, three minutes, or quarter miles... *except* for my bank account.

That shit's like a three-hundred-year-old, one-legged fucking turtle.

She's slow. She's limp. But she's going.

"I can't come down and watch."

"Why the fuck not? You know you wanna."

"I have a boyfriend. I don't know if you got the memo yet, but that means I'm not available to watch you race. That means you aren't allowed to win for me. That means when he finds out I called you tonight, I'm gonna be in a lot of trouble."

"Are you scared of him?"

"Of Shane?"

"Of anyone? I'll take them out for you."

She snorts. "My daddy? Yup." Her answer comes across so casual, but truth rings in the single word. "I'm terrified of him. He'll beat me if he finds out we're talking."

Then he can sit at the top of my list. "What about Shane?"

"Scared of him? No. He's just a clueless idiot."

"You let that clueless idiot touch you?"

My cock thrums with anticipation as, just like I expected, her breath becomes short, her groan barely distinguishable.

That groan's not for him. I know it's not. "Sometimes."

Start at the top. Aim for the honey. "You let him kiss you?"

"Yes."

"With tongue?"

"Sometimes."

I run my tongue along my teeth. First order of business; get the taste of Shane-*I like dicks*-Turdsky out of her mouth. "Would you let me kiss you? With tongue."

Her breath shudders out. "I can't."

"You have a boyfriend. I know. Does he kiss your neck?"

"Mmhm."

"The same spot I kiss it?"

"You shouldn't do that anymore. It's inappropriate."

Second order of business; keep making out with her neck. He's trying to take possession. She's mine. "He touch your boobs? I watched you grow the last three years. A's in sophomore year. D's this year."

"You're a pervert."

"No. More like a guy who can appreciate perfection. Yours are... perfect." I chuckle arrogantly. "You're still perfect, but a couple cups larger. A handful each, if you will."

"Pig."

I make piggy snorts to make her laugh. "You didn't answer my question. Limp dick touch your boobs?"

"Yes."

"Above or below the bra?"

"This is inappropriate."

"Below." I work to keep my voice easy, but inside, my gut churns like pools of lava. It'll spill over and burn him soon. I'm saving it for him. "Would you let me touch your tits, Bert? Under the bra."

"Bryan..."

"Uh-huh. Just like that. When I take your titties in my mouth, get a taste, show you what a real man can do to your body, you'll say my name just like that."

"So inappropriate."

"Mmhm. I hope to get super inappropriate with your body. You sweaty right now? It's hot as Hades for May."

"The weather?"

I stifle a smug laugh. "Yeah, the weather. I'm not talking about your body right this second."

"Yes, it's hot. Yes, I'm sweaty. I'm hiding under my blankets."

I close my eyes and lay my head back on the glass wall of the phone booth. She's sweaty. In bed. In silk. Under the blankets. And she's choosing to talk to me. "Let me come to you. Let me show you what it could be like."

"You gonna go to another girl if I say no?"

No chance in hell. "Maybe, if someone's offering up what you aren't."

"Pig."

"I'm a man. You'll love that about me once you let me show you."

"Shit! I've gotta go."

My eyes snap open. "No, wait! Don't run off now. I'll stop talking about my dick, I promise."

"No, I've really gotta go. Daddy's awake. See ya, Bry."

"Nelly! Wait." But she doesn't. The line falls dead and my world suddenly snaps back to reality.

Like a rubber band stretching, stretching, stretching; for ten minutes, I was right there with her. I was in her bed, sweating under the sheets, sliding my legs between hers and sharing her oxygen.

But now I'm standing at the top end of Gordon Avenue in an orange and silver phone booth as fruit flies zoom around my head. I'm still sweating, but that's because even at ten at night, the temperature's still in the eighties.

I stand in the booth for a full minute in hopes she might call back.

I move out slowly and lean against my car for ten more. When she doesn't call back, I go for a walk.

Six blocks. A hundred and eighty second round trip on foot.

I stop across the street from her place and study the darkness. All the lights are out. No TV lights flickering between the curtains. No cries of pain or *help me.*

He woke up. She had to go.

But she wasn't caught.

Safe for tonight, with my hands dug deep in my pockets, I wander back to my car and drive back to Geo's apartment.

CHAPTER 4

NELLY

I skid out of last period math and practically sprint to the parking lot.

I don't want Shane to catch me. I want Bryan.

Ignoring my friends' calls, ignoring the teacher when she calls me back to discuss my *not-an*-A, ignoring Shane's eyes when I sprint past him to the parking lot; I run, and I exhilarate in the feel of my backpack slapping my butt as I move.

I don't have a car. I've never driven to school.

I drive my daddy's truck on the weekends to go grocery shopping.

I learned on my first lesson how to drive stick. I crunched the gears once.

Once.

The welts on the backs of my legs ensured I never did it twice. It also ensured no skirts that summer, and no swimming at the lake with my friends. Or Bryan.

I emerge from the concrete hall leading out of the main building. With a smile plastered over my face and wings of anticipation battering at my heart, I stop in the middle of the lot with a cry of frustration at the lack of a Mustang.

Bryan Kincaid graduated last year – and by *graduated*, I'm pretty sure he just dropped out at the eleventh hour – but despite the fact he's no longer a student here, he's stood in this parking lot watching me for three years. He wasn't always as bold as he is now. The ear licking is fairly new. The hands on my hips are new.

Just like the phone calls he's been answering the last three nights are new.

My daddy's gonna kill me next month. He's gonna kill me so bad.

But the phone bill is nothing when I spin a full three sixty in the parking lot and find no sign of Bryan Kincaid. The thought that I might see him, the promise that even if I continued to say no – *'because I have a boyfriend'*, thus leaving my conscience clear – he would still touch me; those were the imagined daydreams that got me through the day.

And now, nothing. He's not here.

Tears of disappointment burn my eyes, then a scream of excitement rips from my throat when hungry hands wrap around my waist and tug me from my feet. Like a rollercoaster, I close my eyes and enjoy the wind in my hair as he practically runs, carrying me like a football, through one hall, then another, out the other side of the school to the teacher's parking lot. An explosion of breath bursts from my lungs when he presses me against the brick façade and leans in to rub his sharp jaw along mine.

My chest heaves with excitement. "I thought you didn't come today."

He doesn't kiss me. His lips buzz an inch from my skin. He simply allows his nose to roam my sensitized flesh and illicit goosebumps right down to my toes. "And despite the fact you *'have a boyfriend'*, me ditching still upset you. You suck at lying, Bert."

He's a jerk. He won't let me off free. He won't let me claim innocence. "You're right. I do have a boyfriend, so get off me."

He chuckles, and in response to my feeble attempt to push him away, his knee comes up between my legs, his hips pin mine, and ever so gently, his thigh brushes where I can feel my pulse skittering deep inside. My eyes roll to the back of my head with pleasure and the anticipation of so much more. "You wanna be a naughty girl, don't you? You want me to *make* you bad."

My daddy wants a good girl.

Bryan Kincaid wants a bad girl.

Sliding his nose along the soft skin behind my ear, I can *feel* his smile crackle between us. "I bet you could be bad. I bet you'd go off like a firecracker."

"Umm." I lick my suddenly dry lips.

"You're a good girl for now though, aren't you?"

With a weak cough, I clear the nerves lodged in my throat. "Um."

"Virgin. I know you are." His hands squeeze my ribs. His thumbs stroke the sides of my almost double D's. "I'd bet my left nut you're still a virgin. You've been saving yourself for me."

"I've been saving myself for marriage."

"Uh-huh." He drags his stubbled jaw along my hypersensitive skin. "That's what I just said."

"You're so arrogant."

"Yup. I'm pretty fucking arrogant. I know that. I'm also funny. Sexy. Smart. I can do sixth grade math at a seventh-grade level. I can drive fast, and I never steer wrong. If you only ever get in the car with one person for the rest of your life, make it me. I'm the best driver you'll ever know. I'll keep you safe." His hand comes up to stroke my jaw. "I'd be gentle for you, Bert. Fuck knows, I'd probably eat the headboard in an attempt to go slow, but I'd be gentle. I'd never hurt you."

"Bryan..."

"Tell me what's in your brain right now. What are you thinking?"

"I'm thinking that it's really hard to think when your dick presses against my belly like that."

His plump lips pull up into a smug grin. "You're the only girl in the whole world that makes me hard like this."

My heart hammers between us. I so desperately want to believe him. I want to believe that's the truth, but it's not. He takes other girls home. Nineteen-year-old women, not seventeen-year-old virginal nuns like me.

"Come to the tracks tonight, Bert. Let me race for you."

"Would you let me drive your car?"

Stumped by my question, he pauses for half a beat and his breath moves heavy in my ear. "I mean, you could sit in the front seat."

I've found his kryptonite. "No. Let me race."

"Ha! Not a fucking chance."

"You don't trust me not to crunch your gears?"

"No, I trust you with anything you want. You can have everything you ever ask, but not this. I don't trust the other guys on those tracks. It's not safe. It's not NASCAR, Bert. They're not a pool of morally upstanding men. It's dirty, people get hurt."

I roll my eyes. "Well, that's one way to make sure I worry about you."

He chuckles and goes back to *not* making out with my neck. "You don't have to worry about me. For as long as you're earth side, I'll be here watching..." His fingers go back to roaming the sides of my boobs. "Teasing. Pleading." Finally, his lips press down on the soft spot behind my ear. "I'd sit, stay, beg, play dead. I'd perform any trick you asked just to hear you say yes."

"Yes?"

His teeth graze my earlobe. "Exactly like that."

"What do you want me to say yes to?"

"Everything," he answers instantly. "Yes, you'll come to the tracks." His eyes come back and pin mine. "Not to drive. Just to watch." Leaning back in, his stubble rubs along my jaw. "Yes, to coming to me whenever I call. Yes, to me keeping you forever. Yes, to you keeping me."

"Bryan..."

"I'll be anything you want in a man. Funny. Sexy. Smart. I'll blow your fucking mind in bed. I'll tell jokes and make you laugh every day. And if my jokes suck, I'll do something else to make you laugh. I'll proudly parade you around town. I'll take care of you. Make strong babies with you. Mine, all mine."

"Bryan, you need to stop."

"Don't wanna."

"Chantelle?"

Bryan groans in my ear. "Swear to Christ. Why does he say your name like that? I find a man on you like this, I wouldn't stand there like a fucking pussy and say your name."

"What would you do?"

His serious eyes come back to mine. "Before or after I slammed his skull against the bricks?"

Nerves and excitement skitter beneath my skin. "You're not like Shane, are you?"

"Not even a little bit. Not even fucking close." He leans in and nips at my jaw. "If you want *me* – broke, potty mouth, rough edges, but so much fucking passion your hair will catch fire – come to the tracks. Come find me tonight."

"Bryan..."

"Uh-huh. Keep saying my name like that. Practice. It turns me on."

"Chantelle!" Like Shane found a pocket of bravery he never knew he possessed, his hand shoots out and takes mine. Yanking me from between Bryan and the school wall, he slams me against his chest and commits what may be his stupidest act ever. "Get off her, trailer trash."

Fuck! His head's about to hit the bricks.

As Shane attempts to shove me behind his back, I attempt to step in front of a loaded gun, but true to his word, Bryan's hand shoots out and wraps around Shane's throat. Picking him up and slamming him to the wall without jostling me at all, Bryan presses his hand to Shane's windpipe and squeezes. "If you ever grab her like that again, if you ever *touch* her again, I'll slit your fucking throat, Turdsky."

"Get off me." Shane's words are an attempt at strong, but in reality, are barely a whisper past a crushed larynx. "Get the fuck off me, trash."

Bryan leans in close. "She's not yours. You're holding onto her for me. For safekeeping. But make no mistake, she's not yours, fuckface. She'll never be yours." He turns his fiery eyes to me. "Did he hurt you?"

Bryan Kincaid is a lot of things. Sexy. Confident. Funny. Terrible at math. But one thing overshadows it all. He's scary. And not necessarily the good scary. I'm talking, if it was me he was threatening death, my bowels would've already evacuated. "No."

"He didn't hurt you?"

I shake my head.

"His hand didn't bruise your arm?"

Yes. I think it did. But for the sake of Shane's life, and the fact he's *normally* a pussycat, I shake my head. "No."

He turns back to Shane. "I don't have a three strike system. You're already out, fucker. Don't touch her again." He pushes hard until Shane's head raps against the wall, then he turns to me and winks. "Come find me. I promise you won't regret it."

CHAPTER 5

BRYAN

I stand with Geo on Friday night beside a 1983 Chevy pick-up truck. A dark blue tarp lines the bed, and a shit ton of ice fills the space to keep the beer cold in this unseasonably stifling fucking heat.

I don't drink.

I don't drink, ever.

I can't afford the cost of a beer, nor can I afford the risk. I won't drink and drive; I especially won't drink and race, but Geo's not racing tonight, so he leans against the green truck and sips at his Coors. "She didn't come."

"She might. It's still early."

He leans back lazily and shakes his head. "You need to get your head in the game, man. You can't be thinking about her while you're out there."

"I've been thinking about her for years. Don't sweat it."

"Bry!"

I snap my angry gaze to his. "I didn't start winning *until* I started thinking about her out there. Trust me, George, I've got this."

He scoffs. *"George.* Look at you scolding me like I'm three. Get the fuck outta here, Kincaid." He nods toward the far end of the field. "You're up against JT tonight. You ready for that?"

I look down to Geo's leg. "I'll get him back for you. Don't worry about it."

He scoffs. "I'm not worried about my leg. We all go into these things knowing we could get hurt. It's just part of the game. Hell, I'm not even mad at him. If I'd thought of it first, I woulda pulled the same move. Nobility ain't my middle name, but I'll be pissed if you get stupid and fuck up."

"I'm never stupid."

"No? So what you did at the school with Shane... totally a smart move? You were on school grounds, he's a student, and your ass became an adult last year. Still think you're clever?"

"Fuckin' A. It was my smartest move yet. I got her to admit she loves me."

Halfway through a pull of his beer, he chokes and bends forward to clear his airway. "What? She said that?"

I smirk and thump his back. "Well, not out loud. But she was thinking it." Her untouched core was like an inferno on my leg. "She was definitely thinking it."

He shakes his head. "You're a fucking mess, Kincaid. God knows what you're gonna do when they ask *'does anyone object to this shit'* at her wedding."

"I don't think they say it exactly like that."

"No?" His green eyes meet mine. "You know what I mean! Should I buy her a baby shower gift now, or...?"

Fury rages hot inside me. "It won't make it all the way to the alter. She already wants me. And she'll *never* carry his babies. I'll drag her off to Nantucket before he gets his hands on her."

"Just like that?" He laughs and leans back onto the Mustang. "All our history, all our fun, you ditch your best friend and move to Nantucket for a girl?"

I scoff and force my raging heart to relax. "Just like that. But you can come with us. I'll find you a nice girl to talk into bed."

He rolls his eyes. "I don't need your help. Unlike you, I get laid on the regular. Unlike *you*, I don't become a fuckin' eunuch for an unavailable chick."

"Different paths, Geo. You like 'em fast and loose. I like *her*. We both still smile at the end of the day."

"Speaking of," he murmurs hungrily. His eyes zoom across the lot to none other than Tammi St James. She strides across the hardpacked dirt in a teeny tiny denim skirt and big hair. Tammi also has double D's, but hers don't hold even close to the same appeal for me. With a sequin purse hanging off her shoulder, fire-engine red lips and popping gum, she leaves her arm stretched back as though pulling someone through the crowd.

As though...

"I fuckin' knew it!" I slam my fist into Geo's shoulder. "I fuckin' knew she wanted me." I act badass, I act unaffected... sort of. But today, I sprint across the dirt and swing Nelly into my arms before she sees me coming.

Tammi and her double D's are forgotten as I jog around the back of a VW van and stop with her back pressed against the fading blue paint. Legs wrapped around my waist, her chest rising and falling with shock... surprise... exhilaration? Fuck knows, but she's not mad, she isn't hitting me to let her go, and her arms wrap around my neck instinctively. "I knew you'd come find me." I bury my face in her scented neck and take a whiff. *Mine. All mine.*

"Tammi made me come."

"Uh-huh. Your excuse implies Shane still *thinks* he's your man." I nibble on her rosy flesh and smile. She came for me. For the first time in three years, she dressed up for *me*, she snuck out for *me*. She always looks pretty, but tonight, she did it *knowing* she was coming to find *me*. In nineteen and a half years of life, this moment is legitimately my happiest yet.

And it's only going to get better from here.

"Did you race yet?"

"Not yet. Soon." I pull back to look into her smoky eyes. "I'll race for you. Win for you."

She smiles shyly. And yet, her legs remain around my hips. Her warmth resting against my belly. "What do you get for winning?"

"A little cash. The satisfaction of knowing I'm number one."

"That's important to you?"

"Winning? Uh-huh. I always intend to be number one. I fight? I win. I race? I win. I want you... I *will* win."

Her eyes darken and glitter in the moonlight. "Am I just a game to you? A trophy to collect? What happens after you win?"

I smirk arrogantly and extend one arm to the space around us. "I win. But I keep coming back. It's not one and done. It's win once, win again, keep winning. I'll always work to keep the number one place in your heart, Bert."

She rolls her eyes, but I see her lips shaking. *Tell me yes! Tell me it's okay to taste them.* "You think you're so sweet, Bryan Kincaid. You think you're so convincing."

"I got you here." I slide my hand along her silky thigh. "I got you to watch me race."

"I haven't watched yet."

I smirk against her collarbone. "In twenty minutes, you will. You wanna be in the hot lane? You can release me from the line."

Her fingers go to my hair – feels like they've been there our whole lives – and she pulls me back until our eyes meet. "Let me in the car with you."

"After. You can come for a lap after."

"No. Let me in for the race."

I shake my head and devastatingly knock her hands loose of my hair. "Not a fucking chance, Bert. There's nothing you could offer that would convince me to put you at risk."

"Nothing...? At all?" Her eyes glitter. "What if I said *'fuck me, Bryan'*?"

I groan and drop my head back. "No. Not even that."

Her body jolts like I sucker punched her. "Not that? You don't want me?"

"I want you more than my next breath. But there are a million things betting against me right now. I won't put you at risk. It's dangerous. If you were in my car, I'd drive like a fuckin' granny. And that's *after* I bubble wrapped you."

"But if you're going to race around a track and put yourself at risk, I wanna go with you. If you die, I die."

My eyes snap back to hers as though she returned that jab. "No!" I take her face in my hands and squeeze. "No way. The universe only allows a handful of angels to walk this earth at one time. I've got one of them in my arms. You don't die. Ever. It's not allowed."

"But you put yourself at risk. That's not fair for me."

But you aren't even saying yes to me! "It's the way it is. I'm good at what I do. I'm fast and agile. And if I lose control, it's not a big deal. You just brace and roll with it." I stroke a thumb beneath her eye. "I haven't died yet."

"Kincaid!" We snap straight at my shouted name. I let her slide down my body, not because I'm scared of her being caught or snitched to her man, but because with her legs wrapped around me, her skirt had ridden up indecently high. No one gets to see that.

Reilly steps around the van and smirks. "Shoulda known you'd be with a girl. Five minutes, you're up."

I nod as he turns away. Turning back to her, I stare at her cherry lips and sigh with want. "Watch me race, but you don't get to ride with me." I take her hand in mine and tug her away. We slide through crushing crowds and move back toward my Mustang to Geo and Tammi.

"Bryan?" She tugs on my hand to slow us before we get to the car.

I turn back, but my feet carry us forward. "Why haven't you kissed me?"

My eyes go straight back to her lips. "Because you're not mine yet."

She frowns in confusion. "But you keep saying–"

"Yeah, I keep saying. But *you* haven't said anything yet. The only thing you tell me is that you have a boyfriend. Get rid of him, give me the yes, I'll kiss every last inch of your body. Give me the yes, and I'll give you anything."

Her feet falter as I tug her through the noisy crowd. "Anything? Would you quit racing?"

"For you? In a heartbeat. But you can't claim you worry about me if you're not even mine. The day you say yes, *that's* the day you get all the power. Anything you ask, it's yours. You give me forever, Bert, and I'll give you the world."

CHAPTER 6

NELLY

Rushing across the lot with my heart in my throat and my hand tucked securely in his, Bryan throws me at his best friend. "Geo. I'm up. Watch her."

"Watch her?" My eyes narrow stubbornly. "Wait a damn minute. I'm not a toddler, Bryan, and I'm not yours to boss around, remember?" He wants to play, then so can I.

Playfully, Bryan snaps his teeth. "That's the first time I've seen your fire, Bert. I knew you had a bunch tucked away inside you. Hold onto that thought; let's pick up where we left off in about ten minutes."

"No!" He didn't want to kiss me. Well, he *did*. But he won't. "Take me with you, or I'm going home."

He looks at me like I'm a true toddler, then with a raised brow, nods at Geo. A strong arm slams down onto my shoulders and pulls me in close. "You're mine for ten minutes, pretty girl. Let's see if I can get the yes faster."

"Hey!" No longer smug, Bryan turns back to his best friend with murder in his eyes. "I'm trusting you, Geo. She's the most important thing I have. Do right by me."

Geo rolls his eyes and loosens his hold. "You've got trust issues, man. Go, run. I've got her. Justin's already on the line."

Bryan's dark eyes come back to mine. No longer murderous, now they hold a heady mix of desperation and regret. "Stay here, Bert. Maybe we can negotiate. Soon."

"Take me with you."

"No. I've laid down my terms. You've laid down yours. We'll talk again soon." Jumping into his car, he revs the engine so loudly, I jump back until my back slams against Geo's broad chest. He laughs throatily by my ear. He thinks he's so amazing with a girl under each arm and a dirty grin on his face.

Bryan backs away from us slowly, and as soon as the Mustang clears the crowd and moves toward the line, I elbow Geo in the ribs and step out of his hold. "Get off me! Don't touch."

He lifts his hand in surrender, but his smile remains. "This is how Bry feels, huh? Gets to hug you for a sec, then you turn into the ice princess and flick him off."

"I have a boyfriend. I don't hug Bryan, either."

"Uh-huh, guess my eyes go wacky sometimes." Two narrow dimples pop below his bottom lip and wink playfully. "Stop playing games, Nelly. You know you want him. You know Shane's a pussy. We already know how this story ends. Why hurt him on the way?"

Bryan doesn't look like he's hurting. Mostly, he looks like a tomcat that's having a bunch of fun playing with the scared little mouse.

I'm the damn mouse, and I'm terrified. "My daddy will kill me for being here, Geo. He'll *literally* kill me if he learns of Bry's existence. I can't dump my boyfriend just so Bryan can fuck a girl with a clear conscience."

He rolls his eyes and turns a giggling Tammi into his chest. "If you don't know that he'd protect you with his life, then you don't know shit. Book smarts don't mean a damn thing when you're in our world, and you, my pretty little ice princess, are dumb as shit in *our* world."

I don't get a chance to argue further. I don't even get a chance to find a stick and beat him for his arrogance, because car engines roar and the cheering crowd turns to deafening screams. Geo gets busy dry humping Tammi, so I take a step away, then another, then a third, and when he doesn't reach out for me, I turn and make a break for it.

I sprint for the line. I know I won't reach him in time. I have no chance of hopping into his car to hitch a ride, but I want to be closer. I need to be closer.

Because in *my* world, fifty yards is too damn far away.

I get within twenty feet when the buxom blonde in tiny shorts and super-high heels throws down her silky scarf. The thick black wheels on Bryan's sparkling Mustang skid in the dirt and send rocks bulleting through the air. Both engines roar like pissed off lions, then finding traction, they're off.

I've never been to the races down here before. I've never seen Bryan – or anyone – race in real life, so it's not until they're a quarter mile away before I realize the grass and dirt space the crowd party in is the *inside* of the track.

They circle us, frenzied like sharks, and we're the tiny little feeder fish. I turn as they turn. I follow Bry's car with my eyes. I lose sight of his car every few seconds as people and cars on the inside block my way, but within a millisecond, he's back in my sight.

The roaring sends adrenaline and worry fighting for dominance in my blood. The two cars drift around a loose bend and turn straight on, and when the Mustang skids to the side dangerously, my hands go to my mouth and my heart threatens to explode.

A mile away, they straighten out. Intent on his win, the Mustang speeds up, faster, faster, closer to the midnight blue 'Cuda until sparks rain between them and the Mustang shoves his opponent to the side.

Quarter of a mile away, it's like watching through molasses as they come close enough I can see the rage in Bryan's eyes. The blue muscle car corrects and screams out as it works to make up the inches it lost.

I watch every single gear change, every emotion that passes through Bryan's intense eyes. The nose of the Mustang sits in front of its opponent's the whole time. Barely, only inches ahead, but a win is a win, and I imagine crossing the line first is all Bryan cares about.

Two-hundred yards to go, and my palms sweat. I'm imagining bakeries, cinnamon, icing powder. I'm imagining Bryan's strong hands, and what kind of life I could have if I was simply brave enough to say no to my daddy.

Two words, so simple.

A no for my dad.

And a yes for Bryan Kincaid.

George Blair may be arrogant, he may even be a little too blunt and offensive, but he's right on the money when it comes to my smarts.

For a girl who does pretty well in school, it takes until Geo's strong arms wrap around my stomach and fling my long legs into the air before I realize how stupid I've been. How I'm stupidly standing on the start line, which doubles as the finish line. How I force Bryan to drive right at me, because the other guy would have anyway. How I *force* Bry to win, for fear of the other guy getting to me first and potentially obliterating my existence with one single miscalculated jerk of the steering wheel.

From molasses to sharp reality, the terrifying roar of engines and shouting people turn to individual screeches of excitement and worry.

But it's Geo's voice in my ear that runs loudest. "You fucking idiot!" He swings me around barely a second before the cars pass. As the wind off Bryan's fender blows my hair back with a single powerful *whoosh!* "Are you suicidal? You fucking halfwit! He's gonna kill me." Geo runs me back to the VW just like Bryan did, but at the same time, not at all how Bryan did it. "He's gonna kill me, then I'm gonna kill you!" He slams me against the bus and clutches at his chest. "Are you insane, Nelly? Why would you stand there?"

I'm in shock.

I'm naïve.

"I wasn't thinking."

"No! You weren't! Fuck me, Nelly!" He thumps the side of my head with his thick fingers. "What the hell have you got up here? It's not a fucking brain, that's for sure!"

"I'm sorry." The adrenaline and realization of what I've just done crashes over me and sends tears to my eyes. "Oh my God. I wasn't thinking. I'm sorry!"

Pressing me against the car, he steps back and thrusts his hands into his hair. "Sweet fucking Jesus, woman. I almost had a heart attack."

"I'm sorry."

He runs a strong hand over his leg, a leg I know was covered in a cast not so long ago, and though I'm sorry, and shaking, and devastated that I could be so stupid, it's nothing on the way my throat closes when Bryan strides toward us like a restless warrior in the night.

Rage simmers barely checked. His eyes glint like the tip of a gun in the moonlight. Fisted hands and long strides that eat up the fifty yards that separate us, and when I swear he might hit me, he spins on his unaware best friend and slams a closed fist into the side of his face.

Geo's head snaps around dangerously fast. He drops to a bent knee, shock passes in less than a microsecond, and with a hand cupping his jaw, his light eyes watch Bryan as he steps away and grabs my hand.

"I'm sorry, Bry." Surprising me, Geo doesn't jump up and defend himself. He stays down and bows his head. "I'm sorry."

Spinning with my hand still in his, Bryan uses the other to jab a dangerous finger in his best friend's face. "Her death would've been on your hands, George! You think about that next time you want fast and loose."

"Bryan, no. It's not–"

He tugs me along. "Not a word. Give me twenty seconds, Bert. I'm begging you."

"But Bryan!" I turn away; I turn back to Geo apologetically, but Bryan doesn't release me. "It wasn't his fault."

"Twenty seconds, Nelly. A man in my position deserves twenty fucking seconds." He drags me through the parting crowd until we reach his Mustang. He wrenches the door open and tosses me in. "I swear to God, get in, belt on. Don't move until I'm back."

"Where are you going?"

"To beat the piss out of my best friend."

"No!" I jump back out of the car and throw myself at him. "That was my fault. Not his."

"You would have died, Chantelle! This isn't a game. I say no to taking you in the car, so you decide to stand on the fucking road instead? Were you punishing me?"

"No! It was just an accident. I wasn't thinking."

"Which is why I told him to think for you! Instead, Tammi was offering up blowjobs and you nearly died."

"Bryan, stop." I jump on his back when he turns to walk away. For the first time ever, it's me running to him; it's me forcing my touch on him. I squeeze him tight with my arms and legs, and press my lips to his ear. "Please stop, Bry. You're angry." He's *so* angry, his body vibrates with rage.

I've thought about his body a million times over the last couple years, but never once in all my dreams could I have imagined it would be so hard, so powerful, so angry at me. "I'm sorry. I wasn't punishing you. I promise I wasn't. I just wasn't thinking. I was worried about you; you strap yourself into a death rocket and throw yourself around a dirt track. You were in danger, and I wasn't thinking."

His steps falter, and finally, he slows. "Bert. I nearly had a damn heart attack driving toward you."

"I know. I'm sorry."

"I wasn't aiming for you. I swear."

"I know. You were protecting me. You were sticking closest to me so he couldn't."

He nods and drops his head back. In the moonlight, as stars twinkle above us and spectators take on a somber silence and pretend they're not watching our odd fight; I sit on Bryan Kincaid's back with my lips on his ear, my legs wrapped around his powerful hips, and my forearms choking off his air. I press my lips to his neck. "I'm sorry, Bry."

"Are you eighteen yet?"

I let out a breath of relief. "Two more days."

"How long after you don't get up for breakfast tomorrow before your daddy goes looking?"

"I don't see my daddy until after school every day. I don't see him till he gets home from the mill."

"So, he's not expecting to see you until late tomorrow afternoon? How long after that will he go looking?"

I shrug.

"Cops won't take a missing person's report for twenty-four hours, right?"

I snort and lay my head on his thick traps. "Are you gonna kidnap me?"

"I'm seriously thinking about it." His hands slide around to my ass, not to cop a feel, but to simply support my weight. "That twenty-four hours ends on your birthday, Bert, then we're free and clear."

I sigh and close my eyes. Scary, bold, confronting, he still comforts me.

"Can I ask you something?"

I nod. "Want me to get down?"

"Fuck no." He turns on the spot and walks us back toward his car.

I feel so dumb, so conspicuous on his back, but I don't care. Not really.

"What's your question?"

Tapping my thigh, he helps me slide down until my feet touch the dirt. "Wanna come for a drive with me? A regular drive," he adds with twitching lips. "Regular speed."

"Is that your question?" I let him help me into the passenger seat, much gentler than when he threw me in just minutes ago.

"No. I just don't want all those assholes to know our business. It's hardly kidnapping if we tell the whole world our plan."

I snort. With sparkling brown eyes and a still ticking jaw, he watches me for a moment. Shaking his head and running his hand along the back of his neck, he closes the door and walks around the hood. Climbing in, he switches on the engine and starts nudging people aside.

In minutes, we're cruising along the outskirts of town. "You scared me, Bert. I swear, seeing you there was the scariest thing I've ever experienced in my life."

"I'm sorry."

"It was like you were standing on the train tracks, and I was watching a train come for you. Justin was the train, but also," he shakes his head, "I was the train, too." He looks over at me as we start up the hill. "What if I'd fucked up? What if, in my attempt to protect you, it was me who hurt you?"

"I'm sorry I was so careless. I didn't mean to be. But in my defense, I told you to take me."

He scoffs lightly. "So you're a woman who'll make me pay. For the rest of my life, any time I tell you no, I'll regret it..." His eyes flick to mine for the briefest second. "Is that right?"

"I didn't do that tonight to punish you–"

"I know." He changes gears and reaches out to take my hand. We're not a couple. We're not anything, and yet, I find myself in his car late at night, with his musky scent in my nose, and my hand trapped against his hard thigh. "You already said that. I believe you."

"You do?"

"I believe everything you say... Except the boyfriend thing." He turns to me with a goofy smirk. "It's hardly lying when I know the truth."

"What was your question, Bryan?"

"Well..." He takes a sharp twist and downshifts to get us cruising up the steep hill. "Do you not tell me yes because I'm trailer trash?"

I frown. "You're not trailer trash to me. That's just a shitty descriptive term that shittier people use to make themselves feel superior. I don't care where you live."

He nods. "Is it because I'm not rich like Turdsky?"

"His last name is Tosky."

He snorts. "I know. Answer my question, Bert."

"I don't care about money. I'm poor. You're poor. Unless you're a Tosky or Montgomery, you're poor. Can't miss something you've never had."

"Do you say no because I already finished school? Am I too old for you?"

I roll my eyes. "You're barely a year older than me."

"And you don't actually care about Turdsky, because if you did, you'd never let me touch you. Especially not in front of him."

"How do you know that?" I turn in my seat with a narrowed glare. "Maybe I'm trying to make him jealous. Maybe I'm trying to get him to man up and crack some skulls against the bricks."

"You wanna know how I know?" The dash lights twinkle in eyes that are equal parts playful and dead serious. "How I know *exactly* my future? And yours, too? Because you're not even mine, but there's no chance in hell you'd let any man touch you the way I touch you, *especially* not in front of me. If I stood in Shane's place and another man got it in his head that he could touch you, I wouldn't even have to kill him, because I know you'd do it before I got the chance." His eyes come to mine. "Because you're a fighter. You fight for what's yours. Shane's not yours. You don't give a flying fuck about him. But you care about me." I jump when he slams his palm down on the steering wheel. "And *that's* what makes you mine. At our core, that's what makes you mine. I already know my stars. I know yours, too. I'm not even waiting for you to figure it out, because you already know." He looks to me briefly. "You already know. But until I can get you to say it out loud, we sit in this stalemate where we dance around each other, but we don't get to enjoy the real thing."

I swallow my nerves when he slows at the top of Lookout Hill. "What's the real thing?"

"Me." We stop about ten feet from the edge of the hill and he pulls up the hand brake. "I'm the realest thing you'll ever know. I don't know if soul mates are a thing. I don't know if there's only one person for everyone on this planet. That hardly sounds fair, because what if one of you die? Or what if you just never meet? So there's probably a couple people out there for each person. But we *did* meet, Bert. We're right here, right now, together in the same place at the same time."

"Bryan–"

"And you know it. If you thought what I'm saying was bullshit, you'd have removed my nuts the first time I touched you. You're strong, Nelly. You're strong and beautiful and capable. You don't *need* a man, but fuck it, I need you."

CHAPTER 7

BRYAN

"What do you need from me, Bert?" I thread our fingers together. Hers are so small, so delicate, compared to mine, which are almost permanently stained black from grease and hard work. "How do I convince you to trust me?"

"I do trust you." Her long chestnut hair hangs straight over a delicate shoulder. "I trust you, which is why I'm here. But I don't trust my daddy."

"What about him?"

"He'll kill you, Bry. He'll kill us both."

She's completely serious. This isn't a 'my daddy will be so mad' thing. This is straight up honesty. "He doesn't scare me. Nobody scares me except you."

"He scares *me*." Her eyes darken. "He scares the shit out of me. He'd drive his truck into the river with me trapped inside; he'd kill us both, and he'd take you out as we pass, before he'd let me deviate from his plan."

I stroke a thumb over her thin wrist. "When you're with me, you don't have to live anyone's plan except your own. I'll follow yours, whatever it is. *Wherever*."

"What if I go off to school? Four years is a long time to be apart."

I scoff. "Not once just now did I say we'd be apart. I said I'd go wherever you go."

"It's May, Bryan! You'd pack your shit up just like that and move?"

"We're already in the car, Bert. This is all my shit. This is me. You'd be choosing this over money. You'd be choosing ramen noodles over power, struggle street over prestige, but I tell you what, you'd also be choosing passion over Shane Fuckin' Turdsky. Ten years from now, twenty, no matter which option you choose, you'll be living fancy. You can go their way, get the big house now, easy and fancy and quick, or you can choose *my* lane, work on the fancy with me, team work, and we'd get there. But either way, ten years from now, you'll either be lying in bed next to him and wondering where in the world I am. If I'm happy. If you'd be happier if you chose me. You'll wonder what you gave up. *Or,* you'll be lying right beside me, and I'll have just finished fucking your brains out and reminding you exactly why you chose me."

Her chest heaves with every heavy word I throw at her.

"You're at a Y intersection, Bert. Two roads. Two choices. One of them ends only with money. Money won't keep you warm at night. Money won't tell you it loves you. You'll end up the abused wife of a man who keeps three mistresses. He and your daddy will talk, and *bam!* Shane learns how to keep women in line." I reach across and take her jaw. "Or you could have me. I don't have much to offer you. I don't have the money or houses or trinkets, but I *will*. It'll come with time and hard work. I've never been scared of hard work. I won't let you down. But I do promise to keep you warm at night. *Only* you. Until my dying day."

Her poor abused bottom lip rolls between her teeth.

Could she believe me? *Should* she believe me?

"Can I ask you something?"

I bring the pads of her fingers to my lips. "Anything."

"Do you race because it's fun, or just for the prize money?"

"Both. It's a bunch of fun when the love of your life's not standing on the line. But I do it mostly for the prize money."

She nods thoughtfully. "Money to live on or money to save?"

"Money to save. I already work down at the garage. I have money to live on. I spend only enough that my belly's most the way full, I save everything else."

"What are you saving for?"

"You." I lean forward and drop a kiss barely a half inch from her hungry lips. "A house to put our family in."

"Our family?"

"Mmhm. Haven't you been listening? We've already named our firstborn son."

She snorts inelegantly. "Robert. That's right. I forgot."

"I'll keep reminding you." With the very tips of my fingers, I slide the strap of her top off her shoulder and move in to nibble. Her breath races out on a shudder. "If I promise to take care of everything, would you give me the yes?" I can barely open my eyes. My mouth salivates at how close I am to the yes. Lust and love and hunger and protection war inside me. I'll take care of her; show her how vivid and amazing and passionate the world can be.

"Answer me, Bert."

"Yes." She clears her throat. "Yes."

"Yes, you would give me the yes?"

"No. Yes, that's your yes. Right now. This is your yes."

With the combined strength of a million men, I flip the switch on the soft top, wait the three seconds for it to begin moving, and when we're in the clear, I flick her belt and pull her into my lap. Straddling my thighs, she sits on my hardened cock and moans as she grinds down.

I thread my fingers in her hair and pull her close. Our breath mingles. Her lips reach for mine, but I hold her back and wait for her excited gaze to stop bouncing around. "What? Don't say no. Not now!"

"You're giving me the yes?"

She nods frantically.

"You been drinking tonight? Anyone slip you a beer?"

She snickers. "No. I didn't have a single drink."

"Because being on drugs might explain you standing on the fucking finish line."

She bites her bottom lip and grins. "Nope. That was just me being a dumbass."

I shake my head. So stupid. So fucking stupid. "Don't do it again."

"Maybe next time you'll take me with you." Daringly, she grinds down over my cock. *She's a virgin. She's a virgin!* I have to remind myself over and over again before I whip my dick out and slam deep inside her. "You already said so," she continues. "Wherever I go, you go. Well," she leans in close and stops when our lips feather together, "wherever you go, I go."

"No."

"Yes. I'm a fighter. This is the life you're asking for."

"No. *I'm* a fighter. You're who I fight for."

"Bryan...?"

"Mm?"

With a sassy smirk, she closes the gap between our lips and sets off a frenzy of explosions in my head. Her soft lips, softer than I ever imagined, slide over mine. Her tongue, more playful than I ever dared hope, plays with mine. Her breath rushes out on a gust, scorching its way down my throat and setting my lungs on fire.

No way in hell has Shane or anyone else had her like this. This is a first for her – it's all brand new, so I don't rip her panties off like I want to. I don't even palm her ass *quite* as roughly as my hands want to.

I slide my fingers under her skirt and smile when she quivers in my lap. "Let me touch you. Let me show you what my fingers alone could do for you."

"No." I crash back to earth with a shattered heart from her single *no*, but then she clarifies, "I want it all. Show me what the rest of my life will be like."

"Babe." I groan and rest my forehead on hers. "We're in a car. This ain't a family mover. It's a *small* car! I can't take you in my car."

"Why not?" Her fingers trail along the exposed skin at the buttons of my shirt. "It's just... insert A into B, right?"

I snort so hard, I'm winded. "I mean, there's more to it than that."

"There is?" I swear, she's playing innocent. She knows more than her words imply.

"There's finesse. And probably candles. Tender touches, and slow kisses – *not* fast fucking in the car."

"I bet you could still be gentle and suave even here. I bet you'd know how to make me feel good."

I would. I fucking would. "I swear, my cock's about to break through my jeans and kill us both."

She smirks. "If you die, I die." Leaning forward and latching onto my lip, she bites down hard enough it almost has me creaming my pants. "What was that thing we were practicing the other day? Oh." She grinds down teasingly. "That's right. It was *Bryan*." Like she's Satan in a nurse's getup, she thrusts her tongue into my mouth and has me groaning out from the pain in my jeans. "*Bryan*." She trails her fingers along my chest, over my abs, and stops on my belt. Leaning forward, her lips touch my earlobe. *"Fuck me, Bryan."*

That's it. I'm done. Kill me now.

Forgive me Father, for I have sinned.

She unsnaps my belt and slides it from my jeans. I watch her, and like she's been practicing for this her whole life, she dangles my belt outside the car, and when my eyes snap to her hand, she drops it.

"I don't think I can be gentle, babe. I swear, I'd try. But I don't know if I..." I close my eyes and concentrate on breathing as she lowers my zipper. I can feel Every. Single. Ridge. "I don't think this is what's best for you."

"Don't I get a say in what's best for me?"

She takes me out of my boxers and has me whimpering like a girl. "Not if I think you're wrong." Breathe. Don't jizz like a thirteen-year-old kid who just saw his first set of boobs. "Sometimes what you think is best isn't exactly best."

"Like me standing in front of two speeding cars tonight?"

"Exactly." My voice reaches a new octave when she runs her thumb over the beading moisture on the tip of my dick.

"What if I died tonight and we never got to do this first?" She leans in and seduces my mouth with hers.

All along, I was so sure it would be me talking her into bed. I was positive I'd be making a million promises not to hurt her, to go slow, to be gentle.

She unmans me.

She has me desperate to ask *her* to go gentle on *me*.

"What if you say that pesky word that ruins what we have? What if you say no, then something happens to me tomorrow?" With two hands now, she cups my balls with one and strokes my rock-solid cock with the other. "You'd regret it for the rest of your lonely life, wouldn't you?"

"Uh-huh." I open my eyes when she moves around on my legs. Pulling her skirt up and her panties to the side, she leads my cock to her fiery entrance and stops.

Don't stop!

Don't keep going.

"Don't thrust up the first time. Hold onto something and don't thrust."

I let her ass go. Taking the handbrake in one hand and the door handle in the other, I press my feet to the floor so hard, I wouldn't be surprised if I pushed through to the road outside.

She smirks. "Are you ready?"

To die? Sure thing.

Lining me up and sliding down just half an inch, her playful eyes turn serious. Her seductive mouth turns to a pained O. Slamming her eyes shut, she presses her face to my shoulder and ever so slowly lowers, lowers, until she stops and takes a deep breath.

I know I'm stretching her. I know it hurts. With her pain right in front of me, I gain control over my raging hormones and body.

Taking her hips in my hands, I slowly lift her to ease some of the stretch. "Easy does it, baby. Go up, then move down just a little further."

Nodding, her arms come up to choke me. The ball of her shoulder digs into my windpipe, but I don't dare rearrange her. Lowering another half inch, she groans deep – with pleasure? I wish. It's far more likely pain that has her crying out.

"I can feel you. Hey." I bring my hands up to take her face. Her cheeks are stained a rosy pink, and her eyes are dilated and impossibly wide. "This is the last bit, then we're home free."

She nods. She nods again as though giving herself a pep talk.

Before I get a chance to lift her a little to pave the way, she takes a deep breath, presses her lips to mine, and drops her weight. "Ah!" Her breath explodes into my mouth. "Oh my shit, Bryan!"

"Baby. Why'd you do that?" I bring her back to kiss. To soothe. To ease the tremors rolling through her tiny frame. She's so small compared to me. So delicate. "We coulda gone slower, silly. Why'd you hurt yourself?"

"Because I want to be yours." Breathing through the intrusion, she angles her hips and groans. She's so small, so tight, so *bare*, my balls draw up in an instant. It's been too long. I've waited too long for this. "Now I'm yours forever. No take backs."

"No take backs." I bring her lips to mine and take her mouth on a much rougher journey than our bottom half. I let her set her pace.

She can take whatever she wants. "I love you, Nelly." She stumbles for only a single stroke. "I've loved you since I met you."

"I gave you the yes," she breathes. "Now you need to make good on the forever."

NOW

Like day and night, chocolate brown eyes and mahogany hair, my granddaughter sits beside her blonde haired, blue eyed cousin and they stare up at me, rapt with my storytelling skills.

"So what happened after that?" Bean asks excitedly. I shouldn't tell the girls about my youth. Their parents, my sons, would have a conniption, but these girls have always been older than their years.

At fifteen and eighteen, they're either already seeing boys, or they're damn close to it. Their daddies won't tell them what's real. They'll simply mention what happens to any boy that looks at them for a minute too long.

Skulls against bricks... just like my Bryan.

"Well, after that... I went home."

"You went home?" Evie's angry roar ricochets in my brain and makes me smile. They're related to me. They're definitely Kincaids. "What the hell is the matter with you, Gramma? Why would you go home to that piece of shit?"

"Don't swear, Evelyn. Your daddy'll kill me."

Bean snorts. "I don't think swearing in front of us is a big deal anymore. Uncle Jack says all the good stuff, anyway."

"Uncle Jack is a troublemaker..." When the girls' faces drop – because of course, Uncle Jack is their favorite – I smile. "And his shenanigans keep all the trouble off me. Your dads are so naïve, girls. I swear, they see angels."

Snickering, Evie sits back against the couch in the living room of my big fancy house. The big fancy house that Bryan never got to buy for me.

We lived comfortably. We were happy. And he was right, ten years later, twenty years later, he was still singeing my hair with passion. But it wasn't until our boys were grown men that I moved into the home I'm in now.

"So we know you married him, Gramma, since we're all here today. What happened?"

"I went home that night, I pretended everything was normal, though of course, it wasn't."

"You had unprotected sex, Grandma. Didn't you get pregnant?"

I smile indulgently at my daughter-in-law's clone. "I didn't. I could have, it's a risk I ran, so don't be like me. Don't be dumb. Safe sex and all that." The girls blush at my words. "But I was lucky. I didn't get pregnant that night. I didn't get pregnant until your Uncle Bobby; Robert-with no middle name-Kincaid, and that was four years later. Bryan and I had already been married for more than three and a half years by that point."

"More than three and a half years..." Bean's dark eyes narrow. "So you married that same year." She turns and snatches up an aqua blue couch cushion and tosses it at my face. "Finish your damn story, Grandma!"

I laugh and toss the pillow back. I never had daughters. Just like Bryan ordered, I gave him strong sons. Three of them. But those boys married wonderful girls, and those girls gave them plenty of each kind.

I have eleven grandchildren, now. Eight of them carry Bryan's last name.

We made his name worth something again.

"He dropped me home that night with a promise to meet up the morning of my birthday. We'd have an eight-hour head start on my daddy."

"You ran away?"

I think back to that warm morning, to the exhilaration of knowing our plans, to the excitement of a future that lay out ahead of us.

"We did. We ran away. I waited for my daddy to go to work that morning, even knowing there was a birthday dinner planned for me for seven that evening at the Tosky's house. I waited for his truck to pull out. I packed what I wanted. Bryan's Mustang was parked six blocks away at a public phonebooth, and that morning, I simply went for a walk. I never went home again."

The girls stare at me in awe.

"Now, I trust you both not to be so impulsive. I trust you not to get any hairbrained ideas like that."

Evie scoffs. "Yeah, right. You got out because your father was a piece of shit. No way would Daddy just stay here if I decided to ditch town. Not to mention, most of the time, I actually like being in this family. When Daddy's not being such a caveman."

I think of my sweet middle son. My serious, silent, brooding Aiden. "No, baby girl. He wouldn't stand by. And if Ben even so much as thought about it, his brains would be smeared on the bricks."

She snatches up a second cushion and pegs it at my face. "I'm not with Ben! He's an asshole."

I stare into her blue eyes and simply nod. "Alright."

"Stop saying *alright* like that. You think you're so smart."

I laugh and pass the cushion back just in case she gets pissed a third time. "I know boys like Ben. I know that if he drove up – or rode up – in a Mustang and asked you to hop in, he's askin' for a reason. I know he wouldn't throw those suggestions around lightly."

Bean rolls her eyes. "Can we stop talking about Ben and go back to Bryan?"

"That's Poppy to you, sweetheart." I smile nostalgically and remember him standing against his car in the morning sun. "He waited for me at the phonebooth. He had a bouquet of stolen daisies in his hands... the dirt was still clumped at the bottom. He took my backpack, put it in the back of the car."

Evie sits on the very edge of her seat. "And then?"

"And then he took me in his arms, dipped me back, kissed the hell out of me, and pulled a twenty-dollar engagement ring from his pocket and proposed marriage." I stare at the simple band that still rests on my finger. "We drove three towns over, stopped at the courthouse, made it official that very day, then we moved to the desert for the four years it took me to earn a degree."

Evie's romantic eyes regard me whimsically. "What did he do for those four years?"

Even on struggle street, even so poor that he chose to feed me instead of himself, they were good times for us. "He worked hard. He worked at a garage in town, saved every penny, helped me through school. I graduated in the summer, and by that Christmas, we'd conceived and already named our first baby."

"What happened to your daddy?"

"He died of alcohol poisoning a few years later. It was amazing the power I *thought* he had over me. But the day Bryan married me was the day he gave me my power back. My daddy was a bad man, a bully, but like most bullies, he had no power once I told him no. He found us, he even came to us with a rifle, but Bryan never let him hurt me." Broken teeth – my daddy's. Broken knuckles – Bryan's. "He visited us once. He cried about how he only wanted what was best for me. Then when Bryan refused to relinquish the power we'd discovered, the power he knew I had all along, Daddy never came back again. He went home and drank himself to death. By the time Bobby had arrived, my father was already dead and buried, so we came home. Geo wanted his best friend back, he had a job lined up for

Bryan, and I was pregnant with Aiden. It was time to come home to our friends."

"Where's Geo now?"

"Wait!" Bean shoots up until her spine snaps straight. "What did you say Geo's last name was?"

I smile cunningly. "Blair. George Blair."

She scrunches her nose. "He's related to Mac, isn't he? He's a moron too, isn't he?"

I laugh. "Yes, sweetheart. On both counts. Geo is Mac's grandpa, and yes, he's also a moron. But just like Mac, he means well. He grew out of his immaturity by the time your daddy was born. He'd settled down, had a daughter with a nice woman. She's gone now, too. She passed away right around the time Mac was born. Now it's just Geo, his daughter, and Mac – the car-stealing, adrenaline junkie, trouble-making teenager – left for those Thanksgiving dinners."

Evie tilts her head to the side. "How do you know this? Are you still in contact with Geo?"

"Of course. I see him around all the time. We lost contact for a long while there, while he was settling in with his family, but kismet played tricks on us. The universe brought your Auntie Kit into Bobby's life, and with her, came Geo. It's like we're twenty-some-things living in a crappy apartment all over again. Our houses are much nicer now, but the nostalgia sure feels good."

The girls look between each other, and like they have a million times since Bean was a newborn and Evie was a curious toddler, they link hands, giving and taking the love that began the day Bryan declared me his.

Evie's blue eyes penetrate mine and send my heart thudding with memories, good and bad. "Do you miss him, Gramma?

I nod thoughtfully and spin my wedding ring.

"Every single day, baby." I meet their eyes. "I miss him every single second of every single day. But then when it gets to be too much, I visit my boys and I take a hug from my arrogant Bobby, because he's his daddy's arrogance. Or I hug my serious Aiden, because nobody was as serious as Bryan until Aiden came along. And when I need to laugh, when I'm scared that I can't go on another minute without him, I visit my Jimmy, because his jokes are as bad as Bryan's."

Bryan Kincaid promised me the world.

And for as long as his boys insist on hugging me every day, every time they take me in their arms and press a kiss to my hair, I know that he delivered.

Their hugs are his hugs.

He's too stubborn to ever truly be gone.

Follow the Kincaid's in ***Finding Home.***
Book 1 of the **Rollin On Series.**
http://a.co/d/3AoBjCU

WRITTEN IN THE STARS

THEN

"One!"

Her sweet growl has me smiling before I even open the door.

"Two!"

I stop on the front stoop and press my ear close to the door. I want to know what they do when I'm not around. I want to be a part of their lives, even when I'm not here.

"Three!"

Screams. Squeals. Tiny toddler feet scamper across the creaky floorboards.

"Robert! Get back here and let Mommy put a diaper on you."

"No!" He squeals and bolts across the apartment and has his mom chasing. Our apartment is so small, so old, I know where they are just by the squeak of the floor. The kitchen squeaks one way, the living room another.

"Catch me, Momma!"

"Robert! Get your butt back here! It's dinner time."

"No!"

She whimpers. "I don't want to clean up pee from the carpet again, baby. Come back here. I'm begging you."

More sweet giggles. "No!"

"Bobby, I swear, I'll whoop your friggin ass."

I bite my knuckles to stop the laughter that bubbles in my chest.

Anyone on the outside would swear Nelly Kincaid was the perfect Suzie Homemaker. The perfect mother. The perfect wife.

She is.

To me.

But when I'm not being bias, I can admit she loses her shit on a semi regular basis, rarely makes the bed, never folds the socks together, and her culinary skills are *not* the reason I married her.

And yet, I'd marry her again today.

Tomorrow.

And every day after that.

"Mommy, Mommy!" I know he's doing the doodle dance right now. "Girls have got a 'gina, boys have got a doodle!"

"No!" She stops in the middle of the living room, literally less than five feet from where I stand hidden in the outside hall, and sighs. "Put your penis away, Robert. Then go wash your hands. It's time for dinner."

"I don't wike it!"

"You don't even know what I cooked!" Then quieter, she adds, "You little turd."

It's the summer a year after my firstborn son arrived. I married the one and only woman I ever wanted in a courthouse ceremony that was planned exactly ninety-three minutes in advance – in her head.

I'd been planning it for three years.

I whisked her away. Married up. Helped her finish her teaching degree. Impregnated her. And now here we are, with an eighteen-month-old psychotic toddler obsessed with his penis, a wife with sass and a degree going unused, a bank account that sits in the red more often than the black, and a broken bed frame, because we can't afford to replace it.

But we're happy.

So fucking happy it makes my teeth ache.

I place my grease stained hand on the door handle when I think she's given up on my demon spawn and is ready to run away to the circus – without us – but before I open it, she whispers, "Bobby, honey. Come to Mommy."

Like he has all the energy he stole from us, he bounds across the living room and stops only when Nelly lets out a grunt.

My son is a brute, and I know he just body tackled her. He's the only person in the world I'd allow to be rough with her, and he loses that privilege once he gets big enough to know better.

We're men. We don't hurt the woman we love.

"Yeah, Momma?"

"Baby. Remember our surprise? Remember what we were going to do today?"

"What?"

"Our surprise. Remember Daddy's surprise?"

"What?"

Her sentences are way too long for my son. We're simple men. We use muscle, not brains. It's not his fault he's got a high school dropout for a daddy.

"We worked all day on the surprise, remember?"

Silence hangs for a beat too long, and in my mind, I picture him cocking his little head to the side like a puppy. "I don't know."

"Ugh, forget it." With a grunt, she lifts him into her arms and elicits a new round of piggy snorts and squealing. "I've got you, anyway. Time for a diaper. Daddy will be home in a sec."

"Daddy?"

"Yuh-huh. Any minute."

"Daddy be home?"

She snickers. "That's what I just said, baby. But we have to get ready. You need a diaper."

"I don't want a diaper!"

She grunts across the apartment, and when I know she's stepped into the short hall, I open the front door and step in.

We live small. Humble. A two-bedroom shoebox apartment. Paper-thin walls. Leaky... everything.

It's not the mansion I promised her, but I'm working hard for it.

I'd rather live in a shoe box for five years and save, than live in something bigger and never be able to save for something for us.

Something real.

We worked hard. We got her degree.

That was step one.

Next, we take over the world... but that's for when I have spare time. And that, along with money, is something I don't have.

I work at Chub's garage six days a week. Eight till five, five days, and eight till noon, Saturdays. I love to work with my hands. For a guy who didn't really have a plan beyond 'convince Nelly Robertson to marry me,' I'm happy with the career I've fallen into.

It won't always be so hard.

I won't always have to work at the local grocer Wednesdays to Sundays, eight till midnight to prop up our pay. I won't always have to mow lawns half of Saturday, all of Sunday, and sometimes on a Monday night if I'm hungry and the bread just won't stretch.

Someday, I'll be able to go to bed with my wife. Wake up with my wife. Eat strawberries from her belly button and fuck her until we whip cream...

But that day ain't today.

Because right now, we're broke, and the cost of strawberries have almost doubled in just the couple years we've been married.

Everything else at the grocery store has doubled, too.

I set my hat on the side table and grin at my wrecked living room.

My wife isn't lazy. She's not a slob, either. But my son is a fucking psycho, and she spends all her time chasing him.

She worked hard on a degree that she's yet to use, because I wanted a son more than I wanted her to test out her shiny new credentials.

Condoms are expensive, and maybe I didn't pull out as fast as she wanted. She might not have been quite as excited as I was at first, but it happened anyway.

Voila, my twenty-two-year-old wife was carrying my child.

Power surges in a man as he watches the woman he loves growing plump with his child. It's not my fault the universe likes to test us with an eleven-pound first timer who came out with jumping beans up his ass.

As soon as he's old enough, as in, next year, I'll start working with him in the yard. A little training, a little *kata* oughtta wear him out.

Teach the kid some skills, teach him some discipline, and he'll stop tackling his mom.

Silently, I sit my wallet down, and place my keys inside my hat to muffle the sound. Moving down the hall on my tiptoes the way a man of my size should never do, I creep with a crazy grin on my face and sweet anticipation for who I'm about to see.

I live my life waiting to see them.

All day, I work and look forward to dinner with my wife and son.

All night, I stack shelves and count the minutes until I can come home and crawl into bed beside the most beautiful woman in the world.

Bobby's up before the birds, but that's okay, because the earlier he wakes, the more time I spend with him before I'm off again and the clock resets.

If I was working just for myself, it wouldn't be worth it.

But I'm working for them. Every single cent I earn is for them.

Totally worth it.

"Alright, baby." Nelly's sweet voice carries into the hall and has my smile turning up a few extra degrees. "That's it. Now you can pee."

"Boys have got a doodle, girls have a 'gina."

"Yes," she groans. "I know."

"Daddy's got a doodle."

She sighs. "Yes, he does."

Yeah, I do.

"Catch me, Mommy."

"One second, baby. Sit on your bottom and wait till Mommy finishes tidying up."

I stop at the doorway and peek around the corner. Bobby stands on the rickety old change table I took off the pile of trash at the top end of our street.

It needed three new screws and a new mat for the top.

Saved ourselves twenty-bucks this way.

His chocolate eyes – exactly like mine – light up when I stick my tongue out. "Daddy!"

"Yeah, honey." Distractedly, Nelly folds his clothes by the dresser. "Daddy'll be home in a minute. We need clothes, first. It's rude to eat naked."

He's not naked. He's wearing a white cloth diaper with little pins that he'll likely undo and stab me with in the night.

"Daddy!"

"I'm just getting your shirt. Hold on a sec, baby."

"Catch me, Momma!"

"In a second, baby. Sit on your bottom before you fall."

I step into the room and drop a fast kiss on my son's lips as his body shakes with excitement.

Never in my life has anyone been so happy to see me until my son arrived. And I spend such little time with him, every time I'm here, he practically wets himself with giddiness.

I wink at Bobby, then leave him standing where he is and step up behind my wife. Fast as a flash, I take her hips in my hands and yank her back until my cock sits against her ass.

She tosses a red and blue striped shirt into the air with fright, but as soon as my breath is in her ear, she spins and smacks my chest. "Dammit, Bryan! You scared the crap out of me."

"Sorry, Bert." Diving in, I take her lips with mine as payment for working so hard. As payment for missing them.

My salary's for them.

Her lips are for me.

Her wildly beating heart grows more frantic as I lift her to the very tips of her toes and her arms wind around my neck.

There it is.

Payday.

She groans into my mouth and presses close until we touch from thigh to lips.

"Daddy! No."

I laugh into her mouth and tighten my grip around her torso. "Ignore him. He doesn't know what he's talking about."

Still playing with my tongue, but lowering back to her feet, her arms loosen until she's framing my face with her butt-cream-smelling hands. "Welcome home, Bry."

I smile and don't even freak at the familiar *bub-bump, bub-bump* of my heart breaking and healing in the space of two beats.

It breaks, because she's perfect.

It heals, because she's mine.

Shane Turdsky can go and fuck himself.

"It's so good to see you, Bert. I missed you all day."

Five years of marriage, and she still blushes for me. "I saw you at breakfast."

"Uh-huh. That was *ages* ago."

"Daddy!" Bobby's playful calls turn to a pissed off growl. My little boy *loves* attention. "Catch me!"

"In a second, Bud. Not finished seducing your mom."

"Bryan!" She smacks my chest. "Can you not?"

"What? He doesn't understand."

"But he will one day! Then what? We can't afford therapy."

I laugh against the soft skin behind her ear and pull her body in tight. "He'll be fine, Bert. I'll stop next year. He'll never remember."

"Daddy!"

"In a minute, Robert."

"Daddy, turn around!" His bare feet jump on the plastic change mat and make the slurp noise as sweaty skin leaves non-breathable material. "Daddy. Now!"

"Bud!" I spin to scold him for being impatient, but instead, I come eye-to-eye – for the shortest second – with eyes he got straight from me. Then he's gone as he body slams to the carpet the way a frat boy might belly flop into a pool.

Nelly lets out a squeak of fright. "Oh, shit! Bobby!"

CHAPTER 8

BRYAN

Sitting at the head of my dining table, I feel like a king as my son – my heir to a shitty, non-existent kingdom – sits two feet away with rolled toilet paper stuffed in his left nostril and a giant grin on his face.

He bashes a plastic fork on the already scarred and dented off-the-side-of-the-road table, and adds to the existing *personality*.

My wife moves around us, serving us the way I have dirty dreams about. I mean, subtract clothes, add heels, remove toddler son and banish him to his crib.

He might need duct tape to stay where he's put, but we manage often enough.

She's not wearing the garter or thong from my dreams, nor the heels or apron, but that's okay, because the stained sweats that show off the curve of her ass still turn me the fuck on when she bends in front of the oven to take out the meatloaf she lovingly made for her family.

"Did you guys have a nice day today?" I wait for Bobby's attention to come to me. "Did you have fun with Mommy?"

He slams the fork down and adds a dent to my table. "Momma did a wee."

I laugh. "She did a wee? Tell me more!"

"Oh, shut up." She whips me with a yellow hand towel as she brings the meatloaf to the table. "Bobby, no toilet talk at the table."

He giggles the way only a toddler can. "Momma did a wee."

"I did a wee today too, son. Don't you care?"

He cackles. "Daddy did a wee!"

"Can you stop saying wee!?" Nelly whips me a second time, but squeals with surprise when I hook her around the waist and drag her into my lap. Rosy cheeks, excited breath, wide eyes, she lays across my legs and stares up at me. "Stop talking about my peeing habits at the dinner table."

"Kiss me."

"Daddy, no!"

I grin. "Ignore him. He doesn't know what he's talking about." I lean forward and peck her lips. "He's strapped into his chair. We're good for a minute."

She snorts. "No. We're never good. He's a menace. Let me up."

"No. Kiss me, Bert. I waited all day for you."

She rolls her eyes. "You know, when I met you, I thought you were scary."

My head shoots back like she hit me. "Scary?" I never gave her reason to fear me.

She nods. "So scary. You were all about cracking skulls, racing cars, taking what's not yours."

"And now?"

"Now, I realize you're just a big wuss who likes hugs."

I grin. "Well, you're not wrong. I do like hugs, but only from you and B."

She smiles beautifully. "You don't even crack skulls anymore. Life is so dull."

I lean in and press my lips to hers. "That's because Shane Turdsky isn't here. No skulls need cracking."

Her beautiful eyes narrow. "His last name was Tosky."

"I don't give a damn what his last name is, because *yours* is Kincaid." I slowly lick from one corner of her bottom lip to the other. "Chantelle *Kincaid*."

Her eyes twinkle with fun. "Coolest name change ever, by the way."

"Right?" I stroke the bridge of her nose with mine. "You made my name worth something again, Bert. You made it worth a hell of a lot."

Taking a deep breath, I stare into her eyes with indecision. I came home to talk to her about something. Something kind of big. Something she might not be thrilled about. "Give me a kiss, then sit down and eat."

"Did you have a good day at work?" She's not in any hurry to leave my lap. And for as long as I don't scold my son for scratching designs into my table, he's happy, too.

"I did. Same as usual. But listen, I wanted to talk to y–"

"Uh oh." She shoots up in my lap. "What's wrong?"

"Nothing's wrong. I just wanted to talk–"

"You said 'but listen'. That's a big deal. And you *want to talk*. That means bad shit's going down. Tell me quick."

Taking a deep breath, I look to the popcorn ceiling and hold her tight. "Do you wanna sit and serve dinner, first? We can eat and relax."

"I can't relax till I know, Bryan! Come on, you know I can't take the suspense."

No. She can't. Not since her daddy turned up here with a .22 and a bottle of bourbon. Not since she had to wait for me at the hospital while they patched up my broken hand – a hospital visit we couldn't afford.

Not since we got the call that her daddy had drank himself to death and she'd inherited a shitty, dilapidated house that she insisted would be bulldozed before her daddy was buried.

It's what she wanted.

So I made it happen.

Now we have empty land with a *'For Sale'* sign on it seven hundred miles from where we live, but an economy that means no one's buying shit. Especially not empty blocks of land.

"Bryan! Tell me."

"Are you happy here, Bert?" I look around the small apartment. "Here. In this place. In this city."

She looks up and follows my gaze, but inevitably, her eyes come back to mine. "Of course. I'm happy wherever you are."

I pull her in tight and press a kiss to her brow. "I love you. But now answer that question and only consider this apartment, this city. Take me out of the equation."

Her face drains white. "I will not take you out of the equation! You *are* the equation, asshole. You're not leaving me, Bryan Kincaid. I'll lace your dinner and chain you to our bed before you leave."

My eyes go to the ceiling. How is it I made her fall in love with me? How did I get her to fall *this* in love with me?

Whatever it was, I'd do it again and again and again.

Bringing my eyes back down and my hand to her beautiful face, I stroke my thumb beneath her eye – just because she doesn't work outside the home doesn't mean she's not tired. We're both exhausted at the end of every day. And when I crawl into bed in the middle of the night, exhausted but craving her body more than I'd crave my next breath, she always obliges, because we need each other like we need air.

She's tired. She hardly wants to be touched anymore, because she always has a stinky toddler climbing on her. She's as exhausted as I am, but she never says no.

She never denies us the chance to be joined.

"I love you, Bert. I'll never be out of your equation. When I'm fifty, sixty, a hundred and three, I'll still be in your equation."

"Please get to the point." Taking my hand and pressing it to her chest, her eyes hold mine. "Can you feel that? You're making me nervous. I can't handle it right now."

"I got a call at the garage today."

Biting her bottom lip, she nods.

"It was from Geo."

Her body tenses. "Is he okay? What's wrong?"

I smile. She cares about my best friend, despite the fact she hardly knows him. She knows I love him, and therefore, she loves him. "He's fine. He misses us. Misses B."

"He's never met Bobby."

I nod. "Exactly. He wants us to come home."

Her head tilts to the side. "Home?"

"Yeah, back home. He said he's got a job waiting for me. An apartment big enough for all of us. He wants to know our son. He wants us back."

"You wanna move?"

I stroke my thumb over the delicate flesh of her chest. "Only if you do. I won't go anywhere without you, and I won't make you go anywhere you don't want to go." I press my lips to her forehead. "I promised I'd follow you anywhere. That offer never expires, so this is your decision. I won't get mad if you say no."

She nods and turns to watch Bobby gouge our table. Naked except his diaper. Hair growing into his eyes. Broad chest he got straight from me.

She looks back to me. "Do you want to move?" She nods before I can answer. "You do, otherwise, you never would've brought it up."

"I would like to be near my best friend again. But it's not a big deal. If you're happy here, then we stay here."

Again, she nods and goes back to watch Bobby. "Maybe you need all the facts, first."

My eyes narrow at her doomsday tone. "What facts, Bert?"

"Moving is hard work. It's expensive. Geo's a full day's drive away. That's a lot of gas. A lot of hauling."

"Get to the point, woman."

"Bobby." She waits for his playful eyes to snap up. "Do you remember our surprise for Daddy?"

"What?"

She snickers. "Look at me, baby. What did we do today?"

"Momma did a wee."

Shaking her head, she leans back against my chest. "I did a wee."

"Is that your surprise?" I whisper in her ear. "Because, I mean, I can celebrate that if you need me to. I can get on board. I know staying home with a one year old can be a little... under-stimulating."

She elbows me in the stomach, but that's nothing on how her next words wind me. "I'm pregnant, Bry."

Heart. Splat.

Heart. *Soar!*

"You peed... You're pregnant. Oh!" I bounce her in my lap to bring her face around. "You did a pregnancy test! Bert, you're pregnant?"

She rolls her eyes. "I know you do it on purpose. I know you know how to pull out on time. The two times you're all *'oh damn, baby. I'm sorry.'* Two times I start puking around ten in the morning."

"You're having another baby?" I press my lips to hers. "You're making me another baby?" I stroke her still flat tummy. "Fuck, woman! You're having my baby?"

She laughs softly. "I am. I started puking yesterday. You *forgot* to pull out about five weeks ago – I marked it on the damn calendar. I knew what you were doing. I went to the doctors today, Bobby watched me pee into a little cup. We're having another monster."

"You're having another baby!" I stand and take her with me. The rickety dining chair slams to the floor and reduces Bobby to a giggling mess. He claps his hands and stabs his own palm with the fork. "I totally did it on purpose! Oh my God, you're making me another baby." I press a kiss to her lips.

"I don't know why you did that, Bryan. You work three jobs. Three! You work so hard, and now you're going to add another mouth to feed."

"Making a family is bigger than our bank balance. We're making our future, Bert. Our legacy. Who gives a fuck if I need to pick up an extra job?"

"I do!" She pokes my chest. "I married you because I kinda like you. I'd like to see more of you, not less." Her eyes water with emotion. "I miss you all day. I want you to be able to rest. I don't want you to worry as much as you do."

"Hey." I swipe away her tears. "Are you sad we're having a baby? Because I didn't mean to make you sad."

"I'm not sad about the baby. I'm sad that this will make you worry more. You need to relax. You need to be able to sit down one day and look around and enjoy all the things you work for."

Sitting her on the edge of our shitty table while Bobby's boredom starts to take over, I step in and pull her legs up to wrap around my hips. "Every time you smile; that's me enjoying. Every time we make love; that's me relaxing. Every time Bobby does the doodle dance and falls to the floor in a pile of giggles, that's me justifying my hard work. I don't resent working, Bert. As long as I get to come home to you every day, it's worth it."

"Bryan..." She sighs. "Five years has flown," she clicks her fingers, "like that. So fast. I don't want you to stop and breathe only on your birthdays, and realize you blinked, got another year older, and wonder what it was all for."

"I never wonder. I know what I live for. *Who* I live for." I press a kiss to her lips. "Let's move home, Bert. We can share apartment expenses with Geo for a bit. He told me I'd be on fifteen dollars an hour there. I'm only on twelve, here. That'll open things up for us. It's cheaper to live there. We'd be better off. Then I can get *one* extra job on top and we'd be ballin'."

She giggles through snotty tears. "Ballin'. I don't think we're the ballin' type of people, Bry. We're just us."

"And I love us. Exactly the way we are. If you want to stay, then we stay and you'll never hear another peep about it again, but if you're not opposed to it, I'd really like to go home. We have a new baby on the way. Geo's garage will pay us double what I'm on now—"

She rolls her eyes. "From twelve an hour to fifteen is not double. It's more like..." She shrugs. "I don't know. A quarter? I didn't get nearly as many A's in math as I told my daddy."

I cup her face. "He's gone now, Bert. Going home doesn't mean going back to him. He can't hurt you, and he can't hurt B or the baby." Her asshole daddy fucked her up bad. He beat her. Tormented her. Had her walking on eggshells her whole damn life.

He's the only person I couldn't protect her from... until I could.

"He's gone, Bert. We could go back to be with our friends. Put down some roots. This place is just temporary for us." I point to the bare wall. "There's a reason why you haven't put any pictures up. Five years, Bert. No photos."

"Because we're renting. Not allowed to put nails in the walls."

With a raised brow and gentle hands, I stroke her cheek. "There are eleven nails in that wall alone. They were there before we moved in. There are three nails, and a hole where a nail was over there." I point with my chin only. "You're not settling in, because this isn't your home. I want walls of photos. Millions of photos. I want memories on the walls and family to smile at me in every room. Tell me where to make a home for you. I'll do it. I'll do anything you want. You just have to tell me."

"I want to make you happy."

I smile. "You make me happy by existing. You don't have to do anything else except make my babies and tell me how to make your life better."

Her eyes flash with panic. "Jesus. I won't have to have another eleven pound baby, will I? That hurt so bad."

I grit my teeth. "I'm sorry. Truly I am. It's the Kincaid genes. Broad shoulders. We're fighters. You knew that going in."

She sniffs and looks down. "We can move, Bry. I don't mind."

I pull her face up. "You *don't mind*? Or it would make you happy? Because I don't want you to settle. I want you to actively make choices that'll make your life happier."

Biting her lip, her hands come up to hold my forehead against hers. "I *want* to move. Let's go home."

"Yes!" I lift her from the table and bring her lips to mine. Her arms instinctively wrap around my neck. Her legs around my hips. "You make me happy, Bert. You said yes. You married me. You make my babies. This is happiness for me."

Nodding, she rests her forehead against mine and scratches her nails against the back of my head. "Please lord, give us a calm baby. I love my son, Bry. But if we get two of them, they'll kill us both."

Turning, we stop and watch Bobby sitting on the table with fists full of cooled meatloaf.

"He's yours," I declare. "I want the next one."

CHAPTER 9

BRYAN

Two weeks, fourteen more puking sessions, two poops in the bath, and twelve hours of driving our packed to the brim car halfway across the country with a whiny toddler and a carsick wife, we drive across the train tracks leading back into town, and like this place gives us life, all three of us take a deep breath as we roll onto Main street, then we let it out like a cleanse.

This is home.

This is where I met her.

This is where I saw her for the first time.

This is where I declared her mine before she ever knew I existed.

Home is where the heart is?

Nelly Kincaid, formerly Chantelle Robertson, *is* my heart.

My home is wherever she is.

"It's like nothing's changed." Face-aching smile, Nelly stares into every storefront we slowly pass. "Jonah's is still here." She turns to me with a grin. "You know, his son asked me out one time in high school."

Playful anger in the back of my throat, I hum, "Just like old times... Heads are gonna meet the bricks."

She laughs and smacks my thigh, but she's fooling herself if she thinks I don't expect it. If she thinks I wouldn't shoot my hand down and clasp hers.

Bringing it to my lips, I nibble on her knuckles. "We haven't been here since the day you turned eighteen." I glance her way. "You weren't married yet. But you are now. Seems to me, I better make up a sign for the yard or something. *Mine, all mine.*"

She smiles and lays her head back against the headrest. "No need for signs. People knew I was yours before I knew I was yours."

"Yeah they did."

"Oh!" She sits up with a wide grin. "I wonder if Shane's still around? He's probably still waiting for me to turn up to dinner. We should catch up."

Pulling a U-Turn in the wide street, I head back the way we come.

"What are you doing?" Frowning, she turns and looks back to Main. "Where are we going?"

"Leaving before I kill Shane Turdsky. Fuck it. Geo can come to us."

"No!" She laughs and turns back to the front. "Stop. Turn around and go back. I will divorce you if you make us drive all the way back again."

"No Turdsky, woman."

"I was kidding! Geez, Bry."

I know she was. I know she's blind to other men. But it's my role to play; gruff and possessive. It's who she married. It's who she loves.

The problem is, the woman I married is ridiculously beautiful, and completely oblivious to the hungry gaze of every man she passes.

Turning the car around in a wide arc on the almost empty street, Bobby giggles, and Nelly's poor face turns green. "Don't do that anymore, Bry. Let's just park and get out before I hurl."

"Sorry, babe. Two minutes and we'll be there. Promise."

"No Shane. I'm sorry for teasing."

I take her hand and bring it to my lips. "I know. I was playing, too. Let's go crash Geo's place. Let Bobby tear it up, and make Geo watch him for ten minutes while I fuck you and make you forget you're not feeling well."

The fact she's pregnant means I get nine months – well, seven, now – where I don't have to be careful. Where I can come inside my wife. Where I don't have to spill my seed between her tits.

Not that I don't enjoy that, too.

"Can you stop saying those things in front of him? He's going to remember."

I look in the rearview mirror and watch my son toss little brick blocks out the window like they were a trail of bread crumbs.

Jesus Christ.

I'm gonna have to come out later and collect the damn things. I can't do it now. My poor green wife will kill me if I stop and start and keep swinging the car around.

"He won't remember, Bert. He's not listening to us." I pull around the end of Main and head toward Geo's apartment. "Are you excited?"

She shrugs easily, but I know she's nervous.

It's been a long time since we were last here.

We're not teenagers anymore.

I'm a married man.

A dad.

Soon to have another baby.

Shit's changed since I last knew my best friend.

Pulling into the parking lot out front of Geo's apartment block, I switch off the ignition and turn in my seat. Meeting Nelly's eyes, I pull her shaking hand into my lap. "Hey. This'll be great. I promise."

She nods shakily.

"You trust me, right?"

She nods again and traps her bottom lip between her teeth.

I frown and squeeze her hand. "Better say it more confidently than that, Bert. You're pissing me off."

With a shaky smile, her eyes finally meet mine. "I trust you. I've always trusted you."

"Alright, that'll do." Whipping my hand behind her head and pulling her in close, I don't stop until her lips clash with mine and her breath scorches down my throat.

She groans into my mouth, but green or not, unwell or not, nervous or not, she kisses me back the way she always has.

All there.

All encompassing.

Passionate. And so fucking mine.

"Daddy!" A plastic brick hits the side of my head. "No!"

Pulling back with a smile, I shake my head and press my hand to Nelly's stomach. "Make me a little lady. Make her not a brute. Make her a daddy's little princess that would never throw shit at her daddy's head."

She snickers and covers my hand with hers. "Whatever it is, it's already decided. Too late now."

Leaning forward for one more kiss before my son breaks out of his car seat Incredible Hulk style, I take the liberty of biting her bottom lip before she does it. "We'll keep trying. I could go on forever."

She smiles. "Let's see what we get, first. It's not your vagina they're tearing up, so stop writing checks I can't cash."

I chuckle against her lips. "Say vagina again. It turns me on."

She smacks my chest and turns away to open the car door. "Everything turns you on, Bryan. It's disgusting how much regular shit turns you on."

"Peaches look like asses, baby!" I climb out and move to unclip Bobby. "Bananas look like dicks. *Small* dicks, but dicks nonetheless. How do you expect me not to rock a boner when peaches and bananas sit in the bowl together?"

She slams her door and turns to pin me with a glare. "You're disgusting."

"Vacuum cleaners are literally suckers. How'm I supposed to watch you vacuum and not think of you sucking my dick?"

"Bryan!" She snaps her chin toward my giggling son. "Stop!"

"And when Barbie and GI Joe are in the same toybox... Baby, how do you expect me not to make them hump? I'm a man! That's what men do."

Shaking her head, she walks to the trunk and begins pulling cases out. Tearing Bobby from his seat and holding him like a football, I rush around to stop her. "No. I got it."

She rolls her eyes. "I'm not an invalid, Bryan."

"You're my wife. I'm a man; we literally just covered this. And you're carrying my baby. I got the cases."

"Fine." With a huff, she drops her hands to her hips. "Come to Mommy, B. I'll take him."

I scoff. "No way. He's easily thirty pounds. I've got him, too."

"Oh my God!" She stomps her foot. My very soon to be twenty-four year old wife of almost six years literally stomps her foot like a toddler. "I'm not a child, Bryan. I can carry a suitcase. I can carry my son."

I lean forward and smack a noisy kiss on her lips. "Shush. Your sass is showing. Put it away."

"I'll hurt you, Bryan Kincaid." I swear, she's *this* close to blowing smoke out of her ears. I know she's using this shit as a distraction from her nerves. She used to use Shane the fuckface as a barrier. But now she can't do that, so she'll use sass instead. "Give me something to carry, Bryan. Right now."

"Carry my dick if you want, Bert. It's exhausting carrying that sucker around all day."

"Oh, for God's sake. Forget it." She turns on her heels and moves along the path with her purse slung over one shoulder and a slight duck legged walk.

My pregnant girl's busting for the toilet.

And she's hormonal.

We've played this game before. She'll cool down around the second trimester.

Then when she hits that raging third, gives birth, waddles for a few weeks, finally turns to me and says she forgives me for what I did to her body, we'll make love again, then I'll try for the hat trick.

She won't be mad once she gets used to the idea of three Bobbys.

"Come on, Bud." With Bobby under one arm, and two cases clutched in my right hand, I follow Nelly along the path to the same apartment Geo always lived in. As I pass the *'For Lease'* signs near the front mailboxes, I raise a brow and consider.

We can't live with Geo forever. But an apartment this close to his would be cool.

Close enough, he could watch over my family when I work at night.

Far enough that he won't hear us fucking when I'm home.

I follow her into the shitty foyer with tiles at least three decades old, past a broken-down elevator with a *'do not use'* sign, and up three flights of stairs. By the time we reach the top, I reconsider my resistance to sharing the load.

My son hangs like dead weight, red faced from gravity, but lulled into relaxation from the climb. His diaper is full and desperately in need of a change. His hair won't stop growing. His knee is all skinned up from walking to the park yesterday.

My son has no fear.

Refuses to slow down.

Gives no fucks for what anyone says.

He makes me proud.

Stopping at 334, with a shaking hand and hesitant eyes, Nell turns back to me, but her fist taps the hollow door and has Bobby's relaxed body turning to full alert.

"Cool it, Bud. Lay back down."

"Home?"

"Yeah, but this is Uncle Geo's place. So we gotta be cool. No forks on the table. Actually," I meet Nell's eyes, "no forks at all."

She nods. "It's safer that way. We don't want him to stab Geo and get us kicked out."

I laugh at the thought.

Geo wouldn't kick us out, but he'd probably stab *me* with a fork as payback.

Unlatching one chain, then a deadlock, I scoff at the uselessness of Geo's security. His door's so flimsy, I *know* it'll have a Bobby shaped hole in it within a week.

I'll need a third job to pay for a sturdier door.

The timber swings open, and like no time has passed between the last time we saw each other and now, I come eye to eye with my best friend and his big stupid grin. "Bry! Fuck me, son!" Stepping in so fast, Nelly sidesteps to avoid being bowled over, Geo throws his arms around my neck and squeezes so hard, he crushes my ribs against my lungs. "You're a sight for sore eyes, Bry. Holy shit, I missed you."

Stepping back, he turns to Nell and pulls her in close and crushes her like he crushed me, despite the fact they never had a hugging relationship before.

Everything went down so quick back before we married.

We weren't together.

Then we were.

Two days later, we married and got outta dodge.

"You look amazing, Nelly. Oh my God, I'm so happy to see your faces."

Shell-shocked, she steps back, but he hardly notices as he turns back to me with lit eyes and glances down at a not at all relaxed Bobby in my arms. "No fucking way. It's a little Bryan!"

Nelly's gonna kill me if he doesn't stop swearing so much.

Clapping his hands together as though to warm them, Geo's eyes flick between mine and my son's. "Can I hold him? I wanna meet the little dude."

Laughing, I drop my bags to the floor, since this rude-ass hasn't invited us in yet, and picking Bobby up properly, I bring him to sit on my hip. "Bobby. This is Daddy's friend, Geo. Geo, this is my little buddy. He's my best friend, now. You've been bumped."

Geo's snake-eye dimples pop playfully. "I don't even care. Look at him!" He turns to Nell. "It's like you incubated, but he's all Bry."

She laughs nervously. "Yeah, you're telling me. Maybe I'll get lucky second time around."

"You guys are gonna go back again?"

"Actually." I grin like a fool. "We already did. You need to be more careful when you hug my wife, asshole. That's my kid in there."

"Shit!" Excitedly, he spins and pulls her back into his arms. My poor bride is simply a ragdoll for him to push around. Her cheek smooshes when he kisses it. Her teeth grit when he squeezes her tight. Her toes come off the floor when he lifts her. "You guys! I'm so psyched for you."

Taking his shoulder in my hand, I yank him back. "In fact, you can just stop hugging her altogether."

He laughs and comes back toward me for a hug. "I'm so fucking proud of you, man. Look at this! You've got a family. Your kid's badass. Look at his eyes; he's got attitude."

"He's got so much fucking attitude, Geo. He scares me."

Barking out a laugh, he reaches forward and takes Bobby without asking a second time.

A lot of kids might freak about that. Some kids might burst out in tears and cry for their mommy. But not Bobby. He smacks Geo in the face and giggles like a fool.

"Hi Bobby. I'm Geo, and I'll be your best friend, too."

"Geee-ooooo."

"Yeah, exactly!" Proud as a father, he turns on his heels and leaves Nelly and me standing at the front door to collect our shit and come in.

"Geo, that's my name. Can you speak much, kid? How many words do you know?"

I shrug in answer and cart our bags inside. "He does pretty good. Bert's always at home working on sight cards and shit." I smile as she closes the front door nervously and follows me in. "Gotta put her degree to use as much as she can."

"You can read already, Bobby? You're smart, huh?"

He can't read. But he can talk well enough for his age.

"Did you have a big drive today? Are you tired?"

He shakes his head. "Momma did a wee."

"Bobby!" Nell's face burns red, but Geo simply throws his head back and laughs.

"This is gonna be fun. Kids always tell the truth. Tell me all your secrets, kiddo. I wanna know everything."

Smiling and showing off a not yet complete set of small square teeth, Bobby's eyes twinkle with fun. "Peaches wook wike asses."

"Oh my God!" Groaning, Nelly steps under my arm and buries her face in my chest. "I told you he was paying attention, Bryan."

CHAPTER 10

NELLY

"I invited some friends over for a few drinks." Geo pokes his head into the kitchen with a rueful smile. "It won't be wild or anything. I just wanted to welcome you guys back, you know?"

I clean the last of the water from the sink and wipe my hands on the towel. "It's okay. This is your place, Geo. We're just crashing."

"No, not just my place anymore." He steps into the kitchen and leans back against the doorjamb. "You guys are paying rent. You clean a hell of a lot more than I do. You cook every night."

"My cooking sucks."

He laughs. "It totally sucks, but you're trying. I see your recipe books. And you make a mean steak, so I'm not complaining."

"My daddy was a meat and potatoes guy, so that's all I know."

He shrugs. "I honestly don't care. Food in my belly is food in my belly. You won't ever hear me complain. And I've never heard Bry complain, either. Even if you served up rat poison on the daily, he'd still eat it, because he wouldn't wanna offend you. Then he'd go take care of spewing in private. That man is stupid in love with you."

I laugh. I know this already. Bryan tells me every day what he thinks. He always has. But someone on the outside saying it has my stomach jumping pleasantly. "He's kinda obsessed. He's the first and only person in the whole world who loved me like that."

Crossing his arms, Geo's eyes go to his boots as he smiles. "Even before you guys got together, you know, during his stalking phase..."

I burst out laughing.

On paper, when not in context, it's totally creepy how obsessed Bryan was, and still is, with me. But in my heart, in my gut, it's exactly right.

"... Even when you weren't together, it still felt like you were. I've been looking at you guys forever, and every time I meet a girl, I compare what I feel for her to what Bry feels for you. So far, no one has stacked up."

My brows pull in tight and my hands nervously work the towel in knots. Bobby tears between us completely naked and throws a Matchbox car to the floor. Thank God Geo's place is mostly tile. "You compare it to us? But..." I look him up and down. "You know..."

He grins playfully. "Spit it out, Nelly. If you're gonna offend me, you better own it."

"You like them... you know, fast and loose. It's apples and oranges." My eyes pop wide when I realize how offensive I'm being. "I mean, it's not that—"

He chuckles. "It's okay. You can say it. I don't cry easily. I do like them..." he clears his throat, "fast and loose. But that's only because I haven't found my forever girl yet. I want real. I want what Bry has, but while I wait..." He scrunches his nose. "The not-so-pure women are a fun distraction."

I purse my lips sarcastically. "It's been six years since we left, Geo. Maybe you're not looking hard enough."

He shrugs. "I thought I did. Maybe. But she ditched town. She was kinda a hybrid. Fast and loose and fun, but she also felt kinda real. So maybe there is such a woman that has both." He shrugs. "Didn't find her yet."

"Maybe you'll meet her at your party."

He barks out a short laugh. "That's right. I forgot why I came in here. The party. It's not a *party*. Just a couple friends. Do you mind?"

"Nope. I don't mind. We're not here to inconvenience you. You want a party in your home, then you can have one. Don't make it stupid big, keep the psychos out and away from my son. No drugs. And we've got a deal."

"Seriously, it's not a party. Just a get together for us guys. Just the original crew from down Piper's Lane. Not a party."

I nod confidently. But inside, I'm shivering. "No drugs. No psychos. If they wake Bobby too many times, you're all dead to me."

He grins and pushes off the wall. "Deal. I'm going back to work now."

"Why'd you wait for Bry not to be here to ask? Why didn't you just ask him at work?"

He turns back with a smile. "Because you would've deferred to each other. He woulda said it's up to you. You would've said yes just to make him happy. I wanted a real answer, so I divided..." His head cocks to the side. "Devode? Devud?" He chuckles softly. "I got you apart to get a real answer. But I gotta get back to work now. Catch ya, Nell."

"Geo, wait!"

He spins back one last time. "Yeah?"

"Is he happy there at the garage? He's eating, sitting at break times, not working himself to death?"

He grins knowingly. "What do you think?"

"I think there's a reason you're here right now at lunch time, and he isn't. I think he's working through lunch and smashing down his peanut butter sandwiches while he works."

He taps the wall with his knuckles. "And there you have it. Times that by six days a week, an hour a day, that's almost a whole extra day of pay he's bringing in for you guys."

I get why he does it. I love that he works so hard for us. "I worry that he's always working so hard. When does he get to rest?"

Geo watches on with horrified fascination as I duck forward and whip the mop bucket off Bobby's head as he passes through. "When do *you* stop, Nell?" He points at my son. "You've been here a week. Your kid never sleeps more than an hour at a time. You're baking another. You serve your man, and now that you're here, you serve me, too. You never eat your own dinner when it's hot, because your kid would rather take chunks outta the table with his spoon than eat."

My heart pounds with anxiety. "Does Bobby bother you? The not sleeping. The table. I know he's a handful." *Please don't kick us out. Please don't add more stress to Bryan's workload.*

He laughs softly. "He doesn't bother me one bit. He wakes, but he ain't my problem, so I go straight back to sleep. The table came off the side of the road. The spoons came from the local Salvation Army. I love having you guys here, so don't freak about that. I'm just saying, you're worrying about your man changing sparkplugs and hauling wood, but *you* don't sleep, either. When was the last time you sat down? Legit question." When I shrug, his lips come up arrogantly. "You sat for thirty seconds last night, until Bobby almost peeled his own fingernail up with the spoon. Then you stood and busted your back as you leaned over him."

"I sat when Bryan pulled me into his lap."

"And now you know why he's always pulling you into his lap. All I'm saying is, this ain't the first time I've had this conversation, but last time was with Bry, about three hours ago, and he was worrying about *you.* He was asking me if I knew of anything else going for weekends. He wants more work. More money. He wants to buy you all the pretty things, Nell."

"I'd rather spend my time with him than wear jewelry."

He grins. "Which is why I lied and said I didn't know of anything else."

The following Saturday night, almost two weeks after we moved back to town, I stand in the room Bryan and I share with Bobby, with his crib pressed up against our bed, and the other side of the bed pressed up against the wall.

This apartment is small. It's enough; beggars can't be choosers, and I'm not complaining.

But it's small.

I stand in front of the mirror and smooth my dress over my tiny little pudge belly. I barely showed with Bobby until I was closer to five months along, but closing in on ten weeks now, I definitely have a bump. Second time around, my stomach isn't quite as firm as it used to be, and bloat definitely has me popping out in a sweet little belly that makes me smile.

It makes Bryan smile, too.

And when I walk into a room, when his eyes are on me, *only* on me, and his plump lips turn up into that smug grin of his, that's how *I* rest. That's how I relax.

Rubbing a hand over the soft blue fabric of my summer dress, I watch Bobby in the mirror as he stands in his crib and slams his rarely-used pacifier against the bars.

I give him a pacifier every night, but he thinks it's a toy.

He never uses it for the reason it should be used. And now that I've weaned him off my boobs and onto bottles, he's pissed.

My son wants to make his own decisions in his own time.

Too bad, kid.

Nervously pushing my long hair behind my ears as voices penetrate the walls from the living room, I take a deep breath and turn back to the crib. "Time to lie down now, Bobby. Time for sleep."

"Not tired."

Of course not. "Too bad, baby. It's eight o'clock. It's late. Time for sleep."

"Momma sleep?"

"Mommy's gonna go out and watch TV with Daddy, first. Then we'll come to bed."

"Soon?"

I lean over the crib and pull his face forward until our lips meet. "Soon, I promise. Sweet dreams, baby. I'll be just out the door."

"Back soon?"

I nod and help him lie down. Pushing his stuffed teddy under his arm, and the pacifier into his spare hand, I pull the thin sheet up and tuck him in tight. "Back soon, baby. I need you to lie down and not climb out, okay? No climbing out. I'll be just outside the door. I won't go far, I promise." Kissing my fingers, then pressing them to lips that are identical to his father's, I smile. "I love you so much, Bobby. I promise some day we'll have our own big fancy house. You'll have your own room. And lots of toys. And a brother or sister. We have a whole life ahead of us. Are you excited?"

He has no clue what I'm saying, but since it's me saying it, he nods. "Yuh-huh. Excite."

"Good. But you have to sleep. To be big and strong, we need to eat and sleep." He's got the eating under control. My eighteen-month-old son literally eats more than me most days, but his sleep is awful. "Good night."

"Night, Momma."

I step into the hall a minute later and stop breathlessly when I find Bryan waiting against the wall with a twitching grin and playful eyes. He takes my hip in his hand instantly and pulls me close.

Pushing the long hair off my shoulder with his other hand, he leans in to pepper kisses along my already sensitized flesh. "I love you so much, Bert. Did I tell you that yet?"

I arch my neck to give him room.

Guests can be heard barely feet away at the end of the hall, but they don't come down here. It's just Bry and me all alone for a minute.

It was a good idea to move.

To combine living expenses with Geo.

But the trade off is never having alone time. Ever.

It's tempting to run out to the car and make out all alone, but neither of us would dare leave Bobby alone – even with Geo here. Not on a normal night. Especially not tonight when he has guests over.

Bryan is protective of me. He's careful, and thoughtful, and considerate.

But his devotion is on a whole other level when it comes to his son.

Falling off change tables, notwithstanding.

"You look so beautiful, Bert." His hand snakes down to my thigh and fingers the fabric higher. "Almost inappropriate for company, but I can't bring myself to make you change." He pulls back to look into my eyes. "It's easier to gouge their eyes out than it is to tell you to change from this pretty dress."

My face turns warm. Even after being together so long, his kind words affect me. "You bought me this dress."

He nods. "For your birthday last year. I know."

"So, I'm wearing it for you."

"Yeah?"

"Mmhmm. And I was thinking, since you're not working tonight, and it's Sunday tomorrow and you're not mowing lawn anymore…"

"Uh-huh."

"Well, we can sleep in till Bobby wakes up."

"So, four a.m. then?"

I laugh and turn my face to kiss his palm as it snakes up to stroke my hair aside. "If we're lucky, he'll sleep later than four."

"What are you thinking, Bert?" His dick pulses against my belly. He knows. "You got something planned for me?"

"Uh-huh. I was thinking, it's eight now. We can hang with your friends as long as you want, but with any luck, they'll get lost by ten."

He laughs and presses a kiss to my temple. "Keep going... Depending on what you tell me, I could get rid of them right now."

I smile and lean into his strong body. "No point getting rid of them right this second. Bobby's still awake. But by ten, he might be out cold. Then we can go to bed and you can take this pretty dress off me."

"With my teeth?"

"Preferably."

He smiles. "I wonder what else I could do with my mouth..."

I shrug casually, but inside, my heart races and my underwear slick with want. "Your tongue knows what it's doing."

"You want me to use my mouth, Bert?" His head comes back. "I feel like maybe I should keep studying. Perfect my techniques."

I let out a shuddering breath. "You can practice on me."

"Preferably." He leans in and nibbles on my jaw. "I want you so much it hurts, Nelly. You have no fucking clue."

I lean around him and look down the hall. Still no one there. But voices are close. Leaning back into him, I take his hand and lift it between my legs until he reaches where my heart pulses at my core. We both groan as one.

"I do have a clue." My eyes snap shut as his fingers explore. "I want you so much, I'm ready to explode."

"Explode on my hand, Bert. Show me how much you want me." He pushes a digit inside and robs my body of breath. Leaning down, he takes my lips hungrily and presses his tongue against mine. "There's something they call the seven-year itch. We're at year six. Let's prove them wrong, Nell. Explode on my fingers and make me feel like a man."

My chest lifts and drops heavily as I try to catch my breath. "You're a man." My breath rushes out as his fingers work. "You're my man. All man."

"Mmhmm." He angles his body around to shield mine in case

anyone comes into the hall. "Come on my fingers, baby. You're preg-nant again. All sensitive and shit down there, huh?"

I nod breathlessly. "So sensitive."

"Perfect. Means you'll go off like a rocket. I want you to explode. And do it quietly."

"Bryan, I can't–" He curls his fingers until I collapse against his chest.

"Yes, you can. You saying we can't just makes me want to prove you wrong."

I'd only intended to show him what he does to me. The same way he presses himself against my belly to show me. I didn't expect him to bring me to the edge so quickly.

In the hallway of Geo's apartment.

Looking over his shoulder to check, then back to me with a dirty grin, he brings a second hand down to tap my clit. One single tap, one single plunge of an extra thick finger, has me burying my face against his chest and biting down to ride the wave as soundlessly as possible.

He rips out a low growl in my ear as I come on his hand. As I pulse against his fingers. As his broad palm catches my pleasure, and yet, liquid rolls down the inside of my thighs and tickles my ankle.

"Exactly like that," he breathes in my ear. "So fucking beautiful. So responsive. So *mine*."

I nod breathlessly and allow him to keep me on my feet. I'm weak like a baby and would slide to the floor if he let me.

But he wouldn't.

His strength and protectiveness – along with his wit and kindness – are the reasons I married him. The reason I made babies with him.

He thinks he's so in charge.

So smart.

His *'oh damn, baby. I'm sorry,'* comes *only* after I hold him to me. After I clutch at his back and drive him to the brink of insanity. He thinks he tricks me into babies. He thinks it's all on him.

But he can't know the powerful drive that sits in my heart, in my soul, to make more of him.

More babies.

More Bryan.

More Kincaids.

He's special. What we have is special.

I'd make a dozen babies with him if he asked, because who am I to tell the universe no to more Bryan Kincaids?

Exactly.

Pinning me to the wall and peppering kisses along my jaw, he pulls his strong hand from my panties and pats my dress back down. "Told ya we could do it."

I let out a breathless laugh and melt against the wall. "You sure did."

Lifting his hand to his mouth, he presses two fingers between his lips and cleans the shiny lubrication off with a soft hum of pleasure. "Delicious."

My eyes fight to close from pleasure.

"That's my appetizer, Bert." He leans forward and drags his flavored tongue along my bottom lip. "I'll get the rest in two hours. I promise, I'll get mine."

I let out a shuddering breath and work to not simply melt into the floor. "I wanna go to bed now." I want to feel his skin sliding along mine. I want to fall asleep with my ear over his heart the way we did on my eighteenth birthday.

The way we've slept every night since then; even if we don't go to bed at the same time. I have a permanently kinked neck because I sleep on his broad chest when he crawls into bed after midnight. I don't even care; it's totally worth it.

"Not yet." He drops a gentle kiss on the corner of my lips. "Let Bobby pass out. We'll go out. I'll get you a soda. Show my beautiful wife off. Two hours at the most, then we go to bed and finish what we started."

I look down at the solid length stretching his jeans. "What about you?" I reach out, but he grabs my wrist faster than any mortal should be able to move.

"Don't touch," he chuckles nervously. "Don't you fucking touch, or I might cry like a little bitch." He pulls me from the wall and pats my ass. "Go clean up. Get new panties. Come back out."

"But–"

His dark eyes are like one giant pupil. I can't see where the iris starts or the pupil ends. It's like looking into the eyes of a wild animal, and you *know*, don't trust it, for he *will* attack. "Run."

Together, we walk into the living room to find Geo sitting on the old, worn sofa, with a girl I don't know in his lap, her long legs hanging over the side of the couch, her heels pointing out sexily, and her breasts in Geo's face.

Literally.

If she had no top on, his lips would be nibbling on bare flesh.

I look to the right to find a vaguely familiar face, though I don't bother trying to place it.

Too many people at Piper's Lane.

Too many years ago.

Squeezing my hand gently, Bryan nods toward the friend and grins. "Bert, this is Reilly. Reilly, my wife, Chantelle. You may say hello. You may *not* hug her."

Geo barks out a laugh, but my face simply burns. After all these years, he still insists on peeing on my leg.

Stepping forward, I extend my hand. "Hey, Reilly. You can call me Nelly."

He doesn't stand, since another girl I don't know sits across his lap and refuses to let him up, but he smiles and leans forward to take my hand. "Nice to meetcha, Nelly. I remember you from school."

"You do?"

He nods. "I was one grade above you. A grade below these guys. I was friends with him, which means I knew who you were."

The girl on his lap scowls like a pissed off cat.

"I remember you from the races that one time."

He nods proudly. "Still go down there."

"You race?"

"Yeah. Won a new car last weekend."

"You *won* a car?" I turn to Bryan. "You told me you raced for money."

He pulls me into his chest and buzzes his stubble along my temple. "Different races. Different stakes. But the bet's laid out before you drive up. I raced for money most of the time."

"*Most* of the time? But not always?"

"Not always." He leads me to a love seat and pulls me into his lap. "I raced for pink slips one time. Won a brand-new Mustang."

"You won the Mustang?" I look from Bryan's face, to Geo's, to Reilly's. "It's like I don't even know you!"

Bryan chuckles. "How else do you think I got that car? I didn't pay for the damn thing, that's for sure."

"But what car did you have before that? What did you bet?"

He shrugs and accepts a cup of soda when Geo hands it over. Pressing it to my hands, he drops a kiss on my lips. "I had a '69 Camaro."

"Sexy car," Reilly adds.

"True. Sexy car," Bryan agrees. "But mine wasn't sexy. Mine was trashed. The paint was awful. The body was half rusted away. The seats were torn and the springs ripped my jeans more often than I could afford to replace them. But the engine was sparkling, so it won me a brand-new car. I gave the other guy my Camaro, since I had no use for it and no way to get it home if I took the Mustang." He flashes a fun smile. "And I was for sure taking his Mustang. First time I ever rode in a brand-new car. Possibly the last time, since we have better things to spend our money on now. There was no way I was passing it up."

"You came to school with that Mustang."

"Uh-huh."

"You were sixteen when you started at our school."

He nods. "Uh-huh."

"You took a man's brand-new car when you were sixteen? Jesus, Bryan! I swear, if Bobby's even half as naughty as you, I'm gonna flip my shit."

He winks and lifts my hand, but before the cup makes it to my lips, his eyes flip to Geo. "No alcohol?"

"Just soda, Bry. I knew you'd share with her."

The pettiest, cattiest little throat clearing has us looking up at the girl in Reilly's lap, and it takes the clueless fool entirely too long to catch on. "Oh! Shit. Ann-Marie. Bryan Kincaid. His wife, Chantelle, like you just heard. Maybe don't hug her, he has rules." Bryan smiles. I smile. Geo and his date smile. The final woman... does not. "Guys, this is Ann-Marie Page."

Geo's obviously already met her, so he simply goes back to biting his date's clothed nipples. Bryan peeks around me and nods in the way guys do.

Leaning half off Bry, his hands are the only thing stopping me from toppling to the floor as I reach out to shake her hand. "Nice to meet you, Ann-Marie."

She looks me up and down with a perfectly styled brow, but at least she takes my hand. "Hi, Chantelle."

Leaning back into Bry, I pull my legs up and work to pull my dress down modestly, but still curl in the way Bobby does to me. "You guys been dating long?"

She nods.

He nods. "About eight months, I think."

"Eight months?" My smile grows. "Wow. That's not eight hours. You guys are serious, huh?"

She nods.

He shrugs. "We're having fun. She's normally a lot chattier than this," he pulls her in close, "but she's not feeling so great this week."

I'm a horrible person, because instead of equating her sour mood to not feeling well, my mind instantly jumps to Bobby and how mad I'll be if she gets him sick.

I never used to be a germaphobe until I had a kid.

You spend one single night with a blocked-up baby who already doesn't sleep, and you learn fast; colds are the devil.

"I feel fine," she throws out casually. "Just have nothing to say."

My brows pull in tight.

Reilly's eyes crackle with something akin to anger, but when she climbs out of his lap and excuses herself to the bathroom, he smiles when she turns back to watch.

As soon as she's out of sight, Bryan speaks up.

Of course he does.

"What the fuck, Reilly. What's her problem?"

He sighs and flops back into his chair. Lifting a bottle to his lips, he stares at the roof. "She was fun. She was cool. But..." He leans forward and peeks down the hall. "I want out, man. I need a safe house or something." He laughs. "I didn't invite her here. She pitched a fucking fit when I said I was going out without her."

Mimicking him, I look down the hall, but she's not coming back yet. "Do you live together?"

He scoffs. "Fuck no. She just came over. Told me what we were doing tonight. I told her I had plans. She told me *we* have plans."

I laugh and relax back into Bry's lap. "That'll teach you for hooking a crazy. And I was so excited, too. Bryan's *other* friends," I clear my throat and have Geo biting back a grin, "don't seem to bring the forever girls home. You said eight months. I was ready to start making dinner party plans with her."

"Oh, she's forever, alright." Bry laughs. "She's a fuckin' crazy.

She's yours forever, or she'll break your ankles and murder you in your sleep."

Barking out a laugh, Reilly flicks his bottle cap toward us. "Shut up, asshole. You ditch town without a peep, come back with a wife, a family, and you start bitching about my girl. Get the fuck outta here."

"You just said you were done, anyway. What do you care?"

He shrugs and sips his beer. "Dunno. I get off on arguing."

"But not with her." I laugh. "Are you a battered man, Reilly? Do you need help getting out? We're your friends. We can help."

He chokes on his beer and wipes a muscular arm along his chin. "Don't joke. This is how it begins. She'll start hitting soon."

I giggle and press a kiss to Bry's chest. "I sometimes hit."

He snorts. "Yup."

"I'd also murder you in your sleep if you left me."

He nods and plays with my fingers. "You're fuckin' crazy, Bert. I already knew that. But you're *my* kinda crazy. I wanna keep you forever, and ever, and ever..."

Reilly pokes a finger into his mouth and pretends to gag. "You guys are just so... fucking gross."

Geo snorts. "I gotta live with this shit. They're always making out, then I gotta make myself scarce and hide in my room like a virgin no-friends. Trust me, you'll be fine."

"Yeah. But he's gotta live with the crazy bitch, so really, who's got it worse?"

"Who you calling a bitch, bitch?"

Like fire ants sting every follicle on my head, sharp nails dig into my hair, and a strong hand tugs and snaps my neck back. My eyes meet hers – green, swimming, feral – for half a beat, before Bryan flies from the chair and pulls me from her; even at the expense of a large chunk of my hair.

She dives for us.

Like she's possessed by the devil, she lunges for my face with her teeth bared and her nails aiming for my eyes. "You don't get to talk shit about me unless you're gonna back it up, bitch!"

Reilly flies out of his chair and grabs Ann-Marie as she scratches at my face. Buzzing fills my ears and deafen me, and dots float in my vision as she slams an open palm across my face and pivots my head around.

Grabbing her around the waist, Reilly picks her up and spins her around, but her heeled foot snaps across my jaw with a painful crack that'll leave me with a nasty case of whiplash tomorrow.

Roaring like a wild animal as my body falls limp in his arms, Bryan holds me against him with one arm, then snatches Ann-Marie with the other and slams her against the wall.

Pinning her with a strong hand on her throat, veins bulge in his neck and his breath comes out like a pissed off bull. "Get. The fuck. Out."

"Bry!" Reilly pushes at Bryan's unrelenting arm. "Let her go, man!"

Nausea rolls in my belly and my jaw throbs. People speak around me. Shouted instructions, angry demands, a baby crying. But it all sounds as though I have water in my ears.

"Kincaid! Put her down!"

I've been hurt a lot in my life.

My daddy made it a fun weekly routine the way others might make church their thing, so by the time I was eighteen, I'd become used to it.

Conditioned, even.

It didn't hurt so much, because I was used to it.

But six years of pure gentleness from my loving giant has healed me... and left me unequipped for a fresh beating.

A single tap to my jaw has tears burning my eyes.

A single yank of my hair, something I endured almost daily as a kid, now sends me down a long tunnel almost like PTSD and sends my spotty vision to a cloudy black.

"Nelly?" With his hand still on her throat, Bryan's eyes come to mine. His mouth moves like he's shouting, but the air sits stale in my chest and my ears don't work. My lungs refuse to inhale. They refuse to exhale.

My body simply refuses to *do*.

"Baby! Hey!" Releasing the red-faced Ann-Marie into Reilly's waiting arms, Bry turns as my knees buckle and my brain starts swimming. His terror-filled eyes bore into mine. "Hey. You're safe now, baby. Are you okay?" His strong hand strokes my aching jaw.

Geo sprints to us from the front door and stops mere inches from my face.

A hand strokes my belly.

Another strokes my jaw.

A third squeezes my hand.

And a fourth presses over my chest to find my heart pounding.

The guys shout at me, they shout at each other, but their noise is just noise drowned out by the sounds of my father's rage. *"Next time you'll do as you're fucking told, bitch!"*

"You bring this on yourself."

"If you'd just keep the house cleaner..."

"If your mother was still here, Pumpkin..."

"Being a slut won't get Shane Tosky and his family to marry you, will it?"

"Bert! Come back now. Come back to me, baby. Geo, get my keys."

"No." I blink once, twice, three times to replace the image of my daddy with that of Bryan.

"Yes." He pats his pockets. "We're going to the hospital."

"No." I push away from Bry's arms, only to find myself lying flat out on the floor.

Did I fall? Did he lower me?

He's going to kill her.

Then he's going to kill Reilly.

"Momma?"

Snapping back to stark reality, back to real time, back to the now in all its clarity, I sit up like I was never hurt and catch Bobby as he throws his shaking body into my arms.

Bryan reaches out to take my son, to save me from my 'brute,' but like a raging bear, I spin and snap at his grabbing hands. "Don't touch him!"

Bobby screams in my face. He sobs, and fat tears dribble down his face and stop on a wobbling bottom lip.

How much did he see?

How much did he hear?

With renewed rage, I turn to Geo. "I told you not to let this shit hurt my son! I said you can't let it hurt him!" Standing alone and pushing hands away, I hug my baby to my chest and hold in a sob at the ache in my head. My vision swims and the room tilts, but without assistance, I stumble down the hall, into our room, slam the door, and collapse onto the bed with him in my arms. "Shh, baby."

"Momma cry." Bobby's fat fingers come up to stroke my aching jaw. "Momma sad."

"Mommy's okay, baby. I promise." I stroke his face the same way he strokes mine. She didn't touch my belly, I'm sure of it. I didn't fall, because Bryan would never let me fall.

My baby's okay. Everything's okay.

"Just gotta sleep it off."

"You fall down?"

"Mommy stubbed her toe." I smile, though it's weak. "Silly Mommy."

Bobby's shaky smile matches mine. His long hair hangs in chocolate eyes, and the moisture from his tears sticks strands to his lashes. "Silly Momma."

CHAPTER 11

BRYAN

War.

My body's at war.

Follow her.

Avenge her.

Reilly's V8 roars away down the dark street outside, and the *pop-pop-pop* of his souped up engine calls for me to follow.

He knows.

He *knows* if I had my hands on her right now, I'd hurt her.

I don't hit women... normally. But I'd hit that bitch.

"Bry!" Geo snaps his fingers in my face. "You want me to call an ambulance? What do you want me to do?"

When I don't answer, he slams his fist against my chest. "Bryan! Wake the fuck up, asshole. You want me to call an ambulance?"

I nod.

I look at the floor and nod.

I do the math in my head, but the hundreds and hundreds of dollars an ambulance will cost – money we don't have – barely registers in my mind. "Yeah, call an ambulance."

I jog down the hall as soon as my thoughts realign and crystalize.

Opening the bedroom door, I step into the dark room and barely stop myself from choking on failure at the sound of my world crying.

Both of them.

Quiet cries and jerky breath.

Blindly, I climb onto the bed behind Nelly and rest my face in the back of her neck. Gently, I place my arm over her hips and stroke her belly. "I'm so sorry, baby."

"She scared Bobby."

"Not scared, Momma."

She laughs, but it comes out more like a choking sob. "You're so strong, Bobby. So strong and brave. Go to sleep now, baby. Time for sleep."

As my eyes adjust to the dark, I watch her soft hand stroke his hair.

"Forgive me, Bert."

She stops breathing for only half a beat before she resumes. "Forgive you. What for?"

"For not protecting you. For letting her hurt you. You're my whole life, you and B and the new baby, and I let her hurt all three of you." I stroke patterns into her belly. "I'm so sorry."

Finally, so obvious now, that I didn't even realize she was holding back, Nelly relaxes into my chest and melts against me the way she has every other day of our marriage. "The baby's okay. She didn't touch my belly, she just pulled my hair. The kick was an accident."

None of it was an accident. Ann-Marie Page is a fucking psycho bitch. "Still." I bring my hand up, but freeze when she hisses at my fingers on her jaw. "I'm so sorry."

"It's okay." Neglecting Bobby's hair for only a moment, she reaches up and brings my hand to her lips. "It's just bruised. Nothing I haven't had before. I'm fine."

Sirens wail in the air outside. I hear them, because I'm expecting them, but it takes her twenty seconds longer to figure it out. Her body snaps straight in the space of a single heartbeat. "You did not call an ambulance!"

"I did. Geo did. We've gotta go in, Bert."

She spins in my arms so fast, Bobby whines at being jostled and neglected. "What the hell is the matter with you! We can't afford an ambulance. We definitely can't afford an ER visit. I'm fine!"

"Momma."

Spinning angrily, she sits up on the bed cross-legged and pulls Bobby into her lap.

A knock at the apartment door makes her snarl into the dark.

Then a knock at the bedroom door has her fiery eyes killing me where I lie. "Stupid move, Kincaid. So fucking stupid! Where's your brain?" Standing with Bobby in her arms, she strides to the door and flings it open before the EMT's break it in. "I'm fine! See, I'm standing, I'm talking, I'm fine. Please, leave and pretend you never came here. We can't afford you."

Helplessly, I look up from the bed as the EMT's stare her down.

As she stares them down.

As Geo watches from behind.

There was no right choice for me tonight.

Call an ambulance and spend every last cent we'd worked so hard to save.

Don't call and risk a concussion, or so much worse.

The only right choice was going to bed an hour ago when she asked.

I should've fucking listened.

CHAPTER 12

GEO

I pull up out front of Reilly's shitty apartment and slam the car door.

Running on adrenaline and rage after watching my best friend lose his fucking shit, after watching my best friend's wife get put down more brutally than a mongrel dog, I sprint the path toward his front door ready to smash it down and steamroll in to tell him what the fuck's up, but instead skid to a stop at the sight of him sitting on the front step with his face in his hands and his broad back fighting for breath.

Rage courses within me.

But so does compassion for a broken man.

But rage...

But his chest heaves.

But Nelly and the baby... "What the fuck, Reilly?"

His red rimmed eyes come up and meet mine. World weary after only two hours, pale faced and shaking hands, he looks up at me help-lessly. With my eyes only, I follow his arms to the very ends, until I stop on a long blue strip clutched between work stained fingers.

I'm a twenty-five-year-old man. Practically an old man.

A man my age comes to know what that strip is.

He also knows what those two little blue lines mean.

"You're choosing her."

Shaking breath, he drops his head into his hands and howls like a baby. "I have to, G. I won't leave my baby. Not for you. Not for Bry. Not even on Bry's kid's life."

CHAPTER 13

BRYAN

The wrench snaps away and slams down on my finger so hard it brings tears to my eyes.

Fucking tears!

"Motherfuck!" I spin and peg the heavy wrench across the garage, missing Geo's face by mere inches as he pokes his head up from beneath the hood of a '79 T-Bird.

He ducks again, though the wrench has already passed. "What the fuck, Bry? Jesus, you could kill a man tossing those things around."

I bring my hands to my face and scrub to try and reset my week.

My month, even.

I should've just gone to fucking bed when she asked.

Standing, Geo wipes greasy hands on a rag and steps toward me. "Talk it out, Bry. What's up?"

"Money. Fuckin' money!"

"Mo' money, mo' problems, bro."

Snarling, I spin until we're chest to chest. "This isn't a fucking joke, George! I'm broke. I can work the next two years straight, not spend a cent, and still be fuckin' broke!"

His smile turns to regret. "You got the bill from the ER?"

"Yup! She was right. She's *always* right." I swear, tears of failure burn my eyes. "I fucked up, Geo. I fucked up bad, and no matter how hard I work, I won't be able to pay it off and still feed my family." I slam my fist into the steel beam of the car lift. "I don't know how to dig my family outta this mess."

He sighs and rubs a thumb to his forehead, though that only leaves a smudge of grease where he scratched. "You're already working fifteen, sixteen hour days, Bry. You can't take on more and still keep your family."

"You think I don't know that? You think I enjoy not being with my wife and kid? Fuck, Geo. You spend more time with her than I do. You think I enjoy knowing that?"

He lets out a deep sigh. "You could maybe race again? A couple times. Race for slips. Win a few cars, sell them."

"And if I lose? Then my family's still in the hole. *And* I'll have no car to drive my pregnant wife to the hospital when she gives birth. Oh, and that's another thing! I gotta pull that money outta my ass this year, too!"

"Okay." He takes a deep breath like it's *his* life that's spiraled so far out of control. "Let's just... let's cool it and think."

"Fuck you and your calm shit, asshole." I shove him back a step. "Get the fuck outta my space."

"I'll spot you the money to race, Bry. You race, you win, you keep the cash."

I turn back sarcastically. "Oh, awesome! I race, I lose, I owe *you* money, too!"

"No. I'll spot you the cash, no strings attached. Consider it my new-baby gift. It's my fault this shit went down. I invited them. It was my idea to have people over."

"I should slit your fucking throat, asshole. You're right. This *is* on you. We came here for peace. To make a home. We came because you asked us to! We were broke at the old place, but we weren't in the hole. We come here, you have a party in the home you invite my wife and kid to live in, then look what happens! You're lucky that bitch didn't hurt her more." I step in close to his face. "You're lucky she didn't hurt my kid."

"I know! You think I don't know? You think I don't feel like shit that your girl walks around with a dented fucking face? I can't fix it. I feel like shit. Let me spot you the first entry fee, first race. We both know you won't lose. You keep the cash. You enter another. It'll take you about ten races to pay off the ER. Another ten to pay off the birth. Or if you get brave, one car to pay them both off. You lose your car, I'll lend you mine."

"No! I won't bet the fucking car. I won't let her down like that."

"I'm trying to offer you solutions, Bry. I can't spot you all the money you need. I'm not rich, but I can give you a bit. You're not working weekends except Saturday morning. Shit's changed since you left; races are worth more than they used to be. You said it yourself; work two years and still be in the red. Race ten weekends, or hell, race twice a weekend for five weeks, or three times in a weekend to save even faster. You could be outta the hole in a couple weeks if you roll up to the line."

My heart races in my chest. "She'll kill me. Or worse, what if she leaves me? My fuck-ups are piling up."

"She never has to know." His light eyes hold mine. "I'm not trying to be *that* guy, Bry. I'm not trying to hurt your marriage. I feel like shit that this all went down. I'm just trying to offer you a solution."

I step into our shared apartment the following Monday and stop at the sight of my smiling wife lying on the floor with her eyes closed, while Bobby crawls over her and plays.

He's heavy.

He digs elbows and knees into her chest and stomach, and though she grunts, she laughs and tickles him and sends him into a frenzy of giggles.

I was coming home to lie to her. To tell her I got a new night job. To tell her not to worry anymore, because the new night job pays twenty-bucks an hour and I've got all our troubles sorted.

But it's all lies.

I've got a race set up.

The race will pay five-hundred bucks if I win.

Which I will.

My family depends on it.

Then I can race again right after. With Geo's initial five-hundred, plus a won five-hundred, then a third five-hundred, I could clear out most of the ER bill. I could do that again next weekend, then the weekend after that, then the weekend after that, and we'd be pretty close to set with the delivery, too.

I could keep doing it week after week and set our family up for good.

I just need enough for a house. A reliable family car.

After the new baby arrives, we can't drive the Mustang anymore. Well, we could, but it'd be tight. It's a soft top; that's not safe enough for my family. The engine's been chewed up and shit because of my racing from years ago.

It's still in good shape, because I like to work on it in my measly spare time, but the parts, the belts, the frame, it's all going to shit out eventually.

You can't treat cars the way I treated mine and expect it to last forever.

I was coming home to lie and get our family back on track, but with all the lies comes a ball of lead – also known as dread and guilt – that have sat low in my belly ever since Geo suggested I race.

Every day since then, the ball has coiled and grown until the point it almost chokes me to death.

I don't lie.

I especially don't lie to Bert.

But here I am, ready to feed her a bullshit story to help ease my male ego and the responsibility I feel to provide for my family.

"I can feel you." Her voice feeds me. Lightens me. Relaxes me. "Remember when you were first trying to get into my pants and you said we could *feel* each other." She opens a single eye and pins me where I stand. "You said it wasn't normal. It was special." She inclines her head. "You remember?"

I set my hat and keys down on the side table, move to my hands and knees, and crawl along the floor to stop beside her. As soon as I lie on my side, Nelly turns to hers and clasps my hands.

Instantly adapting, Bobby adjusts his routine and takes turns climbing on us both.

"You remember, right?"

I nod. "Of course I do. It was the truest thing I've ever said."

She smiles. "Exactly. Well, marriage, six years, a monster already here and another on the way... I can still feel you."

I can still feel you, too.

"What's got you sad, Bry?" Her finger comes up to stroke my nose. "Is it money?"

I nod and pretend like my heart isn't breaking.

"So, I've been thinking." Her smile is breathtaking. So sweet and pure and all I ever wanted. And here I am, getting ready to lie to her face. To risk it all. One slip, and she could decide she's done with me. "So we know how much we owe. We know how much you earn. Assuming you don't get fired, and hell, you may even get a raise, so that'll help. Assuming we live on a strict grocery budget, we don't go out ever, and we don't travel anywhere in the car." She smiles ruefully. "We can pay off everything in eighteen months. I know it sucks." Her hand comes to the back of my head like she's scared I'm going to run off. "You'll be working so hard, Bry. I know you work hard, but if you can hold on for eighteen more months, we can pay it all off, then it's all up from there."

I clear the shit from my throat.

Emotion, pussy bitch emotion. "I've been doing the math too, Bert. My math and your math don't match."

She smiles. "That's because you suck at math. And... Because I realized I can help. I should contribute to the family."

And *that's* why she was holding my head. For the inevitable blow-up. "You're not getting a job, Bert! No fucking way!"

"Not a job outside the home," she rushes out. "But I could do stuff here. I was thinking... I have that shiny degree, Bry. I could tutor an hour a day during the week. Those kids would come to me. It'd keep my brain sharp. It would make me feel useful. And it plays into the eighteen-month plan. It's not much compared to what you bring in, but it'd mean a lot to me to be able to help."

"I promised to take care of you, Bert." My heart pounds against my chest. "It's my job to take care of you. It's my privilege!"

"You can't take care of us if you race, Bry. I've had a bad feeling in my gut since the day I found out you race." Her eyes bore into mine. "Back in high school. Those cars are no good. That track is no good."

"How'd you kn–"

She smiles. "I didn't know exactly what. But I know something's up, Bry. And I know money's your biggest worry. Especially after the ER, I know you're hurting." She places her hand over my heart. "I know you'd do anything for your family, and since I know your go-to plan for money is racing... it was the logical solution."

I take a deep breath and close my eyes. "I was coming here to lie to you. You'd never have to know I was racing. You'd never have to worry."

Opening my eyes, I stop on her smile. "I worry about you every single day, Bry. Every single time you drive out in that car, even if it's just to work, I worry. I know you were coming to lie, because you suck at lying almost as much as I sucked at pretending Shane Tosky was my boyfriend. I can *feel* you." She scrunches my shirt in her hand. "I can feel everything you do. When you're right here, right in front of me. When you're gone, at work, with Geo, wherever, I can still *feel* you. It's like..." She shakes her head. "I dunno. It's weird. It's like, my heart is in your chest. And yours is in mine. I can feel you, because you take my heart wherever you go. And you can feel me, because I walk around with yours. I know you've been mad. I know you've been sneaky. I know you're unhappy here." Her gaze beats into mine. "I know that even with how hard you worked back in our old town, you still came home so unbelievably happy. But you're different here. It's different."

"Do you wanna move back?"

She shakes her head. "No. I wanna stay in this town. This town doesn't make you unhappy, Bry. Sharing an apartment does. But I worked an apartment into our eighteen-month plan, too. We need to get out of Geo's place. We need to get out on our own again. That's when you're happiest. Even if it costs more."

"I don't wanna share you with him."

She nods. "And it hurts me when the wrong man walks through the door in the evenings. Bobby gets up and screams '*Daddy*', then he sits down again, because it's the wrong man. We want you back, Bry. So I made the plan to make it work. We can afford an apartment, but twice a week we eat beans and rice. *Only* beans and rice. We can afford the baby, the delivery. We'll reuse the cloth diapers. I'll breast-feed, and if that doesn't work, I'll take on an extra student per week to cover the cost of formula." She brings my fist to her lips. "I'd eat rice and beans every day for the rest of my life if you say yes. If we stick to the plan, we can make it. If we stick to the plan, we can make it on our own."

I close my eyes and thank whatever God is up there for giving her to me. "You think you're so smart, huh? You think you've got it all figured out."

Hesitantly, she nods. "Don't race, Bry. You told me a long time ago that if I gave you the yes, *then* I can demand you quit. You said I'd have all the power. I'm asking you not to race tonight. Or any night.

Ever. For the rest of our lives." She squeezes my hand. "Don't race. Sell the car. Throw it in a ditch. I don't care. I'm begging you to stay with us instead, because every time you get in that car, I worry it's the last time I'll ever see you. I can't lose you, and I can't live without you. So I'm asking you not to go."

I bring her fists to my lips and breathe her in. "Even if we're poor?"

"Money doesn't buy my happiness." She moves in closer and tangles her legs in mine. "You're my happiness, Bry. You and B and the baby are the *only* things that mean something to me. If you remove yourself, if you risk yourself, it's like the stars don't shine as bright anymore." She lets out a shaky breath. "It's not worth it. Choose us, Bry. Stay with us."

NOW

"We lay on that floor. A family of four. My face still bruised. Scratches in my skin. My belly growing each and every day with the baby that would be Aiden." I look up and smile. "My second baby was nothing like the first. The universe had tested us. It knew we couldn't handle another Bobby... yet." I grin at my granddaughters. "We got another one just like him... perhaps even wilder, in Jimmy, but that was a few years away, and by that point, I'd had a couple years rest with my sweet Aiden. By that point, your Poppy had successfully pulled us out of the hole, and we never fell back in again. Aiden never once jumped face first off a change table. He never gouged holes into our table. He never once did the doodle dance."

The girls squeal with laughter.

He's Evie's daddy. Jimmy, the wilder third child, is Bean's.

Jimmy definitely did the doodle dance.

I grab Evie's delicate hand – delicate, yes, but she still walks around with cracked knuckles more often than not. The cycle will not repeat for her.

"Your daddy will tell anyone who'll listen that he's my favorite..."

I laugh. "And he's not wrong. I love your Uncle Bobby. I love Jimmy. He's my baby. But Aiden slept, and Bobby didn't. He didn't climb out of his crib by his first birthday, but Bobby did. Aiden was the one talking Bobby down from stupid shit; he was four, Bobby six, and he'd be the smart one talking Bobby out of dangerous situations. I love my sons equally. But I *like* Aiden the most."

Evie's grin spreads. "He's kinda cool. He's always asking me '*did you think it through, Smalls?*" She lowers her voice dramatically. *"That time you snuck out with Ben and Mac, did you think it through? Or did you do a Bobby and figure you'll deal with the consequences later?* He uses the word Bobby like it's a verb." She laughs. "Did you do a Bobby?" She turns to Bean. *"Did you do a Jimmy? Because he's dumb as rocks sometimes. He woulda thrown himself off a crane, too. Dumbass."*

The girls dissolve into silly giggles.

"So that was how our family began. Bobby first, our wild one. Aiden next, and he came out just fine even after that night, all those beans and rice, all that worry. Maybe that's why he came out the way he did," I ponder. "He knew we were stressed, so he came out prepared to conquer the world... quietly. We were in our own apartment less than two weeks after that day on the floor. We didn't move far from Geo. We stayed in the same apartment building, and the guys still hung out a lot, but as our family grew, and Geo's didn't, they slowly drifted apart. There were no hard feelings. Just different stages of life.

"Bryan was busy working. We had one car, and with the boys, we decided I needed to drive more than he did, so we traded in, bought a truck, then every morning, we'd wake at five. The boys, too. We'd eat breakfast, get dressed. Pile into the truck by six. Drive Bryan to work. We'd come home, do our thing for the day. I'd tutor, and for a while there, I had more than one student per session every day. So I doubled my measly income, and the boys learned math and how to read before they started kindergarten. Bryan didn't want his sons to suffer because he was a *high school dropout,* so they learned. They read. They added and subtracted by kindergarten. Then they excelled in school. Bryan would catch a ride with another guy from the garage to his second job..." My eyes turn sad. "For three years, he didn't come home for dinner between. He would have it no other way. He was going to work, and he was going to save."

"Did he buy you a house, Gramma?"

I smile. "He did. He bought us a small three-bedroom house before Aiden started school. We were in the apartment until then. Then the little house that I never would've moved out of if your daddies didn't insist and buy where I am now."

"Do you still own the little house?"

"I do. I'll never sell it. Not for the rest of my life. And when I die, when it passes onto my children, then onto you guys... I beg you, don't sell it. Keep it. Keep the millions of pictures on the walls. Mow the lawn, because he was so proud of that shitty lawn. He took it from weeds to the greenest grass in the street. He was so proud of that house; I'll keep it in the Kincaid name for the rest of eternity if I could.

"When we were handed those keys, when Bryan finally stepped inside his castle, when he pushed the first nail into the wall to hang family photos, he put cartoons on the TV and gave the boys a bag of chips." I pause thoughtfully. "We never bought chips, that wasn't part of the plan. But he did that day, then he took me to the room, and voila, Uncle Jimmy."

Bean squeals and throws her hands over her eyes. She's fifteen and knows the mechanics of sex, but she still blushes at the thought of Bry dragging me to the room like a genuine caveman.

"So what happened to that bitch? The hair puller." Evie's eyes flash with anger. Not because Ann-Marie hurt me, but because she pulled hair.

We fight. We don't pull hair.

And after she hurt me that day, after things settled down a little, I asked Bryan to teach me how to fight. Not because I wanted to hurt people, but because I didn't want to freeze the way I did that night.

He took me to the backyard every single day from then on out, and he taught me how to fight. He taught me every day until the day he died.

"The hair puller... went on to have her baby. She wasn't lying that night. That test was real. That baby was real. She went on and had a baby girl not too long after I had Aiden."

"Are they still around?"

It's so obvious, so in their face, the girls don't see it.

"Reilly, the guy... Reilly was his last name, not his first. He passed away a while ago. He was sick and died when he was still young."

"That's so sad."

"You don't see it, Smalls?" I wait for her ocean blue eyes to meet mine. "You've visited Reilly before. You've been at the cemetery with Uncle Jack."

"Uncle Jack?" She gasps. "Uncle Jack! Reilly. His daddy?"

I nod. "That was his daddy."

"Which means that baby girl–"

"Is your Aunt Kit."

The hair puller's baby would someday be my daughter-in-law.

"Why didn't you ever say anything?"

I look up.

I don't jump.

I don't startle.

I don't gasp.

I simply smile, because that's karma, and I already know not to talk about people when they're not here.

I smile at my beautiful daughter-in-law. The mother of my grand-babies. The love of my son's life.

And I know she's nothing like her mom.

She's all Reilly; sweet, funny, caring.

Loyal.

He wouldn't leave his baby girl, not for anything, and definitely not for his friends.

Kit steps into the living room and stops on the arm of the couch. She's been through a hell of a lot in her short life, so finding out I knew her mom is low on the crazy-meter for her.

"You sat there that night we met, and you asked about my daddy like you never knew him. You pretended you didn't know my folks."

Heat spreads on my cheeks, but I stand by my actions. "Had I told you I knew them, I would have had to explain it all. Your mom was already gone. Your dad had passed only a few months before that dinner. I wasn't going to tell you I knew her. I definitely wasn't going to tell you I was watching you, to make sure you weren't like her."

She laughs. "I am a little, I guess. He's stuck forever. He'll never escape me."

Leaning across the couch, I take her hand and yank her down beside me. "Do you remember that night we met?" She nods silently. "When I asked you to help me with dessert."

She laughs. "How could I forget? I was scared out of my brains. I hated moms. I was dating your son. I was terrified you'd hate me, and that was *before* I knew all this shit." She fans her face. "Thank God I didn't know this extra stuff. I'd have died before Bobby got me into the car."

"Do you remember what we talked about in the kitchen?"

"Apart from his baby bowel movements. And the fact you told me he bought you this house?" She looks around my grand living room with fresh eyes. Nodding thoughtfully, she answers, "You asked me if I was crazy."

"And you said..."

She snickers and leans in close. "I said yes, ma'am, I am. I'm crazy in love with your son, and I hope you can get on board with that, because he loves us both and if we don't get along, that'll hurt him."

"There are two kinds of crazy in this world, baby girl. There's flat out crazy, then there's us. The ones that can admit it are our kinda people. They're good to come over and hang out with us. It's the people who don't know they're crazy that are dangerous." *Like her mom.* "I wasn't letting Bry go, either. I'd sooner chain him down and break his ankles than let him walk away. But he knew that. He loved my crazy. And you love my son just as fiercely. So much passion. So much selflessness. *Your* kinda crazy is allowed. Because he loves you." I bring her hand into my lap to study the beautiful wedding and engagement rings. "Bobby told me he was bringing a girl home. He told me you were special. He told me he could *feel* it in his heart."

Her smile turns shaky. "He did?"

I twine our fingers together. "He really did. He told me your name, and I nearly had a heart attack. But before I could say anything, before I could even decide if I *should* say anything, he told me I had to be cool, because you were special, and you were afraid of me. You were afraid of moms, because yours was so awful. He begged me to never let on that he told me that, because he didn't want you to get mad that he blabbed, but he made sure I knew, because he didn't want me to screw it up for him."

"She used to beat the crap out of me."

My heart aches for an abused little girl. Ann-Marie's fists weren't reserved only for me. And they weren't the result of a hormonal night or an isolated fit of rage. They came often, and they came especially for the little girl that had already begun growing that night Ann-Marie was in our apartment. "I know."

"She was such a bitch."

I laugh weakly. "But you're all your daddy. Hard working. Loyal. Funny. Caring. Sweet. I hardly knew him; I saw him that one time at the races. Saw him again that night at Geo's place. Saw her once or twice more over the years at the store, but we never caught up again. Bry told me a million times he wanted to make up with your dad, because family's family, you know? And rumor had it, your daddy wanted to make up with us, because he wanted his friends back. But your mom wanted none of it, and there was nothing your dad would risk losing you over. Each time I saw her in the store – and it was only two or three times ever – she'd take your sweet little hand and yank you around and take off in the other direction."

Her eyes soften with longing. "You knew me when I was little?"

"I didn't *know* you. I saw you a time or two. You looked just like your daddy. But Bryan and I had our own family, jobs, house, we had our own stuff to take care of, so after a while, I just forgot about her. We didn't know your mom died until after the fact."

"The guys didn't make up after she died?"

Emotion clogs in my throat. Memories of the worst day of my life flash in my mind and threaten to drag me under the way I couldn't let them when it happened.

I had three young boys to take care of. A house to run.

The measly income I made from tutoring wouldn't feed my family.

Bry took my heart with him to the grave, and I knew it, I knew it the moment it happened.

"They were going to." I pull Evie and Bean onto the couch with us.

We're four women that share the same last name, though not one of us share blood. We huddle on the couch and hold hands.

"Bry reached out to him. They were going to hang out for the first time in a long time, but he never got there." I lean into Kit's shoulder and bite my tongue. "I knew it the moment it happened. He wasn't racing. He promised to never race again, and he kept that promise. But he was still in the car. It was just an accident."

"He was on the way to see my dad when he died?" Her voice breaks with realization. "I didn't know that."

Bobby doesn't know that. No one knows that.

It wasn't an important detail to my sons at the time, and since I've never told my now-adult children I knew the Reilly's, it's never come up.

There are some people I blame for Bry's accident, but not Kit, and not her dad.

"It was just an accident, honey. But somehow in all the chaos, he made sure we got you. He made sure I was set up. He made sure his family was okay. Then more than a decade later, you turned up on my doorstep with a beating heart in your eyes and your hand clutching to my son's like he was your only tether to this world."

"He kind of was."

"I understand completely. I know what it's like to love so deeply, the man you clutch to is the only thing keeping you on this earth. I know that feeling, and even if our time was cut short, I'll never regret it. Bry might've taken my heart with him, but never forget, he gave me his in exchange. I carry him around inside me every single day. He lives on. I can still *feel* him." I press a shaking hand to her flat belly. "Then a few years after you turned up on my doorstep, after you married my son, after you tried for so long to conceive a baby, you gave birth to a brand-new Bryan Kincaid. You named your son for a man you never met, and from your body, came a boy that looks just like my son." I sigh with content. "He looks just like my husband. Bryan would've been stoked with that."

Continue the Kincaid's story in *Finding Home.*
Book 1 of the **Rollin On Series.**

http://a.co/d/3A0BjCU

FULL CIRCLE

THEN

"I can't do this, Bry! I can't. Make it stop."

Laughing, I pry Nelly's hands away from her face and press them down around her hips. Wrapping my arms around her torso, I lock her in and refuse to let her loose. "Just watch him, Bert. Watch him go."

"I can't!" She buries her face against my chest. "I'm not ready for this. You promised!" She rears back and pins me with angry eyes. "You promised you'd never let me hurt. This hurts!" Snapping her arm from my grasp, she slams her fist into my chest until I cough out a laugh. "You promised a lifetime of servitude and happiness, Bryan Kincaid!"

Using my weight – and more strength than I should need for such a small woman – I pin her arms and turn her toward our seven-year-old 'baby' as he steps up to his opponent in the center of a boxing ring.

He's covered head to toe in three-inch thick padding; head gear, shin pads, gloves, body armor.

He'll be fine, but my poor, sweet wife isn't dealing with it so well.

Jimmy is our youngest son. The final piece to our puzzle, and though Nelly cheered Bobby on during his first fight, and she cheered Aiden on in his, she's having a coronary over her not-so-angelic baby boy.

The referee, dressed as though this was a world title fight with a massive purse, steps between the two kids and places a hand on their shoulders. "Boys, I want a good, clean fight. Listen to my commands at all times. Defend yourselves at all times. Touch gloves and step back."

Shakily, the kid in red taps my arrogant son's fist and skitters away like Jimmy's going to whale on him.

Jimmy is smaller than that other kid. Two inches shorter. Seven or eight pounds lighter. But his arrogance makes him a million times bigger.

Plus, his little girlfriend on the ropes screaming her support. "Get him, Jimmy!" She's a fearsome bitty thing, and she's probably the reason my arrogant son is so arrogant. Because if anyone hurts him, *she'll* beat them up. "Legs, Jimmy! Legs. Quick. He's coming!"

I laugh when Jon, my oldest son's best friend, and that little girl's big brother, steps up behind her like a tired parent and tugs her off the ropes. He's twelve, she's not quite six, but it's like a father daughter relationship as he wears the exhausted smile of a parent that's been up with the baby all night – but he wouldn't change it.

I've never met a more responsible or *fatherly* kid until Jon Hart stepped into our family. He was the poor kid at school, figuratively and literally; broke, hungry, cold... And bullied.

I adore my sons. They can do *almost* no wrong. But the day I turned up to school to pick them up for the afternoon and I found my arrogant child teasing the scrawny kid who was clearly missing a few too many meals, I saw red.

We're not bullies.

We're not assholes.

And the day I found Bobby taking Jon's hat and calling him names, was the day they became best friends; because I damn well forced them to. They hugged it out, traded jabs they thought I couldn't see, then because they did that, we went and got ice cream.

I'm convinced that was the first time Jon had *ever* had ice-cream.

He sat in the red and white checkered booth with his eyes drawn low. He refused to meet my eyes. He refused to answer my question when I asked what flavor he wanted.

So I got him Bobby's favorite.

Jon left that bowl sitting on the sticky plastic table the whole time the rest of us ate ours, but it wasn't until his sister, a baby at the time, poked her finger into the melting treat and went crazy with excitement when she put her fingers in her mouth.

She was a baby. A literal, tiny little baby that should never leave the house with a six year old child, but that's what he did.

And who was I to say he couldn't bring her?

Once she tasted it and made him smile with her spit bubbles, he ran his pinky finger through the melting treat, shyly had a lick, and from then on out, he was sunk. Three minutes, two brain freezes, and a full belly later, Jon sat across from me with his baby sister in his lap and his eyes still downcast... but he smiled.

He fucking smiled like he was drunk, and it was because of a two-dollar bowl of ice-cream.

"Jimmy!" Nelly squeaks out in terror and drags my gaze back as my son sits on the other kid's hips and throws wild swings that bounce off red head gear. I laugh as the ref picks him up and aims Jim's kicking legs away so no one cops a stray swing.

"Babe." I pry Nelly's shaking hands from her face, and with a hand under her jaw, drag her face around until our lips are a mere inch apart. I wait until her darting eyes stop on mine before I give her a gentle kiss. "Baby, you need to relax."

"I can't." She massages her chest. "I don't want him to get hurt."

"He's not getting hurt!" I point at the ring. "He's winning. He's winning *illegally*, since this is stand up only, no grappling, but still, he's the kid on top, baby. You never freaked this much with the older boys. What's going on with you?"

"He's my baby!" she dramatically cries. "I never agreed to this."

"There was no way we could stop him, Bert. He's a big boy, now. He wants to be like everyone else. He's gonna fight, so you've gotta get on board."

"I want a divorce. I hate you for encouraging this, Bryan."

Laughing, I press my lips to hers until she gasps out in surprise and sends her breath scorching down my throat, but when I pull back, when I wait for her cloudy eyes to refocus and stop on mine, I know who won that argument.

And I know she doesn't want to divorce me.

"Hush. Find your lady balls, then turn and watch your son kick some ass. This is just the beginning, baby. Bobby told me the other day that he's gonna be world champion. You need to accept that our boys are brutes, then you need to cheer them on."

"I *hate* when you're being logical."

"Yeah? Well I love everything about you, so that averages us out again. I'll carry us until you get back on board."

"Stop being so reasonable!"

"Maybe you should've given me a baby girl like I said that time. I bet you wouldn't be crying about ballet recitals."

"Combo!" Izzy's tiny, five-year-old tinkling voice echoes through the gym. "Combo, Jimmy! Quick. Step out, step in!"

Nelly shakes her head and wipes a silly tear from the corner of her eye. "I think we got a baby girl, Bry. And I think she's going to be a fighter, too."

"So really..." I pull her into my side as the ref picks Jimmy up and separates the boys. "You're shit out of luck. So just buckle in and enjoy the ride. They're going to fight, and they're going to make memories. Did you bring your camera? I want pictures for the walls."

Sighing, she leans forward and tugs a throwaway camera from her handbag. She sighs like my request is a huge hardship, but she's the one who click-click-clicks through those twenty-four images just to get through the roll, then jogs her ass down to the drugstore each Monday morning to get the negatives printed and framed.

We're filling our walls with memories.

Millions of memories that'll stay and remind us of our good fortune.

We're not broke anymore.

We're not *rich*, but I can afford to let my wife buy a new throwaway camera each Friday, and I can afford the prints first thing every Monday.

We have money for shoes for the boys, and tournament entry fees, and gym memberships; even for Jon and Izzy. We have enough money that I'll be taking my family out for ice-cream after this.

Jon and Izzy are our family now, too.

Everywhere Bobby goes, Jon goes. And everywhere Jon goes, he brings his baby sister along with him.

Making memories and a happy family is bigger than our bank account, and even if we didn't have money for extras, I'd simply get another job to make sure Jon and Iz could still come to our home and fill their bellies between bouts of hell.

I don't know that boy's story.

But I know he comes to us all bruised and broken. I know his folks beat him. And I know he leaves Iz with us as often as he can get away with it, because he refuses to let her experience what he does.

But what I don't know is why he keeps going back.

CHAPTER 14

BRYAN

"I wanna watch Space Jam!"

Nelly's dark eyes meet mine across the bedroom when the floor shakes with a literal boom. The sound of fighting children reverberates through my small home and sends a framed photo on the wall swinging off balance.

"Why do they do that, Bry?" Taking the earrings from her ears, Nelly places them on the dressing table with a sigh. "Why do they have to be so rough?"

"Because they're boys. And because Jimmy thinks he's bigger and badder than everyone else."

Laughing and sighing in one, she saunters across the bedroom in a tiny black nightie and makes me salivate at the promises her long legs make. She has an unfortunate tan line stretching across her kneecaps from sitting in the sun in shorts all day.

I'd still bang her.

Crawling onto the bed in an unintended seduction, I peek down her top as she crawls closer and flops into my lap. "No more babies, Bry. I swear, I'm seriously done."

"We're not watching Space Jam!" Jimmy's warrior-like roar

echoes through my home, followed by a second boom and the glass in the china cabinet rattling. "Izzy wants to watch Princess Bride, so we're watching Princess Bride!"

"Jesus, Bry." Nelly looks up in disbelief. "He really loves her. *Nobody* likes that movie except Izzy."

Grinning, I pull her closer and slide my thumb over her nipple. Her breath races out in surprise when, finally, she catches on that I was hoping to use this time to seduce my wife.

Let the kids fight. That'll give me a solid twenty minutes to try and impregnate her again.

"He's stepping up to the big dogs, Bert. Leave him be. He wants to be Iz's hero, let him. He'll learn. Or he'll win." I angle my lips down closer and nibble along her jaw.

Nelly was lazy and pliant like a cat, but now she hums with unre-pressed energy. Her nipples pucker beneath the thin silk material, and when I slide my hand along her ribs, over her luscious hips, then back up beneath the fabric, her breath comes out in excited puffs.

Using my left hand to cup her face, I bring her closer until our lips clash, and when her breath scorches down into my lungs, I use the other hand to slide her panties away.

I grin and nibble, while she whimpers and helps me lower them.

More than fifteen years of marriage, twelve of those with a kid in the house, Nelly and I have become pros at stealthy sex.

"It's three against one!" Aiden shouts. "I don't wanna watch that crappy cartoon, either!"

"Quick," Nelly whispers. "Do it quick before they lose it." Like we have a fire to get to, but instead of speed dressing, we speed undress, she tears my shirt over my head, and I fling her panties across the room. Straddling my thighs on a giggle when her panties catch on a lampshade, Nelly pulls her nightie up enough to keep it out of the way, then we go to work on the drawstring of my sweatpants.

Frenzied movements, shaking hands, pounding hearts, and eagerness to get where we need to go before the boys tear our house apart, she rips my pants down just far enough to pull my cock out, and when her warm hand encircles me, I throw my head back and bury it between the fluffy pillows as she maneuvers herself, lines us up, and slides down over me until our cores touch and my teeth clamp down onto my lips to keep the groan in.

"Bry." My name is just a whisper in the air, a soft whimper and a promise of love. Nelly brings her hands to my chest and pushes up, then on another *"Bry"* she slides down.

"We don't wanna watch that shit," Aiden snaps through my concentration.

I hold her closer to me, force her lower onto my cock. "Keep going, Bert. Don't you fucking stop."

"Let it go!" Someone slams against the wall connected to ours. "We're watching the princess one!"

"No, *you* let it go! Give. Me. The. Remo–" Another house shaking boom makes the floor vibrate beneath our bed, but this time, a feral scream follows until Nell springs off me like a spooked cat.

She pulls her nightie down, and I pull my pants up, and as one, we sprint from our room and slide along the hall until we stop at the door to the bedroom my two younger sons share.

Jimmy lies on the floor with his arm bent at an unnatural angle and fat tears sliding along a face that still holds a bunch of baby fat. Skidding down onto my knees, I run a shaking hand over his good arm. "Oh, shit, buddy. What did you do?"

He screams in my face.

Not the badass kid anymore, but a little boy in excruciating pain as Izzy lays over his chest to *protect* him.

"I'm sorry!" Aiden hugs Nelly around the hips and bows her backwards with his weight. "I'm so sorry, Mom. It was an accident."

"It's okay..." I work to lift Jim to his butt and not jostle his broken arm. He screams with every gentle move I make, and Iz slides off his lap as I bring him vertical.

I look to Nell, but my panic doesn't come like the last time I had to rush someone I love to the ER. "I have to take him in." We're not broke anymore. I worked hard for this. So my family never has to choose between food and medical care again. "It's okay, bud. You'll be okay."

"It hurts!" His long hair catches in wet lashes as he scrunches his eyes in pain. "Aiden threw me!"

"It was an accident, bud. You were all being rough. Let's get up, come on." I raise to one knee, then the other, and help bring him to his feet. "Let's go to the ER."

"No! They'll hurt me." He pushes away in fear and knocks Iz back a step, but she simply bounces back in and wraps her tiny arms around his waist.

Jon works to move in and remove her, but she clutches to my son and unknowingly jostles him more.

"Come on, bud. We've gotta go to the ER."

"No!" He bucks against my hold, but my badass son still only weighs fifty pounds, so I easily flip him up into my arms and leave Izzy growling because I stole her best friend.

Aiden stands against Nell and cries his apologies.

Jimmy screams in my arms and fights my hold.

Izzy shouts in the space I can't see, hidden by my son's body.

Jon snaps at his sister to move out of my way.

Nelly brushes Aiden's hair aside to soothe him.

And my oldest son sits on the edge of his brother's bed with a candy bar and a grin on his face. "Aiden judo tossed him, Dad. It was awesome."

"I'm sorry!"

"Sissy! Get out of the way."

"I'm coming!"

"I'm not going to the hospital!"

The scrunching of a candy wrapper.

"Alright!" I use my foot to push Izzy away. She's little, but she's fucking determined, and she's gonna end up tripping me over. I shuffle her back until Jon has her in his arms, then I turn to Nelly. "We're going to the ER. You guys just stay here and go to sleep. We'll be back later."

"Dad, no!" Jim chokes on snot and tears. "It hurts. I don't wanna go."

"You'll be fine, bud. I've–"

"I'm coming with you!" Iz snaps. "He's *my* best friend. He *needs* me to come. I'll help him when they fix it."

"No, you're not!" Jon snaps. "It's eight o'clock, Sissy. Time for bed."

"I'm not going to bed!"

"I want Iz!" Jimmy cries. "I'm not going if she's not going."

"She ain't going without me!" Jon's on fire. "Sissy. Put your jammies on and we'll watch that stupid movie."

"I don't wanna watch the movie." She shoves him off, grabs my jeans in deceptively strong hands, and pushes me toward the door with my still screaming, still loud son in my arms. "Let's go! Mom, Daddy needs his wallet."

She calls us Mom and Daddy.

She kills me with her love.

"You're not going without me, Sissy!"

"I'm not going without her!" Jimmy adds.

Bobby jumps off the bed and whips on his black ball cap. "If Jon's goin', then I'm goin'! He's my best friend."

"Oh, for crying out loud!" In her black nightie and no panties – I was *this* close to getting laid – my wife wades through the crowd of elementary and middle schoolers and pushes me toward the front door. "You go. You take Jimmy. Izzy, you go to bed. Everyone else, stop talking and watch the friggin princess movie."

Ignoring my wife, Izzy bolts from the room and down the hall. A set of keys jingle against the kitchen counter, then the chain on the front door clangs against wood as she jumps and works to unlatch it.

She's too short, but she's clever.

It won't take long for her to figure it out.

I look to Nelly. "She's coming with us. I'll take her and Jimmy. We'll be back in a few hours."

"No way," Jon rumbles. Slipping out of the room with an air of rage simmering beneath his skin, he rushes into Bobby's room and works to pull on shoes. "She's not going anywhere without me!" he shouts. "She goes, I'm coming, too."

Bobby sprints from the room on a giggle and unlatches the front door. "I'm coming, too!"

As it closes in on midnight, I sit in a hard-plastic hospital chair with a numb ass, pins and needles in my feet, and a sniffling Aiden leaning against my side; he's still sorry. Bobby sits with his feet up on the chair and a Gameboy in his hands, and beside him, Jon reads a ratty paperback book and strokes long brown hair off Izzy's sleeping brow.

Everyone came.

Like a damn circus coming to town, all seven of us piled into the truck and noisily made our way across town. Izzy sat with her *best friend* for as long as she was allowed, but the x-ray technician forbid her from going in and taking the scans for him.

Though she swore she was willing.

Since then, she climbed into Jon's lap and promptly fell asleep. She loves her big brother more than anyone else in the whole world. Because Jon *is* her world, even when she's being a brat about Jimmy.

Electric doors buzz open, and because I'm bored out of my fucking head, I look up and follow thick, beefy legs covered in jeans. A skinny, knobby pair of knees beside him, then an even smaller kid, even smaller than Iz, clutches at the knobby kneed girl.

They're an unremarkable family.

No need to look up.

But I do, and when I stop on a familiar face, warring emotions lance through my heart. Familiarity, and memories of good times. But there's also rage, and memories of a shitty time.

I swing around in my chair in search of his wife, the psycho fucking bitch that she is, and my heart yearns to see *my* wife, to make sure she's okay.

But the room remains mostly empty and silent.

I turn back to the man I know as Reilly and swallow when his eyes lock onto mine. His are red rimmed and weary. He's exhausted. His little girl clutches to his hand, then the little boy, just a toddler, clutches to hers.

Standing, I push Aiden toward Bobby. "I'll be back in a sec, guys. Don't move. Hey." I tap Bobby's knee to take his attention from the game. "You're the oldest. I'm talking to you. Don't move. Don't let the others move."

His eyes shoot back to the noisy Gameboy, but he nods. "I promise, Dad. Won't move a muscle."

I rub my hand through his messy hair – because I know it annoys him – then I step across the large waiting room filled with a billion other ass-numbing chairs, three vending machines, two of which have 'do not use' signs, and stacks of dog-eared and wrinkled magazines that are probably as old as my broken-armed son.

Reilly steps back and warily pushes his daughter behind him, so I stop six feet away and raise my hands in surrender. "Truce?"

He swallows nervously and casts wary eyes around the mostly deserted waiting room. "How pissed are you, Bry? I haven't seen your face in a decade, so that's probably a lot of lingering anger." He hesitates. "If you're looking to get shit straight, let me get my babies into the car. You understand that, right? I gotta protect them."

Charles – Charlie – Reilly has been nervous for a decade. He's been waiting for retribution that whole time, because his wife kicked my wife's ass. While she was pregnant.

All this time has passed while nerves ate at him, and yet, I can honestly say I haven't given him much thought at all. I was angry for a little while, but then I got busy living my life. Time and distance let me forget.

Obviously, Reilly wasn't so fortunate.

I turn and nod toward Aiden. "That kid over there, the one in the dinosaur shirt; that's my son, and he was in Nell's stomach that night." Reilly's Adam's apple bobs as he waits for me to finish. "He came out just fine. Great, even. He's my most sensible son." Lifting a hand, I give a quiet chuckle. "He hasn't jumped off the roof once, so you can relax, everyone's fine."

I tilt my head to the side and catch a glimpse of a shaky hand snaking it's way around her daddy's belly in search of his. The little girl. The baby Ann-Marie was carrying that night. "She's yours? I heard Ann-Marie was pregn–"

That little hand snaps away and goes back to hiding, and when I look into Reilly's red eyes, I frown. Like he did a million times back in the day, he coughs, and when he brings his hand up to catch the cough, he runs his finger along his lips in the universal symbol to shut the fuck up.

So I do.

A decade apart doesn't negate a simple request to shut the hell up.

I'm not mad anymore.

I'm happy. I have a happy life. A happy family. A happy wife.

So long as that bitch isn't in another room beating on my wife right now – and even if she was, no one has trained as hard as Nelly, so Nelly's ass isn't the ass that'll be kicked – then we're good.

Trying again, and nixing the subject of Ann-Marie, I lean around Reilly with a 'daddy' smile and wait for bright blue eyes to meet mine.

Well, shit. "You got a baby girl that looks just like you, huh, Reilly?"

He's wearied. So fucking tired, but he smiles. "My baby girl." He reaches back to bring her head around. Long blonde hair hangs almost to her butt, and though the ends are combed and kind of straight, there's somewhat of a rat's nest on top, as though she's been sleeping fitfully. "Kit, baby. This is Daddy's..." He clears his throat. "Um. This is Daddy's friend from school. Do you wanna say hey?"

She buries her face between his ribs and arm, and though she watches me, she shakes her head and makes me wonder if she's mute.

Sighing, he jerks out an exhausted shrug. "Sorry, Bry. It's, ah... well, it's a shitty time for us. My kids are exhausted, so don't take it personally."

"No big deal. I don't take much personally these days, because I know what kids are like. If I got bent outta shape by mini hellions, my boys would destroy me every damn day."

Still wary, but with a twitching lip, he looks over my shoulder and watches my kids as they read and play games. He frowns when he counts them out. "You had them close together. You didn't know how to watch TV and leave her alone?"

I laugh and turn back to him. "Two of those are mine. The two on the end, the boy and girl, they aren't mine... technically."

"That your oldest?" The little girl glances around me as Reilly nods toward Bobby. "I met him before."

"Yeah, that's him. A lot changes in ten years. I'm not mad, by the way." I wait for his eyes to meet mine. "You can relax. I'm not gonna hit you."

Like my words are as powerful as *abracadabra*, his shoulders come down a fraction. "I was worried."

Laughing softly, I run a hand across the two-day stubble on my jaw. "Nah, we're good. I mean, what went down was bad, but I'm not gonna hit you. Where is she?" I look around him. "Can't say I'd be thrilled about seeing her–"

Again, he coughs and shushes me. "Do you think..." He shrugs. "Maybe we could catch up sometime? Have a beer. Talk."

Talk... when his kids aren't right here, listening in.

Nodding, I look around the waiting room in search of a pen. When I find one on the desk twenty feet away, I jog across the room and snatch it up, and when the woman behind the computer scowls at me, I scowl right back. "I'll return it, *Debra*. Relax."

Moving back across the room, I grab Reilly's arm. "This is my house number. Call up and we'll hang out. Don't freak if Nelly answers, she's not mad at you, either. You can leave a message with her if I'm at work, she'll pass it along. Or you can call after seven at night. I'll take your call, I promise." I look up and meet his eyes. "We'll hang out. Have a beer. Break down a motor."

His smile twitches. "Just like old times."

I nod. "Just like old times."

When I finish writing and put the cap back on the pen, he digs his work-stained hand into his pocket and scans the waiting room. "I have to go. My kids need their beds. They need to rest." His eyes stop on my boys. "You guys all good? Everyone's healthy?"

"Yeah, we're all good. My middle son broke my youngest son's arm. He's getting patched up now."

He laughs softly and reaches around to pick up his toddler son. "A broken arm. Happens to the best of 'em."

"True. It's a rite of passage when you have a household of fighters."

He nods. "Alright. I'll catch you later, Bry."

"Hey, call me. It's been too long."

He nods and leads his shy little girl away. "Will do."

When the automatic doors whir open and he escapes into the midnight dark, it occurs to me I didn't ask why they were here. If they were healthy and okay. But another whirring door at my back makes me spin and smile at my wife's long legs in mini denim shorts. Then my son as he wears a fresh cast and a goofy grin. He raises his arms above his head like he's holding a giant trophy. "I'm alive!"

I think he's stoned, too.

CHAPTER 15

BRYAN

Reilly didn't call me that week. He didn't even call me that month. But with my family in my home and my wife dancing around my kitchen, I didn't put too much thought into it.

I gave him my number.

He didn't give me his.

So if he wants to hang out, he can reach out.

In the meantime... "Bryan!" Nelly slaps my hand away and flitters from my groping hands. "I'm cooking dinner. Stop it."

"The kids are fine. They don't need to eat anyway."

"They're not fine!" She slaps my hand again, but she's only playing. We've fucked in the kitchen before. She just wants me to work for it. "The boys are in the yard. They could walk in at any moment."

"Just one thrust, Bert. Just the tip."

She bursts into piggy snorts and flees my hands. Turning on me with a wooden spoon as her only protection, she shakes her head. "No. Let me cook this dinner. Then after, tonight, you have permission to use your mouth."

"Oh, well..." Laughing, I step forward and pin her between the cabinets and my groin. I press my hardened dick against her stomach and lean in to nibble on her neck when she drops her face to my chest. "You give me permission to use my mouth." I bite the sensitive flesh and groan when my dick jumps in my jeans. "I'll use my mouth, Bert." I run my tongue along her neck. "I'll fuck you with my tongue. Does that sound nice?"

Whimpering and tossing her wooden spoon aside, the hands she was using to push me away only a moment ago now clutch at my back and pull me closer. "Uh-huh."

"You want me to turn you around, bend you over the bed, and use my tongue until I make you scream? I'll make it so your voice doesn't work tomorrow."

Fuck this 'later' bullshit. I'm getting mine now.

Peeking out the kitchen window and finding my three boys playing in the yard, then little Izzy sitting on the stoop with her head on her knees and her eyes pointed at the fence, I come back to my wife and pick her up.

"We have two minutes, babe. Two minutes to make you cry. You ready?"

"No!" *Yes. She's saying yes.* "We can't."

"Yes, we can."

"Bry." The breath explodes from her lungs when I slide my finger between her legs and inside her hot pussy. "Bry..." Her eyes roll into the back of her head. "Not in the kitchen."

"Okay." One last peek out the window, Aiden and Bobby are grappling, and Jimmy now sits beside Izzy.

I pick Nelly up and swallow her sexy squeal, and running to the bedroom, I stand her on her feet at the end of the bed and yank her pants down. "Hold onto the bed, Bert. Hold on tight." She whimpers and spreads her legs wide. Bending my legs to get lower, I unsnap my belt and tear the zipper down, but when she whimpers and pushes back against my groin, I instead drop to my knees, bury my fingers in her pussy, and my tongue in her ass.

She screams and latches her teeth onto her forearm to stay quiet. Her thighs shake, and her pussy squeezes my fingers tight.

She's no less tight today than she was the first day we made love, and her vise-like grip on my fingers makes me groan for the pleasure I know I'll get in just a few minutes.

"Be quick, Bert." I slide my tongue from her pussy back up to her ass. "Go quick." With a loud crack, I slam my open palm over the soft flesh of her ass and send her pushing back against me. "You like that, huh? I had no clue my little virgin bride would like to be spanked."

Whimpering, she nods and braces against the end of the bed. "I like it." I slide my thumb into her ass until she convulses around my digits. She cries into her arm, and my dick jumps and twitches with want as she explodes into my hand. Standing tall, I push my jeans down a few inches, slap her ass a second time, and when she cries out, I slam my cock deep inside and ride out the wave of her clenching pussy and crackling orgasm.

"Bry! Oh…" She whimpers. "Bry."

"Mmm." Slowly, I start moving. Build her up. Make her come for me again. I push her top along her back and smile at her sexy arched spine.

"Don't come inside me, Bry."

"Don't worry, baby. No more oopsies, I promise." I slam inside her and send the headboard slamming into the wall. Bringing my hand up again, I swing it down and crack against the already pink skin of her ass. "I love you, Nelly." Slam inside her. Slam the headboard against the wall. Crack my hand against her ass. She cries out each time, and yet, pushes back and asks for more. "I love you like I loved you the day we married."

"Bry," she cries against her arm. "Hurry up. I'm ready to go."

"I'm not ready, baby. Hold on." Slam inside her. Slam the headboard against the wall. Crack my hand against her ass. "Don't go yet."

"Bry!" Bringing her head up and looking over her shoulder, she pins me with an angry glare. "Don't make me wait."

I lift my hand. She thinks I'm gonna slap her ass, so she turns away to prepare, but instead, I slide my fingers around and stroke her clit until she cries out and squeezes me impossibly tight.

"Dad?"

My heart stops at the sound of tiny kiddy feet running along the hallway floorboards. Picking Nelly up and throwing her onto the bed, I yank my jeans up and rush to the bedroom door before Jimmy or Iz can run in. Sliding through the smallest gap possible and stopping Jim from rushing into my room, I'm almost woozy as I stand and look down at my curious kids and my orgasm pulls back inside my body and promises to never ever come out to play again.

Like my old Mustang, there's only so many times you can race it and flog it before the engine starts to die. Similarly, there are only so many times a man can have sex and not come before it'll just stop coming to the party.

I'm doomed to little blue pills and an existence of never having an orgasm again.

"Dad?"

I swear, dots swirl in my vision, but my oblivious son smacks me in the belly with his casted arm and demands my attention.

"Yeah, Jimmy. What?"

"Can we have ice-cream for dinner?"

He wants ice-cream for dinner.

He wants ice-cream for dinner!

He just ruined my orgasm because he wants something he *knows* we'll say no to anyway. "No! Go outside and play with your brothers."

"But, Daddy." He's only seven, but like how Reilly does the *shush* thing with his eyes, Jimmy does something similar and subtly draws my attention to the little girl clutching to his hand. "Izzy's not feeling great. So I thought maybe ice-cream would make her feel better."

I look down at the little girl's sad eyes, then when I look behind her and *don't* find Jon hovering, I get it.

He's not here.

The door opens at my back, then Nelly ducks under my arm and brushes long hair from Iz's eyes. "Yeah, baby. If Daddy's okay with it, you can have ice-cream. We're allowed to be silly sometimes."

I nod and pull my wife into my side and press a kiss to her temple. "Later, Bert. Swear to God. We'll come back to this."

She snickers and steps forward. "Come on, Izzy. Do you want sauce on your ice-cream?"

***

We sat around the kitchen table eating spaghetti Bolognese and ice-cream that night, but what is usually a fun and messy time of the day, was quiet and sad as one of our dining chairs remained empty.

Bobby's best friend was conspicuously missing.

Izzy's big brother was missing.

Jimmy's best friend was sad.

I don't know how to help Jon.

I don't know why he keeps going back.

He never comes to us with black eyes. No broken arms or legs. No marks that we see. But he limps, he's withdrawn, and can barely breathe through a coughing fit in the winters.

Every time I ask if his parents hurt him, he denies it.

Every time I ask what hurt him, he denies hurting.

Then he hurts himself more as he pretends he isn't hurting.

Every time I even look at him when he's clearly in pain, he clams up and hides in Bobby's room for days.

My children sneak food from our kitchen.

They think we don't notice. They think we don't know they're feeding Jon and Iz when they come to us hungry.

We know.

Of course we know, but there's not a damn thing I can do about it, because he *refuses* to talk.

Jon and Iz sleep in my home a few nights a week. Iz, a little more often than Jon. They go missing for a few days, turn my hair gray with worry, then I find out they're back in my home only because the *secret* jars of peanut butter are gone from the pantry and I hear crying in the night.

Not Izzy.

But Jon.

I bet he doesn't even know he cries in the night. And I guarantee Bobby never brings it up.

Lying in bed and stroking Nelly's shoulder, I breathe in the scent of her hair and stare at the ceiling. She runs patterns against my chest with her pointer finger as she, too, worries.

"Bry..."

"I know, baby." Bobby's room is barely twenty feet down the hall from ours. Our house isn't large, so when the bedroom window in his room slides open and the counterweights tap against the frame, I hold my wife as her heart breaks.

We know Jon's climbing through my son's bedroom window right now, though he's welcome through the front door any day.

I know he'll be hurting.

I know I'll hear tiny Izzy feet tiptoeing down the hall in a moment because, when Jon's not here, she goes to Jimmy, but when he is, especially when he's hurt, she goes to him.

She'll sleep cuddled up against his chest tonight, and she'll sneak Band-Aids from our cabinet and try to help him.

"We can't let this go on, Bry. We'd never allow our boys to go there, why are we letting Jon?"

I sigh and pull her closer. "Because he won't talk, Bert. He refuses to answer when I ask. Wayne Hart has legal power here. They could yank them back any moment." I press my lips to her brow. "I can't push until I get Jon to talk to me. I can't make it stop until I know what's going on."

"But if he never talks, he might never escape this."

Lances of pain slice my heart. She's right; we would never allow our boys to go through whatever it is Jon goes through. We consider him one of ours, but we don't have the same power when it comes to him.

We can't yank him unless he wants to be yanked.

And he keeps going back.

"I know an abused child, Bry." Pushing up onto her elbow, Nell's dark eyes bore into mine. "They hurt him. They hurt him really bad, a million times worse than anything I ever got. And I think he goes back because he's protecting Izzy. Like they're his parole officers or something; if he doesn't check in, they come looking. He's keeping them away from here."

"That's why he leaves her here so often. He's keeping her away."

Nodding softly, she drops her eyes to my fingers that play with hers. "I don't think he'll ever tell us. I was never going to tell anyone. I didn't tell anyone until I told you, and I was nearly eighteen by then."

"Bert–"

"He's twelve, Bry. You want him to come back here every third day starving and beaten for the next six years, or do we do something about it and fix it?"

"Baby. I don't know how to fix it. He won't admit it, and they're not leaving any marks. We know what we know, we know he's hurt, but unless I catch them mid beatdown, how else am I supposed to fix this?"

She stares into my eyes for a long beat. Her stare makes my heart race, because I know she revisits her abusive daddy every time she thinks of Jon.

She admits, whatever Jon gets is a million times worse than anything she ever got.

"Fuck."

She nods. "So we catch him. That, right now," she points at the wall, "tonight is the last time he sneaks into our home in the middle of the night with whatever injuries he's wearing. Next time he says he's going home, hell, next time he says he's going to the fort, we follow. We have to end this, Bry. He can't go on like this."

CHAPTER 16

BRYAN

"*One two! One two! And through and through.*" My green-haired son – dressed as a tree – waves his arms and pretends to be a creepy willow on a stormy night. "*The vorpal blade went snicker-snack!*"

I cough and hide my laughter at my always-serious son and his terrible – *woeful!* – acting. It's talent night for my son's fifth grade class. We've been here for an hour and a half already.

We've seen shitty magic tricks.

Shittier dance recitals.

One reasonably awesome Kata demonstration. And now it's Aiden's turn.

"Bry!" Nelly slams her elbow into my ribs and has the breath exploding from my lungs on a snort. "Stop it. Watch him."

"Babe," I hiss out on something of a hybrid angry laugh. "He's a fuckin' tree! His hair is green. That shit ain't gonna wash out for weeks."

"*He left it dead, and with its head. He went galumphing back.*"

Bobby slaps his thigh and brushes his crying eyes on Jon's shoulder. "He's so bad. It's *so* bad!"

"*He took his vorpal sword in hand, and* chopped his brother's head off if he doesn't stop laughing!"

Bobby howls and kicks the chair in front of him. His laughter echoes in the auditorium and leeches into what was an unsmiling Jon.

Jon's been so serious, like he *knows* Nelly and I have been watching closer than ever, but he's been careful. He's not telling us where he's going. He's not limping.

But Iz has been at our house less.

As in, he's getting spooked, and he's taking her with him, because that's what he does.

If he runs, he runs *with* her.

"*So rested he by the Tum-Tum Tree. And stood awhile in thought.*"

Aiden brings his plastic sword down over his play-mate's head, but not before pointing it right at Bobby – despite the show lights blinding him, and the fact the audience is in the dark.

His promise comes across loud and clear.

I'll be paying more ER expenses in the next twenty-four hours.

I swear, the clock says Aiden was on stage for only ten minutes, but it felt like an eternity. Between Nelly's dangerous jabs, and her twenty-four roll of disposable camera film, she snaps the last on his bow, then she swings her handbag and slams it against her first-born son's face. "Robert! You're *this* close to being grounded!"

"Mom!" The crowd stands and applauds as excitedly as any crowd you might find at a fifth-grade talent show. "It sucked, Mom! It's sucked rotten eggs."

"You don't laugh at him! That's mean."

"Dad was laughing."

I spin on my traitorous son and pin him with a glare.

He swallows dramatically as I silently mouth the words '*snitches get stitches.*' "Yard. Tomorrow."

"Dad."

"Five a.m."

"Dad!"

"Fifty burpees first."

"Dad!" He stomps his foot like a spoiled child, but his lips twitch anyway. Tomorrow we rumble, not because he laughed at his brother, but because he snitched on me.

"Honey!" As soon as Aiden reaches us in the crowd, Nelly pretends like we didn't just organize Sparta in her backyard. Throwing her arms around his broad shoulders and pressing embarrassing kisses to his face, she leaves red lipstick all up and down Aiden's already rosy cheek. "I'm so proud of you! The way you chopped that boy's head off. It was amazing."

"Aww, Mom. It's no big deal."

"It was a huge deal! What do you want to do to celebrate? It's your night, honey. You deserve roses and a standing ovation."

Bobby gags and pokes his finger inside his throat, setting Jon on a silly bout of giggles. I throw my elbow back and catch Bobby's ribs, then stupidly, without thinking, I do the same to Jon and send him buckling and his face draining white.

"Fuck." Leaving an oblivious Nelly to smother Aiden, I turn to Jon and help a now serious Bobby push Jon's head between his knees. "Shit, buddy. I'm so sorry."

Hair that's grown a little long for his face hangs in his eyes, and a line of drool spills from his lips and lands on the toes of his white sneakers.

Bobby's sneakers.

It's like they think we don't notice the missing bread and peanut butter.

We do.

Just like we notice Jon wearing Bobby's shoes.

Shallow panting breaths whistle through his lungs as his white skin turns a shade of green. "S'okay. Gimme a sec."

"It's not okay!" I don't dare speak loudly. My lips are barely two inches from his ear as I crouch down. "It's time to get serious, Jon. Talk to me, let me fix it. I'll fix it, I swear to God, I will. I'll end it for you. I just need you to give me the yes."

He shakes his head and reaches up to hug Iz to his side as she crawls into the non-existent space between us. "Nothing to fix. I'm okay."

"Jon!"

Fiery dark eyes snap up. He's twelve, but his eyes speak of a man's experience. "Leave it alone, Mr. Kincaid."

Mr. Kincaid.

He's running.

Even as he sits half a foot in front of me, he's running.

I bring my hand up to his hair. "I'm sorry, Jon. I didn't mean to hurt you."

He shakes his head, but he's too weak to speak. He swipes a tear from his cheek and stares at his shoes.

"Come on." Bobby works to help him to his feet. "Quick. Mom's gonna turn around in a sec. Get up."

Shakily, Jon pushes to his feet and clutches at my steadying hand when his eyes roll into the back of his head. "Jesus Christ, kid. You're killing yourself over these secrets."

He shrugs and swallows down a bubble of gas. "S'okay. Come on, Sissy." He turns gingerly. "Where's Sissy?" She wraps her arms around his hips and steps forward with him and Bobby. Nodding, he holds her close. "Okay. S'okay. Let's go to bed." His eyes come to mine. "I just wanna go to bed. Please."

His weary spine snaps straight when Nelly slides under my arm with a smile. "We're going out for ice-cream. Aiden's choice."

"Actually." Bobby wipes a shaking hand over his face. "I'm not feeling so good, Mom. I'm just gonna go to bed."

"Bobby!" She leans in close. "You need to support your brother. This isn't funny anymore."

"No." He's not joking anymore. "No, I'm serious." He looks to

Aiden. "Sorry. I'll make it up to you tomorrow, I promise. I just wanna go to bed."

Nelly's eyes come up to mine. "Bry?"

"I'll take Bobby home to bed. Make sure he's behaving. Put the princess movie on for him. We'll drop you and the others off at Dixie's on the way, then I'll pick you up when you're done."

"You don't have to stay with us, Mr. Kincaid." Jon's glassy eyes clear with determination. "I'm tired, too. I'll go with him. It's time for bed for Iz, too."

She doesn't argue.

Unlike when Jimmy broke his arm, her loyalties are with her hurting brother. She yawns dramatically, because her entire life has been built on being her brother's alibi and going along with whatever he needs to do to survive. "Yeah, I'm tired. I'm gonna go to bed."

"We have to go home tonight," Jon adds. "I told my folks we'd be home tonight. They're expecting us."

My gaze snaps to his, and without words, I promise that if he leaves my property tonight, with or without Izzy, he's in trouble. "Maybe you could sleep over again tonight," I add through gritted teeth. "It's getting late, Jon. It's too late to walk home with your sister. *Too dangerous.*"

Breathing through his nose and nodding, he limps past me and leans on Bobby as they move down the aisle.

Twenty minutes later, after dropping Nell, Jimmy, and Aiden off at Dixie's ice-cream parlor, though they were like pathetic puppies in the window – Jimmy was looking for Iz, Nelly was looking for me, and Aiden was simply worried because everyone else was – I walk through the front door of the humble home I finally bought for my wife, throw my keys down on the narrow hall table, and watch Bobby and the two Harts stumble down the hall to the bedroom.

I have an abused boy in my home.

Day in day out, he comes home to us all beaten and bruised, and I can't do a fucking thing about it.

In all my worries when I was younger, the worst of it was not having enough money. If I could just get another job, a better paying job, all our troubles would be solved. Just a little extra cash, and everything would be okay.

There was nothing money couldn't fix.

Until now.

Now I have a little boy in my home that I consider a son, but I let this boy walk out of my home every day to face the devil.

And I don't stand in front of him.

I don't stop it.

Moving down the hall and silently moving into the kitchen, which just so happens to be off the hall that leads to the bedrooms, I slide a chair out, bury my face in my hands, and listen.

I'm betraying their trust, but I listen anyway.

Because the only people who know what happens to Jon are three kids who refuse to talk to me.

Even my firstborn son.

The boy I've called my best friend since the day he was born.

He knows.

But he won't tell.

"Wayne?"

Someone grunts – *Jon* grunts – then the sound of a rustling beanbag echoes through the hall. "Yeah."

"Why?"

Silence stretches out, then instead of answering the original question, Jon replies, *"Can you get my bag? I wanna read."*

"Jon." Bobby's voice rumbles through my hall in the same tone I used on the boy only half an hour ago. *"Reading won't fix it. Why don't you tell my dad? He can fix anything."*

"Nothing to tell. Gimme my bag. And a pen."

"Jon! My dad already knows something's up. Just tell him, he'll fix it so you never have to go back."

Just say the words, kid. *Why* do you keep going back? What power do they have over you?

"*I go back because I have to,*" Jon vaguely answers. "*Because I have to. Now get my book. Then I'm going to sleep. Sissy, get your jammies on. I'm not going to sleep until you're in bed, too.*"

She doesn't argue, because she knows it's what she needs to do tonight. Tired or not, missing her best friend or not, she walks into the hall with the yellow and pink pyjamas Nell and I got her for her last birthday. She steps into the bathroom and closes the door with a soft snick, and in the silence she leaves behind, my son tries once more. "*Talk.*"

"*My folks are gonna beat someone, B. It's either me or Iz. It's just the way it is. If it's not me, they'll come looking for her.*"

"*Jon—*"

"*They'll never touch her. No one will.*"

"*So you walk back to your place and willingly take a beating? It doesn't have to be that way, Jon. My dad can fix it. My dad can fix anything.*"

"*Then put a target on his back, too? On your mom's. You're gonna put your brothers on the block?*" He lets out a grunt as the beanbag compresses under his weight. "*Nah. This is my problem. I'm fine, and I'm keeping their poison contained. I didn't die yet.*"

CHAPTER 17

BRYAN

It takes a week for Jon's limping to ease, for the gray pallor to leave his skin, and for his hands to stop shaking. It takes an entire week for that boy to stop watching me like I'm the enemy, then to accept a bowl of ice-cream and join our family at the kitchen table again with a smile.

On the eighth day, he watches me from the corners of his eyes, and when he thinks I'm not watching, he makes a run for it.

His parole officers are waiting, and he either has to check in, or risk them coming here. So this brave twelve year old runs toward Hell to save the rest of us, when I wish he could realize that Hell doesn't scare me. I'll run with him, I'll run in front of him. If only he'd trust me to take care of it.

Jon runs through the woods, cuts across the outside of town, and darts between the trailer park, the fort, and my house as easily as if it were just a stroll through a park. In reality, it's an eight-mile trek, but he makes it easily and never mentions his hardships when my boys ride around on bikes.

Unable to cut through the woods, but knowing where he's going, as soon as the boy ducks into the woods out of sight and leaves his baby sister sitting on my back step with sad eyes, I run to my truck and slam my foot onto the gas so the engine roars.

I need to fix this for him. I can't let him keep going home to them, so I don't give it a single thought as I reverse away from my home and look through the dust as I slow and put it into drive. Nelly stands at our front door with grief in her eyes, but she knows what needs to happen.

She doesn't want me to go, but she needs someone to be Jon's savior, so she draws in a brave inhalation until her chest rises, then she lets it out again and rushes back through the door when Aiden comes out to see what all the fuss is about.

I will protect Jon. And to do that, Nelly needs to protect our babies.

Driving across town, but not rushing, since I need to get there when Jon does, I pass through Main Street and think back to high school, back to the good old days of knowing my future bride was betrothed to someone else, and all I had to do to secure my future was to steal her.

It's my thing, right?

Steal, lie, cheat. A man who has lived my life ain't too proud to hit below the belt if it's what I need to do to win a war. I only participate in wars I deem worthy, and if I deem it worthy, then I already deem it necessary to win. There is no second option.

Pulling off to the side of the road at the entrance of the trailer park, hidden by overgrown trees and a wrecked truck, I peek through my windshield and the truck's windshield and wait.

I don't know my game plan, but Jon can't go on living like this. So I wait, I tap my fingers on the steering wheel and sing a Bryan Adams song under my breath. It's the song that was playing over my radio the first night Nelly came to me all those years ago. The same song we dance to in our kitchen every time it comes on the radio.

It's our song, because everything I do is for her. For my family. For the people who hold my heart.

Today, in this trailer park, everything I do is for a broken boy and his sweet baby sister who shouldn't know the things they know.

Eventually, about forty-five minutes after leaving home, Jon pushes through the thick tree line and emerges amongst long grass. He stops and casts a scared glance across the open park, but he doesn't see me here. He'd never expect me to follow, and if I did, he'd expect me to be running behind, not driving around.

With tears on his face, because he already knows going into that place will hurt him, Jon bolsters his bravery and steps forward with broad shoulders. Nothing I've ever endured in my life required as much bravery as Jon shows when he walks toward the front steps and opens the shitty door to his derelict home.

As soon as he steps in, the shouting starts, like his bitch of a mother thinks he's *late* for his beating. Pushing out of the cab of my truck at the first thump and Jon's cry, but leaning back in with the rage pulsing in my blood, I grab a tire wrench from behind my bench seat and roll it in my flexing hand.

I don't own guns.

They're too fucking dangerous for a guy with too much at home to risk, but I have my fists. I have my wits, my strength, my speed, and I have fucking rage sizzling through my blood and a heady cocktail of mourning and injustice for an abused little boy who took a beating time and time again because he was trading himself for his sister.

To keep her safe, he risks death or permanent disability every time he steps inside this place, but today, it ends.

Storming forward and ignoring the shitty Ford that drives in behind me, slams on its brakes, then backs the fuck up again, I head straight to the door Jon moved through and almost rip it off its hinges when I tear it open.

It's dark inside, almost pitch black until my eyes adjust from the middle of the day sunlight outside, but then I see it, I see Wayne-Fucking-Hart with his pockmarked face barely an inch from Jon's, and his strong hand holding my boy around the throat and a full foot off the floor.

Jon's body spasms, his eyes bulge, his feet kick out in search of something to stand on, and his hands tear at his dad's skin. But the man squeezes the life out of a little boy until I roll forward on a roar and slam my tire wrench over Wayne's broad back.

Jon's mother screams when her husband drops. Jon falls and slams his head on the kitchen table. The way his eyes roll into the back of his head when he's knocked unconscious scares the fuck out of me, but in my fury, I consider it a kind of blessing, because while he can't see, I take my wrench and slam it over Wayne's body. Bones break. The sound of crunching cartilage spurs me on, and when blood shoots from the man's body, I toss my wrench and use my fists instead.

It's an unfair fight. The man can't fight back, but then again, Jon couldn't either, so I call it even and let my fists rain over this prick's ugly face with zero remorse.

I might go to prison for this. I might hurt my family by taking care of this man, but I can't let Jon come back here again.

"They're mine!" I break his teeth beneath my knuckles. My fists shatter Wayne's eye socket, but I take pleasure in the possibility of popping the fucking eyeball out and letting it roll away. Jon's mom screams and throws fists at my back, but she's no more than an annoying mosquito. "Mine, motherfucker!" He remains conscious and staring into my eyes, but his hands hang limp. "They're coming with me, and they're never coming back here again!" Pushing up, I toss Shirley off my back, uncaring when she slams against the feet of the table and cries out.

"I'll call the cops on you," Wayne spits through broken teeth. "I won't let this go."

"And I'll take your son straight to the police station now and have him press charges, you piece of shit." My muscles bunch and release, my knuckles hit bones stronger than they are, they break under my strength, but I consider it the price for my boy's freedom. "He will not come back here again, or you'll have me to answer to." Standing, I sink my boot into Wayne's ribs. Once, twice, three times, and take pleasure when they collapse under the force and blood spills from the man's mouth. Dropping down again, I grab Wayne's jaw and bring his eyes around to mine. "I'm taking them both, and they will never come back here again."

"Get the fuck out of my home."

"I won't be back, but neither will he." I glance up when Jon squirms on the floor. "Neither of those babies will be back, and there's not a damn thing you can do about it."

"They belong to me," he lisps past broken teeth. "They're mine."

"If you come looking for them, I'll slit your fucking throat. I'll do it painfully, slowly, and let you watch yourself bleed to death. If you come for them, there's nowhere you can hide from me. If you cross me, I will be the living embodiment of your worst nightmares."

"I'll kill you." Coughing, he spits blood onto the filthy floor beneath us. "I'll end your miserable life."

"Then I'll haunt you, motherfucker. Because nothing scares me, least of all a pissant who beats kids for fun." Leaning closer, I wait for his terrified eyes to meet mine. "Cross me. I dare you. But you will *not* get past me to get to those children again."

Slamming my fist into his face one last time, I snap his head around and send him to sleep just as Jon dizzily sits up and knocks his head on the underside of the table. "Dad?"

"I got you." Ignoring the blood on my hands and the howling bitch I have to step over, I take Jon's much too light body from the floor and help him stand on his own two feet. "Don't look over there." I grab his face when he wants to see his father. "Hey." I bring his eyes back to mine. "I'm gonna take care of you and Iz from now on, okay? You have my word."

"Don't tell Bobby."

My heart stutters in my chest. Pulses. Stops. Then beats anew.

He shatters me, because he doesn't want his best friend to know his weakness. "I won't tell a soul about this. From one man to another, you have my word."

"Tell Mom I fell down." His eyes spill over, but he doesn't cry. His voice doesn't break, and his breath remains even. "Don't break Mom's heart."

"I won't." Pulling him close, I hold him straight and let him walk. To feel like a man, he needs to walk out on his own. "Sometimes we have to lie to those we love. If it's super important, if it's to save them hurt, we can keep the secret."

"That's what I was doing," he whispers as I lead him toward the door. "I was saving Iz from the hurts."

"I know you were, bud. I know what you've been doing. But you don't have to do it anymore. Come on." I lead him into the sun and catch him when he almost sprawls. "I got you, buddy. Come on."

It takes us ten minutes to get him into my truck and his seatbelt secured so it doesn't hurt his aching body. I waited outside barely a minute from when he walked in, and yet, Jon aches in ways that hurt my heart.

Backing away from the trailer park and heading toward town, I say nothing when he curls up on the bench seat and covers his face. He makes it look like the sun is bothering him, but in reality, I know its something else. Something that makes him feel like less.

"You trust me to take care of you, right? Jon?" I tap his leg and grit my teeth when he jumps. "I won't ever hurt you. You're coming to live with us now."

"They're gonna come back and get us. They're gonna be extra mad, so they'll hurt Iz to punish me."

"No they won't. Hey?" I grab his face and bring it around. "I swear to you, I'll make sure they never come back again. Do you think for a sec I'd let anyone hurt Bobby?" With wobbling lips, he shakes his head. "Aiden? Jimmy?" Again, he shakes his head. "What about Mom? You think I'd let anyone hurt her?"

"Definitely not," he whimpers.

"Exactly." I put on my brave face and steel my spine, because this boy makes me want to weep for him. "You're one of us now. You may as well change your name to Kincaid, because I'll protect you like I protect them."

CHAPTER 18

JON - NOW

"He never knew what was *truly* happening to me in that place." Sitting in Mom's living room decades after that day in the trailer park, with my sweet Izzy sitting across from me, and her baby girl – who's no longer a baby herself – sitting right beside Bryan's soulmate. Mom watches us all with pride in her eyes, even if that pride is shadowed by grief. "He never knew they sold me, he thought taking a beating was the worst of it, but I'm actually really thankful for that. He would have killed them." Holding my wife against my previously broken ribs, I press a kiss to the top of her head. "He would have murdered them in cold blood, and I didn't want that on my hands. So I kept the secret from those I love."

"But you still hung at the fort," Izzy says. "And after that, even when I was sixteen, seventeen, eighteen, you told me if they speak to me, to let you know."

"I didn't know that he'd taken care of it for real." Meeting Mom's eyes with a smile, I add, "I worried, because having him stand in front of us was protection, right? But then he died, and my shield was gone again."

"So you worried they'd be back?"

I shrug. "It was a logical worry. I figured everything would go back to how it was just as soon as Dad was buried."

"I promised you it wouldn't," Mom murmurs. Sitting between my nieces, her granddaughters, and snuggling in close, Nelly Kincaid still looks as beautiful and fearsome today as she did back then. I never should have doubted my protection, because Bryan wasn't even the strongest of the two. "We promised to take care of you, and that job didn't end just because... well..."

CHAPTER 19

BRYAN – THEN

"I don't think I can do it legally, Bert. But I don't think they're smart enough to know any different." Whipping a yellow envelope from inside our closet and pulling the flap open, I present highly fabricated and super illegal documents that make it *look* like I'm going to adopt those babies. "We just need the signature, right? It's enough to make them think we have the control."

"I dunno, Bry." Sitting on the end of our bed just days after Jon's last beating, Nelly sits in tiny sleep shorts, bites her nails, and watches me pull my Padres ball cap on. "I just don't know what to do. What if they come back for them? You can beat on those jerks as much as you want, but the law is the law."

"Which is why we need signatures." Snapping the envelope closed and folding it in half, I stuff it into my back pocket. "I'm doing this, okay? But I need your permission, baby. I need your blessing."

"Of course." Standing, she walks forward and doesn't stop until our chests touch. "You have my blessing. They're ours, and we aren't letting go. But I don't know about your plan; it'll only take them a second to call our bluff. And if they take these papers to the police, it might be *you* that gets into trouble, not them."

"I gotta do it, Bert. We need to fix this, so this is what we have to do. Trust me to get the job done."

"I trust you." Standing on her toes, she presses a kiss to the underside of my jaw. "I trust you more than anyone else in the world, so I trust you to take care of this."

"Okay." Grabbing her hand, I head toward the door and into the hall. "Walk me out, Bert. This feels kinda like race day, huh?"

"Don't say that!" She smacks my arm and slows our steps toward the door. "That makes it feel so much worse. You know I never wanted you to race."

"I promise to drive under the speed limit the whole way there and back." I press a kiss to her jaw. "Pinky promise."

"Movie night tonight?"

"Yup. You'd think the Neverending Story would go for longer than an hour and forty-five, but we'll make do with what we've got. I really need that hour forty-five with you, Bert." I let my eyes widen until she giggles. "My balls are blue without you. Blue!"

She wraps her arms around my hips and snuggles in. "We'll be on the clock, and we'll use every single minute that the kids are glued to that movie."

"Yes, please." Tilting her head back, I press a kiss to Nelly's plump lips, then another, and then I just decide *fuck it*, slide my tongue in, and hold her up when she wants to melt into the floor. "Tonight, baby. Tonight, we make up for all the interrupted times."

"Ugh!" Bobby skids on the hallway floor and shields his eyes. "Dad! Let her go."

"Nope." Chuckling, I press another kiss to her lips. "Never ever. Go out the back and play with Jon. Mom and I are talking."

"Jon's at the fort. Ugh!" He cries out again when he opens his eyes and finds us in exactly the same position as a minute ago. "Stop it! Seriously, you gotta respect her in front of us. That's my mom!"

"And she was my wife first, son. Lucky for you, I'm heading out for a bit now. I've got business to take care of, then I'm gonna go see a friend."

Dropping his hands, Bobby tilts his head curiously. "Which friend?"

"A guy I used to go to school with. You met him when you were small, but then we got busy and forgot each other."

"Can I come with you?" He steps forward as though I've already said yes. Usually, I would. He's my best friend and comes with me almost everywhere I go.

But not today. Not for this. Because I made a promise to Jon, a promise I intend to keep. "Not today, B. You gotta stay here and take care of the family." Finally turning away from Nelly and chuckling when she sways, I turn to my son and toss my hat against his chest. "You're the man of the house till I get back."

Pulling the hat on and squishing his too-long hair down, Bobby flashes a handsome grin and broadens his chest as though wearing it makes him proud. "I got control of the place, Daddy. I've got your back."

"Good boy." Turning back to Nell, I hold her jaw and bring her eyes up. "I love you."

"Love you."

"See you soon."

"No racing."

Chuckling, I press my lips to hers. "I promised I would never race again. You gave me the yes, so now you control my world. See you in a bit."

Walking out my front door and sliding into my truck, I sit in the front seat and stare back at my house for a long minute. The family I fight for is in there, and the other two play at a fort the group of them built years ago for somewhere else to play.

I was never a rich man, we never eat steak or drink fancy wine, but noisy nights at the dinner table, and five snoring children crammed into a three bedroom home is all I need.

I need pictures on my walls, smiles everywhere I turn, and a warm wife to climb into bed with each night.

A long time ago, I was lost, but I didn't even know yet that I needed to find my home. My true north. But then I looked into a dazzling pair of eyes framed with dark hair and a sassy smile, and there she was. My world realigned, my priorities straightened out, and my home was found.

Chantelle Robertson was everything I needed, and through her love, gave me everything I didn't even know I wanted yet.

But now it's time to complete that circle. Jon and Isabelle Hart belong to someone else according to the law, but in my heart, I know they're mine.

Finally starting my truck, I back out of the driveway and smile when I catch Nell's eyes through the front window. She gives a gentle finger wave, then laughs when Bobby climbs over her lap and looks through the window like a puppy with his tongue lolling out. He wears my hat, and makes his mom laugh. He's as strong as an ox, and more responsible than any other twelve-year-old I know... bar one.

Heading across town with adrenaline zinging through my blood and the yellow envelope sitting beside my thigh, I cruise through the single set of traffic lights in town, past the town hall, around the park in the middle of town, and turn right at the end of the block. Heading out, I cross the train lines and move closer to the trailer park.

I'm going to hurt a man today, but I won't be sorry.

I'm going to reclaim what is mine, and more importantly, I'm going to reclaim what is Jon's, and I won't feel a lick of remorse for a single thing I do.

Pulling up outside Wayne Hart's home and cutting the engine, I study the closed-up place with narrowed eyes and wait for the dust to settle around my truck. The windows are closed, the curtains drawn, the door is closed. Even the pile of worn and tattered boots that littered the place earlier this week are tidied.

Climbing out of the truck with the envelope in my hand, I reach behind my seats and pull out my newest purchase. Something I never once, not for one single second considered taking inside my home. I took my ass to a sporting goods store the day before yesterday when this idea came to me, dropped way too much money, and walked out with a Winchester shotgun and ammo.

I never told Nelly I bought it, not because she'd get mad about spending money, but because I know she has the deepest, darkest hatred for guns. The same kind of hatred she had for me racing my car back in the day. The same hatred she had for me working three jobs, when she'd rather a little less money, but more time spent as a family.

Closing the truck door and resting the barrel of my gun on my shoulder, I walk toward the home that looks all but deserted and swing the front door open.

I don't knock. I don't show them a single ounce of mercy as I bring my leg up and my steel capped boots smash their flimsy door in.

"Wayne!" Shirley Hart screeches in the dark, with her hair in curlers and her ratty nighty on, even in the middle of the day. Bounding out of her chair and knocking a bottle of bourbon over, she pounces behind Wayne's recliner and shakes the shit out of him until the bruised man wakes with a start, looks around for the problem, then stops on me when I cock my gun.

His face is swollen to hell and back, his lips split, his brow taped from left to right. He doesn't move a single muscle as I stand in his doorway and point my gun.

"You're both going to sign these papers." Reaching back, I tug the envelope from my pocket and toss it into Wayne's lap, and because my wife is smarter than anyone I know, I smile when he pulls the papers out and a pen drops onto his thigh. "Sign them, give those babies to me, then never step on my side of town again."

"You can't do this!" Shirley screeches. "This isn't legal."

"I assure you it is. I paid some fucker who charges five-forty-five an hour to draw those papers up." *Lie, lie, lie.* "It's already done, now you just gotta sign and I promise to leave you be."

"And if we don't?" Wayne's voice is raspy, broken from a beating and too much alcohol to stave the pain. "You can't just take someone's children."

"Yes I can. I will. I already did. Sign those papers, or you'll find out what happens."

"Bullshit." Pushing the footrest back into the chair, Wayne grunts and inches forward. I take great pleasure in the pain I know he feels, and the way his breath whistles through faulty lungs as he works his way to his feet. Standing taller, but still not tall enough for me not to look down my nose at him, Wayne Hart dares me to prove my point. "I'm calling bullshit. Then I'm calling the cops and getting my kids back here."

"Bullshit?"

He nods.

"You sure you wanna risk it?"

Pursing his lips, he stares into my eyes and nods again.

Aiming just an inch above his shoulder, I shoot off a round until the ball bearings leave a hundred little holes in the wall and Shirley races around the room like a fuckin' lunatic. Bringing my aim back to Wayne's face, I lift a brow in challenge, even while Shirley runs through the rays of sunlight now peeking through the wall. "Want another demonstration?"

"I want my lawyers to look at these papers." Turning, Wayne picks up the envelope and folds it as through this is something he can put aside at his leisure. So I turn and shoot out his television until sparks fly into the air and the papers magically reappear between us.

With my gun in hand and every fucking intention to shoot these pricks dead if that's what it takes to walk away with those children, I aim at Wayne's face and watch him sign his children away like they're worth nothing more than a TV. "Shirl. Shirley!" He grabs her arm and drags her hysterical ass closer to us. Pushing the pen into her shaking hand, he draws her name for her and looks back up with unfiltered anger in his eyes. "It's done."

"Good. Those are my children now. If you so much as speak to them ever again, I will shoot you between the fucking eyes and watch your blood turn black. Do we have an understanding?"

His wide jaw ticks, and his heavy brow pulls low. If the fat fuck took care of his body, his life, and stopped drinking, he'd actually look decent.

"Do we have an understanding?"

"Yes!"

"Don't come near them again. If you see them in the street, its your responsibility to turn the other way and get the fuck outta there. If I find out different, I'll remind you what my fists can do."

Snatching the papers back and shoving them into my pocket, I fire off my final round and blow out their box fridge. "Fuck you assholes for hurting those sweet babies."

Walking away with a whole new world in my back pocket, I climb into the cab of my truck and smile when a Bryan Adams song comes on the radio. It's like the soundtrack to everything good in my life. Like the universe is sending me a sign that this was right.

That I risked a lot coming here, but that it was worth it, because they signed, and even if the papers in that envelope won't stand up in any court, I know in Wayne and Shirley's hearts and minds, they think they will.

They think I won, and I won't ever tell them different.

Taking a detour across town and pulling into the house the locals call Popcorn Palace, I climb out of the truck in front of the rotted away home and head around the back with my Winchester in hand.

It's not a lie if Nelly never finds out, right?

It doesn't have to break her heart.

It's a lie I tell to protect those I love. So I bury the hardly used shotgun as deep as I can dig before my shoulders protest, push the dirt back over top and do my best to make the ground look undisturbed, then I head back to my truck and head toward home.

Because home is where I need to go.

It's where my heart is, and where I belong for the rest of my happy life.

CHAPTER 20

NELLY – MUCH, MUCH LATER

I've been a widower since before I turned forty.

Unable to move on from the only true love I would know, unable to let go of the one and only man I could call my soulmate. I made a happy life for myself while I raised three wonderful boys that looked just like my Bry, and I held on tight to my bonus babies, because they, too, were Bry's gift to me.

The day Bry told me he'd be back soon... was a lie. Because he never came back to me. Police reports speak of an accident at the traffic lights in the middle of town, a ran red light, no malice, just a tragedy that implied the universe had declared Bry's purpose fulfilled.

In my heart and soul, I knew it wasn't fulfilled, because I was still waiting for him. Every day, every night, every lonely breakfast, and every noisy dinner, I sat in my seat, and the chair at the head of the table remained empty while the family he helped build waited for our nightmare to end and for him to come home.

But he never did.

I found the envelope filled with signed papers in the wreck of his truck once it was cleared and I was allowed in. The truck was a write off, but I was allowed to take the Saint Christopher's medal that used to hang from the rearview mirror. I refused to think of how it ended up beneath the bench seat, so I took it and hung it on a chain around my neck every day from then until now. Because though Saint Christopher never kept my Bry safe, maybe when it's my time to go, he'll take me to my husband so we can be together again.

I took the yellow envelope from the truck and cried in my bed for days, because they were signed. They were stupid, illegal, and essentially useless in a court of law, but they were signed, and from that day forward, I neither saw nor heard of Wayne or Shirley Hart again.

Bry's purpose had been fulfilled.

He saved me, and then he saved two little Harts who then grew to be the amazing people they are today. They both gave me grand babies, they both continue to sit at my dinner table whenever I need a little company, and through their love and devotion to me, they tell me every single day how much they appreciate me and *Daddy*.

Izzy was still so small when Bry was taken from us, but she doesn't forget, and when I want to cry for my loss, she sits with me, she snuggles in and holds my hand, and she cries, too.

Because she's my baby girl, and she misses the man who traded his life for Jon's.

The years have passed since then. Lots of years, and lots of tears. I've changed, of course, and so have my babies. Weddings have been celebrated, as have anniversaries. Babies have come into this world – one of them is now named Bryan Kincaid, who lives up to his grandfather's memory every single day just by being himself. My children have made lives for themselves, legacies that Bryan would be truly proud of.

My children have made memories, happy memories that last a lifetime, and for Bryan, they had them printed and mounted on the wall. Because that was Bry's thing; pictures on the walls. Every wall. Every space. So there would always be a smiling face everywhere he walked in our home.

But being in a home filled with memories, even the happiest of memories, still hurts when the man who owns your heart is no longer here with you.

We were supposed to grow old together. We fought for each other, so it's not fair he was taken because of someone else's mistake. If they'd left just a minute sooner, or a minute later, it wouldn't have happened. If he'd just left a minute sooner or later, my whole life would be different.

But that's not how my story would be told.

Now I'm an old woman. Not frail in any way, but weary. So unbelievably weary as I drift through my years without my heart in my chest.

Sitting on the edge of my bed in the darkness but for the television lighting the pictures of my children on the walls, I hang up the telephone because my grandson wanted to talk to Grandma. To say goodnight before he went to bed, to tell me he loves me, because it's his job as his generation's Bryan Kincaid to remind me that I'm loved.

But when the line is disconnected, when he's gone back to his family, his life, his photographs, I'm left all alone with mine, and the chain around my neck.

A long time ago, on my wedding anniversary long after Bry was stolen from us, my son danced with me. He's tall like Bryan, handsome like Bryan, speaks, smells, and acts like Bryan, so on that special day, he danced with me, told me to close my eyes and pretend it was Bryan.

It was the most magical day of my life since before his daddy was taken from us, because for those few minutes, with my eyes closed, my husband's cologne filling my senses, and a familiar song playing for us, I was with my one true love, and I held onto it for as long as I could, for I knew it was the only time I would have until the day we were reunited.

I miss my husband so much more with every passing day. It's

supposed to get easier, but it doesn't. The pain is supposed to dull, but that's a lie.

How can I possibly live, when my heart is buried in a cheap casket in the cemetery in town?

Lifting my tired legs from the cold floor and lying back in the bed I shared with my husband for the short time I had him, I clutch to the medallion around my neck and close my eyes.

I dream of him.

I pray for him.

Walking away from my home in the early morning sun on the morning of my eighteenth birthday, I walk the few blocks between my daddy's home and the phone booth that is Bryan's and my meeting point. We talked about it last night. Planned it. We promised we'd meet here and begin the rest of our lives.

And just as promised, Bry leans against his shiny Mustang as his dark eyes shimmer in the sunlight and his smile is bigger than anything I've ever seen on his face before.

Holding a bouquet of stolen daisies in his left hand and ignoring the clumps of dirt still stuck to the roots, Bry steps forward and pulls me against his chest.

"About time, Bert. I've been waiting forever for you to arrive."

ONE MORE
A CHRISTMAS NOVELLA

CHAPTER 21

NOW

A PERFECT CHRISTMAS

The ground outside is covered in perfect white snow. The wind has turned mild after last night's storm. Half of the town is without power because of downed electrical poles, but here we sit, in my son's living room, toasty warm in front of the fireplace, while I balance a cup of tea on the tip of my knee.

We have no electricity, but so much love.

It's Christmas morning once again – breakfast, gifts, family and laughter – and though we've done this fifty times in the past, the traditions remain mostly the same. My boys now own a gym, a world-class, world-famous gym, at that. Which obviously wasn't something we had half a century ago, but the family breakfasts, the gift giving, the pancakes and laughter and teasing; it's all something I've experienced many times before.

The faces change over the years; from the youthful grins when my boys were just babies. Then my babies had babies, so many of them, so many smiles. Now their children are having children, and the family Bryan and I began so long ago when we ran away from this town and started our own world is coming full circle as Westley, my great-grandson, named for the evergreen love from a princess movie, kneels on the plush rug at my feet and tears through wrapping paper and cardboard boxes. He doesn't much care for the toys that came in the box, for the baby sized boxing gloves that came in another. He merely chews through green and gold paper with his single tooth, and grins while his family watch him like the treasure he is.

The roaring fire and dozens of people inside this one room are plenty to keep us all warm, even without electricity for heating. And though my grandsons grumbled about having to cook pancakes on the barbecue outside in the cold, our breakfast was still made, and water was boiled for my tea.

It's a regular Kincaid Christmas in a home bursting with love.

"How are you doing, Nelly?"

My newest granddaughter-in-law, Madilyn, lowers onto the couch beside me, slow, controlled movements, as she's careful not to spill my tea or hers, and tucks her bare feet beneath a cushion to keep them warm. She wears black tights, much the same as mine, and an oversized sweater that hides her trim shape well.

I love all of my family dearly, my sons, my bonus kids, my grandchildren, my great-grandchildren. But a couple years ago, Madilyn came into my life, burrowed her way into my heart, and now holds an extra special piece of it.

It's not entirely normal that I should create this attachment to a woman I had no clue existed even a few years ago, but I do. And I'm not ashamed of it one bit.

Though of course, that could be nostalgia talking.

Maddi's long, dark hair dangles and brushes against my arm as she makes herself comfortable, and when she's finally settled in, she looks to me and grins. "You doing okay?"

"Of course." I lean a little to the right so we rest against each other, and inhaling the beautiful scent of her perfume, I luxuriate in the perfection that is today. All of my family in one room, warm, fed, smiling. "Christmas is my favorite day of the year."

"Yeah?" She tucks her arm around mine and breathes out a sigh of content. "Why?"

I smile when my oldest son walks through the room on his way to do – something. Most likely, he's going to harass his wife and ask her for a hug, because he's a little high maintenance like that, just like his daddy was. But as he passes, he looks to the couch and grins for his mother and his daughter-in-law. His chocolate eyes sparkle, and his grin turns crooked and handsome. He shakes his head as he goes, and chuckles under his breath at the sight of two women huddled together.

No doubt, he assumes we're gossiping.

"Because," I explain on a sigh of happiness. "I see my family every single day of the year. Someone is always at my house, or I'm at theirs. Or I go to the gym, or you girls drop by and try to get me drunk on a Tuesday night."

Maddi sniggers at that.

"All those visits are so nice. But on Christmas, I get you all together in the one space, at the one time. I love seeing everyone together like this. It's my happy place."

"And to think," she smirks and looks around the room the way I do. Her eyes lock onto Bryan's, my grandson's, for just a moment. And for that moment, she's lost to me. They stare, Maddi nibbles on her bottom lip, and when Bryan lifts one hand and presents her with a signal we all know means he loves her, she replies in silence and burrows herself further into the couch. Happy, she rests her cheek on my shoulder, and continues, "To think, all of these people here, all of these kids, all of this love..." I bring my tea to my lips as she speaks. "It wouldn't be possible if you didn't get laid that first time."

A burst of tea explodes from my nose and lands on my pants so that dozens of eyes come up to check out what's going on. "Maddi!" I giggle like I'm still twenty-something, and not decades more. "Filth."

"Well, it's true," she snickers and passes a tissue from the box on the little table beside the couch. "You think I don't know the whole story. When you and your Bry met at school, to when he was trying to steal you away from that other scoundrel."

"That scoundrel..." I finish mopping up my mess and turn to Maddi with a crooked grin. "As in, your grandfather?"

"Yes! Him. I heard about the car racing on the weekends, Piper's Lane, Grandpa Bry's crude words disguised as charm. You think I haven't picked up the stories since I've been here?" Shaking her head and resting back against the couch, she places a hand on her stomach and goes back to watching her Bry play with his niece on the floor. "I got my own crude loudmouth," she continues. "And fifty years from now, it would be cool if I was sitting where you are, studying a hundred faces, and knowing that it started when two people fell in love."

I sigh and watch as Kit reenters the living room with Bobby's hand in hers. They've celebrated decades of marriage already. Three children. A dozen arrests and posting of bail; their own, and for their kids. New house, big fights, tantrums in the yard, and birthdays, so many wonderful birthdays.

Bobby pulls Kit into his side at the doorway, buries his face in her long blonde hair, and makes her throw her head back and laugh when he whispers something in her ear.

CHAPTER 22

THEN

"Come into the bedroom with me, Bert." Bryan's large hands have always made me feel small, delicate... protected. He wraps them around my hips and pulls me in close so his lips feather along the bottom of my ear. "We can bang it out in two minutes flat, and the boys won't even notice we're gone."

"Charming," I drawl to hide my laughter, and wrap my arms around his neck. It's Christmas morning almost ten years after we wed, Bobby is four, Aiden is two, and despite the fact there was a storm last night that knocked a tree into the powerlines up the street, stealing our power while the linemen work in the snow to restore it, here we are inside, toasty warm and surrounded by the heat from the fire Bryan built. Our boys sit under the tree they cut down themselves a week ago, eating the popcorn we used to decorate it, and make faces that their treat tastes somewhat weird. But they smile while they play with the new Hot Wheels cars Santa brought them this year. Bobby is especially loud as he crashes the diecast car against the foot of our couch, whereas Aiden is still our observer, our quiet one. "Does it bother you that this year, we can finally afford our electric, but the storm took it out anyway?"

Bry snorts and drags me toward the kitchen. He's looking for his own Christmas gift, and he's hoping it's filthy. "There's a lesson in there, I'm sure," he jokes. "Something about staying humble, about not taking things for granted. We couldn't afford shit for the longest time, Bert. No power, no gas for the car, no money for diapers. Now we have a few dollars in the bank, and maybe I splurged and bought you something that glitters."

I look down at my hand, at the ring he gave me just an hour ago, and the promise that, although we're already married, and though we already have a family, he won't ever forget the promises we made to always love each other.

Marriage and home life will never make us forget that we choose this. We choose each other.

"The universe saw me splurge, Bert. And it doesn't disapprove, but it's letting us know to be mindful." Without a word of warning, he grabs me around the hips, lifts me without a single worry for how heavy I am, and plops me on the counter so he can step between my legs.

My heart thrums, and my stomach jumps at his display of strength. He always catches me by surprise when he lifts me, though it really shouldn't. We're young, fit, healthy. Bryan is turning thirty soon, and though in his mind that seems old, in the grand scheme, he's only just approaching his prime. His strongest, his healthiest decade.

Bry presses his lips to mine, once, twice, three times, and massages my thighs. "So, I've been thinking."

"Uh oh," I snicker and kiss him back when he stretches his lips forward. "That's going to either be really awesome, or really bad."

"Zero faith." He runs his fingertips along my ribs in threat of tickling. "So we have Bobby, right?"

I burst out in laughter. "Right, we have Bobby."

"He's our crazy one. That punk is going to cost us a fortune in food and bail, right?"

"Yes." I wrap my legs around Bry's hips, my arms around his neck, and nibble on his lips while he speaks. "Bobby is going to do a little damage. We're in agreement."

"And then we have Aiden. He's the one who'll keep Bobby out of prison. They'll get a night here, a night there, but nothing that'll scar them for long. That's gonna be Aiden's cross to bear in life."

"He's two, Bry."

"Right, but he's an old soul." Bryan stops massaging for a moment, and smiles. "Bobby got the Kincaid genes. But Aiden is like his momma. Gentle and quiet, smart and mindful."

"Does that mean Bobby also got the smooth-talking genes, the lady killer smirk, and the ability to talk his way into – or out of – anything he wants?"

"Well," Bry answers with a sly grin. "Of course. It's in the blood."

"What's your point?" I mock-sigh like this discussion is exhausting, though in reality, my husband works so much, so many hours, that we hardly get to see him. Anything he wants to say to me, ever, for however long it takes, I'm going to be here, his captive audience with nowhere else I would rather be. "Get to the point, Bryan."

"I think we should have another baby." He tosses it out so easily, so friggin casually that I choke on...nothing! Spit. Air. Something. But whatever it is, Bry laughs and pats my back to clear my airways. "Wow," he chuckles and rubs circles between my shoulder blades. "You sound thrilled."

"I mean..." I swallow down the ache in my throat, the tears in my eyes. "Just..." I angle my body to the left, to the doorway, until I catch sight of the boys still happily playing. It takes Bobby all but a single second to make things explode. It's like a superpower for him, which means I never get to look away for more than a minute. Coming back to Bry, I study his sparkling eyes, his square jaw, his twitching lips. "It's just..." I swallow and peek down between us. "You do realize how far my vagina has to stretch to get those kids out, right?"

He snorts so hard that my hair flicks back. "Yes, Bert. I know that you stretch a little to get them out."

"A little!" I lean back and shake my head. "A little is this," I lift a hand and separate my finger and thumb just a fraction. Then I use both hands and hold them a foot apart. "*This* is a lot. And this is how far I stretch, because your babies are *massive*."

"Ten pounds is hardly–"

"Bryan Kincaid," I growl the name I've growled a million times in our ten years. "I will shove a watermelon up your puckered asshole if you finish that sentence."

He stops, grins, and grabs my wrists. "I love you, Bert."

"I love you too," I grumble. "But my vagina already hurts thinking about this. And what about our finances?"

He tilts his head a little to the right and frowns. "What about them?"

"You already work so hard," I murmur sadly. "You're working yourself to the bone for us, out early, home late, and maybe we're okay now. We're making rent, and the electric wasn't cut off because we didn't pay the bill. But still..."

"You don't want another baby?" He presses a gentle kiss to my wrist and batts his lashes, because he thinks he's cute. "You don't remember how awesome the first two are?"

"I do," I answer on a whisper. "They're amazing, and you're amazing, and–"

"Putting me and you together," he inserts with a sly grin, "makes for some amazing kids."

"That is true," I concede on a sigh. "I just miss you when you're working."

"I miss you too." He wraps an arm around my hips and slides me closer on the counter until his hardened crotch touches my core. "I think about you all fucking day, Bert." He feathers his fingertips along my arm, over the ball of my shoulder, and when I shiver, he grins and runs his fingers over the side of my neck and up to my chin. "From the moment I leave in the morning, I'm thinking about you. I fix cars, I work with my hands, but the whole time I'm gone, I'm thinking about this cute little nightie."

"Bry!" I squeak and try to bounce back when he fingers the thin material I've yet to change out of, since it's still early. He's stronger than me, more determined as he moves his hand up and cups my sensitive breast. Now, instead of squeaking, I sigh, "Bry."

"I think about how you taste," he murmurs and leans forward to take my lips with his. "Here, and down there."

"Bry, stop. The boys—"

"Have Hot Wheels and each other to play with." He buries his face against my neck and groans when I buck closer. Maybe I said stop, but my body says *yes please*. "I spend all those hours at the garage, Bert, but I think about you. I wonder what you're doing." He smiles against my skin. "I wonder if you touch yourself when I'm not around."

"No!" I exclaim and try to pull back. "What?"

He chuckles and threads his fingers through my hair to hold me close. "I know you don't. You save yourself for me, but I still think about it."

"We go to bed together every night," I breathe out and close my eyes when my brain finally gives up on arguing. "You often work late, so I'm already in bed. But eventually—"

"Eventually I get home," he finishes and bites the sensitive skin on my neck. "I go to bed, and there you are, toasty warm and pliable as a pretzel."

"And you have your way with me."

He breathes out a throaty chuckle and slides his hand along my ribs and down to my hip. "You don't mind, do you? I know you're tired, but—"

"But it's not home until we've touched." I let my head drop back, my neck stretch, and groan as his teeth nip at the pulse in my throat. "I would probably cry if you didn't wake me up when you got home."

"No crying allowed." He smiles against my skin, and slides two fingers past my panties until I sigh and turn to jello. He doesn't need to warn me, no need for any more foreplay. He simply slides the digits inside and catches my heady breath when he hits all the right spots. "Jesus, Bert. You lie about all the stretching you do to get the babies out."

I snort and roll my hips in the same breath. He's already in, already started. And the boys are happily playing. "Charming," I whisper and try to swallow down my groan. "Damn, Bry."

"Fill my hand, Bert." He works faster, harder, and draws me closer to the edge. After ten years together, he knows my buttons. He knows my triggers. So what used to take a little while, he now knows how to accomplish in a minute flat. "But don't make a sound."

"Not your hand," I whimper and reach out for his shoulders, but when my hand drops forward without making purchase, I crack my eyes open and find his chocolate eyes staring deep into mine. I jolt, then frown. "What?"

"Not my hand?"

I lick my dry lips and shake my head. "No."

"Bedroom?"

I giggle and throw myself forward so I can grab onto him. "Yep. But quick. You know Bobby will come looking if we're gone long."

"Deal." Bry scoops me off the counter with one sweep of his arm, crushes me to his chest, and without a single hitch in his breath, he runs across our outdated kitchen and into the hall. "No fighting, boys!" He jogs into our bedroom, spins back and slams the door, then because we have no lock, he presses me against the thick timber and sets me on my feet only long enough to push my panties down.

I know in the movies, the hero tears his leading lady's panties off and thrills in the sound of snapping threads. It's surely a show of being the alpha, the strongest. But we're poor, and ruining things just for the sake of ruining things isn't a turn on for us. So he drops to one knee instead, slides my panties down and lets them flitter to the floor, and though he lifts my nightie and takes a long, penetrating look at what he finds, he doesn't touch. He doesn't taste.

His chest lifts and falls. Quickly. Powerfully. Then he glances up and meets my eyes. And that one look, the way his eyes dig deep into mine – this is the look that reminds me every single day why we're here. Why we choose each other. Why we work so damn hard to make sure we're good to each other.

"I'm so in love you with you, Bert." Bry slowly pushes to his feet, slides his hands along my thighs, and drags my nighty up so the soft ends tickle my sensitive flesh and send goosebumps racing along my spine. "There hasn't been a single second since the day I met you that I doubted you were it for me."

Smiling, I lift my arms around his neck and pull him closer.

"Even when you get on your period and turn into a psycho, I still love you."

"You're an ass," I snicker, and yet, when he lifts, I let my legs wrap around his hips and cinch tight.

"Even though your driving is..." He ponders with a teasing smile, only to finish with "mediocre."

"I'm not a mediocre driver!" I burst out, but it's broken with a whimper when he reaches down and places the tip of his bare cock against my opening. I didn't see him push his pants down. I didn't feel him pull his penis out. But the fiery heat and rock-hard length brings me to a startled silence.

"You are so fucking mediocre when you're driving, Bert. It's terrifying, really." He nudges forward, slowly, torturously. And when my breath comes in short, sharp pants, he stops and waits for my eyes. We stare in silence for a moment, mingling breaths, synced heartbeats. Then when I don't think I can bear the wait any longer, he slams his way home and steals my breath when I cry out at the pleasure and pain. "You make it a sport to not stay in the lines."

"Dammit," I whimper and shamelessly dig my nails into his shoulders. "Jesus, Bry."

"Did I hurt you?" He holds me up so easily, so strong, and slowly begins moving in and out.

"Little bit," I breathe out. But at the same time, I ride him, and let him soothe away the ache to make room for a different kind. "Jesus, that feels good."

"This is the best Christmas gift ever." His movements turn faster, rhythmic, so my tailbone claps against the door and sets us on a deadline. The boys will hear us soon, they'll come to investigate, and if we don't emerge fast enough, Bobby will find another way in. "You're so tight, Bert. So fucking tight."

I press my head back against the door and close my eyes. Every time I *think* about sex with my husband, I plan to be more active, to pleasure him, to make it exciting.

But every time we *actually* have sex, I'm reduced to nothing more than a blob as I feel the sensations that roll through my body. I'm a willing captive, powerless to do anything but close my eyes and absorb whatever he does to my body. "You didn't open your present yet," I whimper and squeeze him tight. "I worked really hard on it."

His hips stop moving, his hands turn firm on my thighs, and when I open my eyes, I'm met with his intense stare.

I look around the room – left, then right – before frowning and coming back to him. "What?"

"You got me a present?"

"Yes." I let my grin creep up and taunt. "It's Christmas. Of course I did."

Hesitant, he lets his eyes flicker between mine. "Under the tree?"

"Yes!" I laugh. "Where else would it be?"

"Well, first of all," he begins moving again. "You didn't have to get me anything. Christmas is for you and the boys."

I drop my head back and groan as his tempo picks up.

"And second." He reaches up and grabs my jaw with his calloused hand. Yanking me forward until our eyes meet, he smolders and turns my stomach to nervous goop. "*You* are my gift, Bert.

Every. Single. Day." He thrusts forward and slams me back against the door on each word. "And lucky for me, I don't have to wait for December to unwrap you." His hips piston in and out, faster and faster, but while he does that, he leans forward and pushes the top of my nightie aside – *unwrapping me* – and nibbles with punishing bites that make me hiss. "You're the best gift I ever got." His head whips up when a crash sounds from the living room. Something heavy, something that likely put a hole in the floor. Then he looks to me and grins.

It's the grin he gets when he speaks of racing cars. The grin that says "challenge accepted." He pounds into me, harder, faster, until my tailbone hurts and my breath explodes out until I turn woozy.

Bry's hands are rough, painful, but it's the best kind of pain.

He attacks my neck with his teeth, biting, then laving, and all the while, the coil of lava sitting in the bottom of my stomach grows hotter and hotter.

"I'm gonna go, Bert." Bryan's movements turn more desperate as he teeters on the edge of oblivion and another crash sounds from the living room. "Come on, baby." He squeezes my hip so tightly that it hurts, but instead of my brain focusing on "ouch", my orgasm runs with it and sprints toward the finish line. "You're so tight," he groans and buries his face against my neck "Fuck!"

A third crash sounds from the living room, then a "*schwoop*" that makes my heart skip with nerves, but then Bryan smacks me. One sharp, cracking smack, and my heart leaps into oblivion.

I cry out, though I know I shouldn't. I scream, but try my damned best to cut it off. Bryan slaps a hand over my mouth and smothers the sound, and while he does that, he comes so violently that his legs shake and our foundations begin to crumble.

"Jesus," he pants and releases his hand when I bite. His breath races to the same tune as mine. "Jesus, Bert. I think I'm gonna fall."

I burst out in giggles that turn to a groan when aftershocks zap my nerve endings and another zinging orgasm ripples through my blood. "Godddddd," I breathe out and squeeze him closer. "Merry Christmas to me."

Snorting, then slowly pulling back, Bry breaks the grip my legs have around his hips, and gently, he pulls away until only the tip of his cock remains inside me. "You ready?"

My throat is parched, and my lips feel abused. Licking them, I nod and make a face when Bry pulls out and his semen dribbles along my thigh. I cup my core and snatch up one of his shirts from the bed to clean myself up before dripping to the floor. While I do that, Bry fixes his pants and swaggers to the end of the bed.

"Don't look so pleased with yourself," I grumble and wipe the excess from my skin. "You know your post-sex arrogance annoys me."

He barks out a loud laugh and grabs me as I walk by to pull on my panties. He wraps an arm around my stomach, yanks me against his body, and slams me to the bed so I'm half *on* him, half *beneath* him. He presses a fast kiss to my lips and chuckles. "You love my post-sex arrogance."

"Do not."

"Makes you wanna have more sex."

"Does not."

"Do you think you got all that cum out onto my shirt, or did a couple swimmers sneak in and make a baby?"

"Ugh!" I punch his shoulder and squirm beneath his hold. It's all a game, an act, because he can hold me down for the rest of my life, and I'll never complain. "We need more than one single kitchen discussion for it to be a *thing*, Bryan Kincaid. Did you forget how far my vagina stretches to get a baby out?"

"No farther than it stretches to get my dick in."

"You are a pig." But still, I giggle while I smack him. Another crash sounds from the living room and makes my heart jump. "We have to get out there before Bobby sets the house on fire."

"Why do you automatically blame Bobby, huh?" Bryan releases me, and takes my hand as soon as we're both on our feet. "You declare

Bobby is all Kincaid, and suddenly, he's the scapegoat for all bad behavior."

"*You* said he's all Kincaid!" I follow him to our bedroom door and into the hall. "Not me. And because it's true. I love my son, Bryan. But he's a damn handful, and you know it." We stop at the living room entrance and catch sight of the Christmas tree laying on its side, the very top just half a foot from the fireplace, and Aiden sitting on his brother's chest while Bobby thrashes beneath him. Aiden still wears last night's diaper, his binkie is being held between his teeth the way an old gangster might hold onto a cigar, and though he's smaller than his brother, he still manages to drop his weight and slow down the arson Bobby no doubt had planned.

"Bobby Kincaid!" I snap out with my mom voice. It's rare I ever have to use it. Rarer yet, that I use it *loudly*. In an instant, Bobby stops fighting, and instead whips his gaze to me and his father.

In his left hand, he clutches to a narrow box, giftwrapped in green and gold.

"Naughty!" Aiden demands around his binkie. "Beebee is naughty."

"It's a present!" Bobby wails and waves his hand. "Present for you, Daddy!"

"For me?" Bry's face lights up as he continues his post-sex swagger and makes his way over the fallen tree. He pushes it back up to stand, pinches off the very tip as it smokes and threatens to destroy our home. Then he grabs Aiden from Bobby's chest and tosses him at me.

Literally.

All forty pounds of solid toddler are thrown at me to catch, and as I do that, Bry lowers to his knees beside his Kincaid-kid and accepts the small gift with a smile.

They're partners in crime, Bry and Bobby. Colluders in this war of boys versus Mom.

Bry studies the wrapped gift for so long that my stomach dips, but rather than opening it, he turns on his knee to study me as I stand eight or so feet away. "Mommy got me a present?"

"It's just..." I settle Aiden on my hip and try to shrug the gift away. "Homemade. Not a big deal."

"Mommy's nervous." Grinning that way he does, Bry twists back to face Bobby, but he extends his arm in silent invitation. We don't often get to exchange gifts in our home. We just don't have the money, and though we're comfortable now, we make sure not to splash out and make tomorrow tight.

The fact Bry got me a promise ring is a big deal. The fact he now gets to open a gift is bigger yet.

I take a single step forward, and pray my wobbling knees don't give out.

"Why are you shy, Bert?" Bry hooks a hand around my hip and pulls me down to sit beside him. He studies my eyes for a long minute, frowns, and tilts his head when I uncharacteristically break eye-contact first. Concerned, he looks to Bobby and fakes the grin that all three Kincaid men own. "That's weird, huh? Mommy is never this nervous, is she?"

Bobby is older now, his vocabulary is advanced, and despite his lapse in judgement with the Christmas tree, he's smart as a whip. But he only lifts and drops his shoulders to explain his knowledge of what's inside the package. I hid this gift from him, because if he knew, he'd spoil it in a heartbeat.

"Bert?"

"Just shut up and open it," I grit out. I can't take the suspense. The worry. The nausea.

Bry's brows wing up in deference to my snapping tone. Thankfully, we've been together long enough to know the difference between angry snapping, and nervous snapping, so making sure Bobby is stable on the edge on his knee, Bry slowly peels the tape back on the paper to reveal a plain white cardboard box inside.

"Is this, like..." Frowning, he continues to slowly peel the box open. Glancing up, Bry's eyes meet mine. "Is this bad?"

"What? Why the hell would I give you a *bad* gift for Christmas?"

"Momma!" Bobby scolds and draws his brows together. "Don't say hell."

"I'm sorry, baby. It's just..." I exhale and look to Bry. "Open it before I take it back and toss it into the fire."

"You would destroy my gift, just like that?" He shakes his head and tears the end of the box open. "You went to all the trouble to–" He pauses. Frowns. Then turning the box upside down, he empties the contents out so they rain into his lap.

One. Two. Three.

"Positive..." His frown makes way for a moment of confusion, then a wide grin as he spins to me. "Homemade! Bert!" Bry throws himself across my lap, saves Aiden and me from smacking against the floor, then he drops dozens and dozens of kisses all over my face. "It's gonna be a boy! A Kincaid. He's gonna be awesome!"

"Bry!" I cry out. Happy tears, terrified tears, laughing tears. "Get off me!"

"He's gonna be hell on wheels," Bry proclaims. "But it'll work out, I swear."

"I'm having a baby," I cry. "Maybe it's a girl."

"It's totally a boy." He scoops one arm under the arch of my spine and pulls me up so my eight-week-pregnant stomach pops a little. Grinning, shaking his head, he presses a kiss just above my navel and takes a moment. "Jesus, Bert. We're having a baby." He presses another kiss higher up. Then another over my heart as he makes his way along my body.

Aiden lays with his head in the crook of my arm, so as he passes, Bry presses a kiss to Aiden's nose. Then he comes to me and stops so our breaths mingle and our eyes meet. "Thank you," he breathes out. "I love you so much, Bert. For the rest of my life, and even after that."

CHAPTER 23

NOW

"We have an hour left until we have to go to the gym," my grandson stops at the doorway between the living room and the kitchen. He looks just like the first Bry, almost carbon copies, right down to the smirk and crude mouth. And today, he watches Maddi the way my Bry used to watch me.

Perhaps, if I wasn't thinking on my own past, I wouldn't notice the words they speak to each other in silence, the looks, the smiles. Maddi remains right beside me, nervously sipping at her empty tea cup, while Bryan's eyes flicker between his father's, his mother's, and Maddi's.

He's nervous when he so rarely is.

Taking a lone, wrapped gift from beneath the tree, he visibly shakes as his eyes flicker back to Maddi's. He's not nervous about her. Rather, he looks to her for support.

I smile and act none the wiser when she rests a hand on her almost-flat stomach and huffs in an effort to sit forward. I take her teacup, and press a hand to the small of her back to help, and I think, perhaps she's so distracted by what she and Bryan have planned, that she doesn't even notice that I help.

Finding her feet while Bobby and Kit are caught up in their own bubble of love, Maddi makes her way across the crowded living room until she stops by Bryan. They whisper for a moment, unnoticed by everyone but me and their niece, Alyssa. Then they each take an end of the small box and make their way to the grandparents-to-be. "Mom?" Bry murmurs with a shake in his voice. "Daddy. We, uh..." He coughs away a lump of nerves when Kit extricates herself from Bobby's arms, so when she turns and tilts her head, Bryan pales.

"Baby?" Kit looks between the couple with a furrowed brow. "What's wr–"

"Here." Bry thrusts the gift forward so fast that Maddi stumbles and he has to catch her. "Merry Christmas. We... uh... it's homemade."

WORTH FIGHTING FOR

A KIT AND BOBBY NOVELLA

CHAPTER 24

CURRENT DAY

Pulling into my family's gym parking lot and stopping in the same slot that's been allocated to me since the day my husband and I started dating, I switch the engine off and mourn the epic chorus that is Taylor Swift and that dude from *Panic!* as they sing of being awesome.

It's kind of appropriate, I guess, for that song to come on the radio just as I think of my husband. Bobby Kincaid has been mine for almost fifteen years, the amazing father to our three children, the best life partner since Bryan Kincaid passed the reigns, and the best fighter I know.

And I know a bunch of them.

Almost a decade and a half ago, I was insecure and terrified, a wallflower with too much weight around her midsection and a dress that was the bad kind of tight and, in my eyes, definitely not sexy. When Bobby walked – or more accurately, *swaggered* – into my life, I was a twenty-four-year-old accountant who wasn't sure how she'd find the strength to go on another day with the weight of the world on her shoulders.

But then I was found, saved, cherished by this man and made to feel like a goddess.

A good man's love is all I need in this world, the kind where I can feel his heart beating in my own chest, and from the moment I told him yes to a simple dance at Club 188, I've been living the kind of life women would kill for.

Not everyone gets to feel what I do, or be treated the way I do. Not everyone experiences this, and I know it. I know how lucky I am, and not yet in all these years have I taken Bobby—*with no middle name because he has mommy issues*—Kincaid for granted.

But as of today, things kind of have to change. If only for a short time. It's time to spice things up, and to do that, I have to get creative, lie to my husband without lying, and try not to break his gentle-giant heart in the process.

There's no one on this planet that holds his heart the way I do, so I vow to be gentle and to do this as trauma free as possible.

Swinging my car door open and grabbing my bag, I slide onto the gravel driveway and brace my stupid knee before it decides today's a good day to fail on me. It's been weak since my early twenties when I stretched the tendons out and allowed my knee to pop in and out at its leisure. It hurts like a bitch every time it happens, and brings tears to my eyes when I have our athletic trainer push it back into its rightful place.

Bobby has been on my case about it for a decade. *Wear your brace, baby. Wrap it up tight, baby. Let me carry you everywhere you gotta go, baby.* But he obviously has a lot to learn if he thinks I'm going to allow him to mother me that way.

Nobody mothers the mother, dammit!

"Baby?" As soon as I walk through the gym doors, my husband and his youngest brother race forward and skip to a stop in my face. "Babe! Tell Jimmy that thing you told me."

I look between the two men who look disgustingly alike, but where Jimmy sits at a comfortable two-hundred and ten pounds,

Bobby has always outweighed him with an additional fifty. Both men are heavy, and so are the rest of the guys in this gym, but none are fat. Heavy-weight champions of the world, mutli-year winners, and respected among other athletes for their clean image and wholesome lifestyles, *my* guys are the best... but they whine like babies. "What thing?" I push past them and head past the regulation size boxing ring where our current contender pants and watches the show.

My husband isn't a competitor anymore, but he trains men and women who show a lot of promise and a hunger to get to the top. Right now, that person's name is Knox, he's eighteen, and hungry for the belt. Lucky for him, he stumbled – *hitchhiked* – his way to our gym where *my* guys remind him that it takes more than lip service and a pocket full of arrogance to win. They work him hard, they work him so much, my husband is gone as much today as he was when he was the one training for the belt.

Knox isn't our only contender, and the belts that belong to the Kincaids aren't the only belts that have come back to our gym. We're the best, because nobody trains as hard as we do. And there isn't a gym in all fifty states that is a family like ours.

Nobody has what we have.

Moving toward the offices in the hall – well, technically Bobby's office, but marriage means what's his is mine and all that – I slow just inside the door and lift a brow. "I don't have time for you guys at the moment. I have calls to make, so... We good?"

"We are not good, woman!" Jimmy is our jokester, our idiot, and the easiest of them all to love. "Tell me the thing, then we'll go. Bobby's been going on about it all day, so unless you can back it up, I'm going–"

"No, go away."

I try to swing the door closed, only for Bobby to catch it with a heavy hand and barge his way through. "What calls you gotta make, baby?" He walks through the doorway and doesn't even stop when his bare shoulder hits mine and pushes me back a step. It's May, but ridiculously, unseasonably hot, which means it's hot as Hades outside and necessary for the guys to work out in only shorts or risk heat stroke, but that also means Bobby's sweaty shoulder passes over mine and leaves a sheen of moisture on my already clammy skin.

"Just business." Walking away with a scrunched nose, I grab a towel from the stack on the filing cabinet in the corner and wipe my shoulder. "But it's kinda personal, so can you go away for a bit?"

"Personal?" Chocolate eyes stop scanning the pictures on the walls and snap back to mine. Just like always, my husband dials in on my shitty attempt at lying and steamrolls across the office when Jimmy tries to come in. With a heavy shove that sends his brother tripping back into the hall on a muffled curse, Bobby slams the door in his face and turns back.

He demands my attention. Stalks forward with a thick brow, sweaty hair, and bunching muscles. After all this time, he still makes my stomach tingle. He makes my heart race, and my palms clammy. Because when there's someone else on this planet that can see your soul, you're kinda screwed when you want to lie to their faces.

I'm wearing my usual tank and cut offs today. Hair up, spaghetti strap top, and short shorts that moms probably shouldn't wear, lest they embarrass their kids. But it's so friggin hot, I can't resist. I wear flip flops despite my angry athletic trainer declaring them bad for my knee. All of that to say, it's hot as hell, and when my husband doesn't stop until his chest touches my chest, his thighs touch my thighs, and his steamy breath fans my face, I'm overwhelmed with thoughts on how to capitalize on this moment, but also, how far away is the nearest lake full of ice?

"Baby?" His body warmth radiates from his chest to mine. His sweaty skin rubs off on my shirt, and his nearness makes my heart run that much faster, which only heats me up more. "What private shit you gotta do that I can't know about?"

"I'm just making appointments and stuff." I glance down at his throat rather than his eyes, since I can't stand under his glare. "Regular stuff."

"Why can't I know about it?"

"I never said you can't know about it." Playing my first card, I lean forward and press a kiss to his muscled pec. Right over the ink dedicated to our relationship milestones. "I said it was personal stuff. As in, lady doctor stuff. Not stuff Jimmy needs to hear."

"Oh..." Relaxing, he nods and leans closer until I drop a second kiss on his chest. "Everything okay down there? I'm kinda your lady business professional, so if you've got questions or concerns..."

"I'm fine," I laugh. Resting my hands on his hips, I push him back a step and meet his eyes. "I've got to make those kinds of appointments. And I think it's time for Brookey too, if you know what I mean. She's not a baby anymore, so we've gotta be prepared for when she..." *Play it up, Kit. Mess with his head.* "She's probably going to get her period soon. So you kinda have to be prepared for that, you know?"

"Brooke?" And there I go, breaking his heart. "But she's my baby."

"She's ten, Bobby. Almost eleven. I'm not saying it's going to happen today, but you need to prepare yourself."

"Prepare..." He's like a big old puppy who's been kicked while he's down. "What do we have to do to prepare? Jimmy never said anything about Bean."

"No," I roll my eyes. "That's because Izzy and I took care of it. Jimmy was spared, but you're not a wimp like him, right?" *Lay it on.* In my head, I imagine myself hitting the kitchen table and chanting *lay it on, lay it on.* "Everybody knows Jimmy's a little bitch, so we saved him the drama. Aiden's kinda perfect though, right?" I bite my smile when my jealous husband starts spinning out about his wife crushing on his middle brother. "He and Tina have Smalls totally under control with the girlie stuff, but Brooke's starting to get a little moody, and that sass..." I shake my head. "All I'm saying is that you have to be prepared for what's coming, babe."

"Okay." White as a ghost, clammy all over, but not from working out, his Adam's apple bobs with nerves. "Shit. Fuck. Okay." He rubs a hand over his chin and makes the short stubble crackle. "Fuck, baby. I'm not ready for this."

"I tried to protect you. I tried to make these calls without you in here, but you followed me in and wouldn't go away." *Keep going, Kit. Let's victim blame now, too.* "We've been married a long time now. It's time you learned when to listen to me. I was only trying to protect you."

"Right. You're right." He blows out an explosive breath and nods. "Fuck, okay. This is gonna be okay." Stepping back, my poor, sweet husband jumps on the balls of his feet as though preparing for a fight. "We're gonna make this all better, okay? I got it, baby." He slams his fists together. "We got this. I'm gonna be my baby's hero!" Spinning on his feet, he rushes out of my office door with a battle cry and zero fucking clue.

Shaking my head, I turn back to my desk and plop down. Bobby Kincaid is the sweetest, kindest, most selfless man I know, but I swear, females make him so dumb. Picking up my cell, I call my sister-in-law and prepare her for what's coming.

"Yeah?"

The sound of cars and cicadas buzz through the line. "Iz, I told Bobby a lie." Standing, I move back to the door and peek into the hall to make sure he's gone. "Bobby thinks the whole world is falling down."

"Bobby *always* thinks the whole world is falling down," Iz smarts back. I hear the school bell ring, then kid's screeching at their excitement about the end of another day. "What did you lie about?"

"You know how we're planning that thing?" When she makes noises of affirmation and the car doors open, I assume our kids are piling in. "Well, he was starting to sniff, so I told him I'm going to get a pap smear, and that Brooke is probably gonna get her period soon."

She scoffs. "Brooke got her period last summer."

"I know that! But now Bobby's freaking out. Probably warn her before you come back here. She's walking into an ambush."

"Ten-four, big chief. We're coming back now. On a scale of one to crazy, how's he–"

"You're gonna need to prepare my daughter, Iz. I tossed her under the bus. I'm a terrible mother."

Laughing, I hear her switch the engine on again as the kids' screeching turns to ear splitting levels. Between us, we have ten kids to shuffle between the school and gym every day. Bobby and I had three and declared that plenty, but then you add Iz's two, Aiden's three, and Jon's twin boys, and we've got our hands full of mini fighters and a hell of a lot of sass. And that doesn't include the babies that aren't yet in school. "You're so mean to that man, Kit. Swear to all that's holy, he's gonna have a heart attack before his time."

"I tried to protect him! I was trying to sneak in and get shit done, but *no*, the second I walk in here, the idiots are up in my face demanding answers."

"What did they want?"

Sitting back in my chair, I study my nails and smile. "I told Bobby last night that I secretly loved the pineapple joke. I admitted that I've loved it all along and only say I don't because I'm teasing. I guess he told Jimmy, and Jimmy didn't believe him."

"But you hate the pineapple joke. You said it was the lamest shit you ever heard."

"Don't judge me, Isabelle! I said what I had to say to get him out of my space. I'm trying to organize something special, but he's always up in my space."

"You used to love that about him. Oh! Brooke, honey." It's like I can hear Iz turning in her seat. "Your mom told a lie to your dad, so now you gotta pay the price."

"Ugh!" In my mind, I see the daughter who looks just like me throw her head back with exaggerated dramatics. "What did you do, Mom? What now?"

"She said you're turning into a woman. Like, with your period and shit. So now your daddy is freaking out."

"I'm sorry, honey! I'll make it up to you, I promise."

Five minutes after hanging up with Iz, and a couple minutes after hanging up with another friend that'll play an important role in my ultimate deception, I head out of my office and into the hall when I hear the Kincaid van pull up outside. The van itself is as silent as they come, one of those new, state of the art luxury models because *if the guys have to drive a mom van, then they want it to be slick as hell.* No, the van is silent, but the children are heard everywhere they go. That's the problem with lugging so many of them around in a small town.

I hear Bobby's deep voice, then Jimmy's. I hear Aiden, the third brother join the fray, then I catch sight of the front entrance when the crew walk in and the gym essentially shuts down.

Because my daughter is turning into a woman.

CHAPTER 25

BOBBY

"Brookey." I push away from my brothers with a racing heart and sweep my oldest daughter up into a bone crushing hug. My baby is only ten, I swear she was in diapers just last week, but now my wife is talking periods and growing up and all that crazy shit. "I'm not ready for this, baby." I drop a kiss on the top of her blonde hair. Then another. Then a third until she smacks me for messing up her ponytail. "I swear I'm not gonna be weird about this. I'm gonna make it okay, and I promise it won't hurt. I'll get you Tylenol or something, okay?"

My daughter, her mother's twin with the single dimple, the big eyes, and the long ash blonde hair looks at me the exact same way Kit does when we're mid-argument. "Dad, you're being weird about it by saying you're not gonna be weird about it."

"Nope. I swear!" I drop one more kiss on her forehead, then release her until she can stand on her own two feet again. "I've got this under control, okay? I'm gonna show you how a real man acts, so when it's time for... to...." The words literally clog in my throat. "No, just know that I'm all the man you'll ever need. Ice cream?"

"Ice cream?"

"Yeah? I'm going to the store. Want a snack?"

Dubious, my daughter looks from face to face as everyone watches on. Doing a full one eighty, she locks eyes with Kit, who tilts her head in the smallest nod, then Brooke turns back to me with a wide grin. "Thanks, Daddy. Caramel swirl, pretty please."

"You got it, princess. You okay for now? Wanna sit down or something?"

"Yeah. Maybe." Less exuberant than she was a second ago, Brooke takes my hand and leans heavily against my side as her cousins part the seas and let us through. "I'm in so much pain, Daddy. Maybe get me some M&Ms to have with the ice cream?"

"Of course, baby. Come on." I pass Jimmy and his daughter, then my best friend while he watches us with narrowed eyes. The women – Kit, Izzy, and Jon's wife, Tink – snicker as I help my groaning daughter along the hall and into the office I sort of share with Kit. "Daddy's gonna take care of this, okay? You can pull up a movie on the flat screen." I snag the remote on the way through and flip it on to the music channel. "Sit on the couch and chill out." Brookey groans and squeaks when I lower her to the leather couch and fix a cushion under her head. I grab the throw blanket off the back, but stop again at the sight of my daughter's gym shorts and remember its way too hot for a blanket. "You want an air conditioner brought in here?"

"Yes please, Daddy. And maybe a soda?"

"Of course." When she's comfortable, I drop a kiss on her forehead and race out to the kitchen. Swinging the fridge door open, I snag her Uncle Jack's Pepsi, only to jump three feet into the air when I close the fridge again and Jon scowls. "Jesus, Fart! You scared the shit outta me."

"Somethin's fishy, B. I don't know what's up, but I'm saying something is weird."

"Yeah, my fuckin' baby is going through *the change*, and I don't like this shit one bit."

He follows me out of the kitchen and into the hall. "I'm just saying, you might wanna slow your roll for a minute and reassess this situation. You know the women are always trying to punk us, so what's Kit's game today?"

"There's nothing to reassess. There's no game. My daughter is in pain. You don't hear her?" Right on cue, Brooke groans and sets my blood on fire. "You remember when this happened to Sissy, right? It hurt her, too. Now it's time to show my girl a real man ain't gonna run away when shit gets messy and PMS is running rampant." I storm through my office door and gently pass my daughter the icy cold soda. "Here, baby. I'll be back soon, okay?"

"You're going to the store?"

"Uh-huh. You want ice-cream and M&M's. Anything else?"

"Do you think they have any of those apple pies left in the frozen section? I really liked those."

"I'll look, okay?"

"Okay. And maybe a bag of gummy bears, too, just in case I want something sweet later."

When my sweet baby is laid up in my office, cooling down with her uncle's soda and a refrigerated air-conditioner I rolled in and set up, I drag Jon through the gym and snag Jimmy on the way past. "Come to the store with me."

"Nope!" Jon slides out of my grasp at the front desk and draws Aiden's eyes up. He's counting receipts behind the desk, making sure everyone is putting in their hours and preparing the students for grading. "I'm not coming for this," Jon snaps. "I didn't have daughters for a reason. Been there, bought that, dealt with aisle three already. Take Aiden."

"Take me where?"

"To the store. We gotta go buy Brookey supplies for her... *menses*."

His scrunched nose illustrates just how I feel saying that word. "You're being weird about it. It's not a big deal. Just buy her the shit, toss a candy bar into the room, then hang out in the hall for a week and deliver anything else she asks for. It's not so hard to figure out."

"Exactly. So you gotta come with me. We gotta buy all the stuff, and I don't know what's what."

"Just go to aisle three and pick one of each. It's seriously that easy. The girls will pick what they need from that stash, then you pay attention to the trash can. All that stuff comes with wrappers, figure out which wrappers are being tossed, then you know what she likes. Then you hit re-order every third week for the next fifty years. Kit and the girls will sync up soon, so that'll make ordering easier, then you set up an auto purchase thing online. My girls are all set, and I never have to worry about PMS again."

"See? You're a pro." I grab his collar and drag him around the desk. "Let's go. It's your duty as my brother to have my back on this. Then after today, we set up the auto-buy and the world is back in order." I drag Aiden and Jimmy into the blistering heat outside, only to remember the fact I'm shirtless when the lava-like sun sizzles my skin. Snagging a tank from the front desk and slipping it over my shoulders, I slide into the front seat of the van and switch the engine on.

"We got this." I turn the music up and bob my head when Fort Minor plays my song. It's like an omen, a sign from the universe. We're going to war, and we're going to win. "Aisle three," I murmur. "Aisle three is where we gotta be."

"And don't forget the ice-cream," Jimmy adds. "Women can get kinda psycho around this time of the month."

"I know!" I catch his eyes in the rear-view mirror. "I know. You think I don't know? I married the queen psycho. You see the sweet princess, but I know the monster that comes around the twentieth of every month. You think I don't know about that storm?" I pull onto the street and head toward Main. "You think I don't feel it in the air. The fifteenth hits and I fear for my life. From the fifteenth to the twentieth, I hide away and hope I survive another month.. She's like

Jaws, and I hear the *dun-dun, dun-dun* as she walks the halls. Those are the scariest days of my month, man! By the time the twentieth actually hits, she's usually more mellow, and then ice-cream and candy fixes everything."

"I don't believe that Kit is a monster," Aiden grumbles. "She's always so sweet."

"To you!" Jimmy pushes his face between the seats. "She's always sweet to *you,* because she thinks you're the bee's knees and *oh so sweet,*" he mocks. "But I see the real Ursula beneath that Ariel. I see the psycho that Bobby fears. You don't remember that time I broke Jack's nose? Fuck me sideways, I thought she was gonna peel the skin from my face. And now there are two of 'em!" My youngest brother brings his gaze back to me. "You probably need to get your affairs in order. Update your will, send out the thank you cards you still didn't do since your wedding, all that shit. Then go tell Mom you love her, because Brookey is a mini Kit, and now we're all dead."

"So fuckin' dramatic," Aiden grumbles. Sitting back in his chair, he runs a hand over his jaw and shakes his head. "Why you gotta be so dramatic? Kit is a sweetheart. Brooke's a cherub. And Knox is cooling off at the gym when he's supposed to be sparring."

"Knox can wait." I pull up into the parking spaces out front of Jonah's store and swing out of my seat. "Knox came to our gym knowing we're a family. That's *why* he came. He wanted family. Now my family is mid crisis, so he can go outside and flip the tractor tire for an hour. In fact." I grab my cell, since it's only the beginning of the month, and text my wife: *Send Knox out the front to flip the tire. I want him going non-stop till we get back. Get Jon out there to watch him, and remind them to drink water. Please, baby. I love you.*

Locking the van when the back door slides closed, our three man army walks through the electric front doors of Jonah's small store and the buzzer above us draws eyes. We've lived in this town our whole lives, and though a lot of people do their groceries elsewhere, since the selection here is both limited and grossly overpriced, we still come here to support local. They know us here, and world champion belts or not, people rarely make a big deal about us walking this store.

But then there's two-bucks-a-blowy Belle. Jonah's daughter, single, fake-tanned and lonely, she's been pining after Jimmy since they were kids and Belle realized she stood no chance. Jimmy has been married almost as long as I have, but still, this bitch slides on into whatever aisle he's in and bats her fake lashes. But not when Izzy's around; *oh, no. Definitely not when Izzy's around.*

"Don't even look at her," Jim grumbles. "If either of you fuckers says hey and invites her over, I'm sending Iz and Bean to sleep at your houses on the fifteenth, because you know they're all synced now. Don't make me be that guy who begins the end of the world."

"I'm not saying shit," Aiden rumbles. Taking the lead, he grabs a cart and heads toward aisle three with more confidence than any man should have in such an aisle. But he does it, and his confidence sets me at ease. "Grab one of each, B. Don't look at the price, 'cause they got the pink tax on everything women buy and it'll only piss you off."

"Hold up." I grab a packet of razors that look just like mine, but pink. "These fuckers are twice the price of mine."

"That's what I just said! Pink tax. It's criminal if you ask me. Grab the rainbow packet there." He points, so I grab. "See the thingy in the bottom corner, the blood shaped drop?" I feel my blood pressure drop at his words. "See how there's the empty drop, then the middle one, then the full one? That'll tell you what kind is in that pack. So you got the light, medium, and heavy."

"Which one do we need?"

"Fucked if I know! Get one of each."

And I do. I grab every packet with a droplet shape on it, and in my mind, the cost piles up before the cart is even a quarter full. "This shit is expensive, guys. Someone should write a letter to the politicians or some shit."

"Kit's been buying this shit with your money for a long time, B. Get over it." Aiden stops beside a new rack, and even he starts to pale.

His worry nearly sends me into a tailspin. "These are tampons. Don't overthink it. Just grab some and move on with your life."

"Which kind do I get?" I lean closer and try to ignore what they truly are. I look at the droplets and feel just a little bit more at home. I know this code now. Droplets. Let's work with the droplets. "Some are super long, and some are short."

"Get the long ones," Jimmy says. "They... uh..." Blowing out an explosive breath, he turns and walks away. "They're applicators," he murmurs over his shoulder. "To help them get them... well... in."

"But–"

"Just buy them!" he screeches. "Just buy them all. Why are you dragging this out? Why do you want us to live this nightmare longer than we have to? We all have daughters, and now all of them are... you know! I don't wanna talk about this shit anymore. Just buy the shit and let's go."

"Fine." Moving my arm to the back of the rack, I sweep everything into my cart in one go and nod. "This is enough. This is plenty."

"You guys can't take all of those!" Belle – all two bucks worth – stops at the end of the aisle and chews her gum. "I mean, you can, but then we gotta get more stock in, and maybe some poor chick is desperately in need of tampons right now, but there are none left. That's kinda shitty, ya know?"

"You're probably right." Nodding, I stare into my cart and wonder which to sacrifice. "Come here a sec."

"Bobby!"

"Go look for the apple pie thingies." I look up to Aiden. "Go with him. Get all the apple pies." When Belle stops beside me and practically whimpers as Jimmy escapes around the corner, I cough to bring her attention back to me. "Which ones don't I need?"

"You don't need the maternity pads, for starters." Leaning into my cart, she takes the jumbo packs out, but pauses. "Right? Nobody just had a baby?"

"Nope. No babies."

"Right." She restacks the packets, then glances back into my cart. "And you probably don't need the tiny travel cases. You bought the saver packs, so keep those and put the travel packs back." I help her restack what we don't need. "Are these for your wife or your daughter?"

"My daughter." My voice quivers with pain. Why does she have to grow up? Why must she grow up so fast? "She's only ten. That's too soon, right?"

Blowing a bubble with her pink gum, Belle shrugs. "Can get your period from about eight, I guess, so it's not too young."

"What's the oldest? Kit said it was happening soon, but not necessarily today."

Again, she shrugs. "I dunno. My friend got hers when she was fifteen or so. So I guess there's a big window there. You got time."

"I got the pies!" Jimmy shouts across the store. "Saddle up, B. We gotta go."

"Hey, before you run." Belle grabs my arm and pulls me to a stop when her nails dig in. She looks every single day of her thirty-five or so years. She hasn't been kind to herself with the bleach blonde and the extra-long fake nails. I'm not against body modifications – I'm the guy with a billion tattoos that people probably judge and snicker about behind my back – but Belle has a natural beauty that she ruined with her sour attitude and homewrecking ways. "Um... about Jimmy."

"He's still married." I yank my arm from her grasp. "And he's really uncomfortable coming in here because you can't take no for an answer."

"No, it's not that." Bringing her pinky finger up to her lips, she nibbles contemplatively. "It's... uh... well, it's not a secret that I've always kinda had a thing for him."

"Nope." I pop the P and take another step back. "Not a secret that you kept his phone calls a secret when Iz was in labor. And it wasn't a secret when you confronted Iz when her baby was brand new. It's not a secret that you're kinda a shitty person and you wouldn't say no if he brought his married ass to your home and offered himself up. Even knowing he's married, and knowing he has kids, you'd still take what he's offering. That's shitty of you."

"That's the thing," she murmurs. "And I don't wanna say it to him. I'm gonna leave him alone now, I promise."

My brows lift with suspicion, so she continues. "This isn't high school anymore, and I'm not a teenager anymore. Back then, it's just breaking up a stupid high school romance, right? It doesn't count."

"It does count! For them, it counts."

"No, I know." Her brows pull in tight while she thinks. "I meant, back then, it didn't count. Not in my mind. I saw him, too. I get she saw him first, but I saw him, too, and why should she get automatic dibs, ya know what I mean?"

"No."

"Back then," she huffs. "That's what I was thinking back then. And I was a nice person. I was skinny, and my hair was long like hers. I was blonde and she's not, but maybe he was just defaulting, ya know? So in my mind, it was just a matter of showing him I was around, and maybe he'd change his mind. If he just *saw* me, then maybe he'd want to date me."

"It was always Jim and Iz, Belle. Always. It was written in the stars, so your stunts were wasted. Izzy nearly died the night she had that baby. You blocked his calls and maybe he would have missed it. They were all stunts for you, a game, but the rest of us weren't playing."

"I'm not playing anymore," she whispers. "That's all I wanted to say. I won't go up to him and tell him or Iz. They wouldn't believe me, anyway. So I'm telling you; I'm going to leave him alone. I'm too old for games now, and too proud to keep wanting a man that was never available to me. So this is me saying I'll be good. I literally won't even talk to him except to give him his change if he comes through my register. I promise."

I'm usually a pretty easygoing guy so long as my family isn't threatened, but my cynicism toward this bitch just doesn't go away so easily. "Twenty-five years, Belle, and you're quitting like that? It's really that easy?"

"Not easy." She gives a soft laugh. "It might be the hardest thing I've ever done. You don't get it, you think I'm stupid and desperate." Glancing down, she toes the floor in four-inch hooker heels and skin tight jeans. "If you would just think of it like you and Kit. Say you wanted her, but she said no. But you knew in your heart you wanted to be with her. Think about it from *your* heart, from *your* soul. You kept coming back because you just knew, if she'd just listen for two seconds, you could be together. That's me and Jimmy." I open my mouth to object, but she's faster. "He's a non-participant in this scenario, I get that now, okay? I do. But keep thinking of it as you and Kit. And now, after all these years, you finally realize that you have to walk away." Her voice wobbles. "I know it's dumb to you guys, and I know I'm the butt of most of your jokes in your house. But you be me, and make Kit Jimmy. Then think about your poor heart when you finally acknowledge that it's time to let her go."

"Belle..."

She smiles right in the very moment my heart breaks. "I know it's dumb, and I know he never once returned my feelings. I brought this on myself, but that doesn't make the hurt go away. I promise I'm stepping away now, but maybe remember me next time y'all make me your dinnertime jokes. It sucks being me, it really does. It sucks spending your whole life wishing for something that'll never come true." She lays her hand on my arm. "Anyway. I have no ill will toward you guys, and the least I can hope for from your camp is to not be openly mocked. I promise to stay away from now on."

"I got the M&M's!" Jimmy snaps. He knows I'm standing here with Belle. But he doesn't know how my heart hurts for her. How maybe we were a little harsh. "Let's go, B! Fuck."

Her lips wobble, but she puts on a brave smile. "I'm done now. I said everything I needed to say. Pass it on, or don't. But as the patri-arch of the Kincaid family, I wanted you to know."

"You gonna be okay?"

"Uh-huh." And yet, her voice cracks. Swiping a hand beneath her nose, she looks up through fake lashes and nods. "I'm leaving soon."

"Going home for the day?"

"No." She clears her throat. "I mean... I'm leaving town. It's time for me to move along and leave my father's home. I spent so long on pause, waiting, I forgot to live my life. I didn't go away to college, because that would be too far away. I stayed nearby and learned a trade, because I wouldn't need a high paying job anyway. Not with the Kincaid money supporting me. I didn't leave my daddy's house, because what's the point when Jimmy would realize his mistake soon, ya know?" She smiles when I chuckle. "I didn't want to go to the trouble of renting when I was so sure I'd have to break the lease just as soon as your brother woke up and dumped Iz. I left my life on pause, while everyone else kept moving forward. I've wasted time, but hey, we aren't dead till we're dead, right?"

"Kinda morbid," I laugh. "But I feel you. I get what you mean."

"Yeah." Studying the floor, she nods and draws in a long breath. Letting it out on an exhale, her eyes meet mine. "Ya know what? I said you could tell him if you want to. I said it was whatever. But I changed my mind."

"What do you mean?"

"Don't tell him. Let him go on hating me."

I frown. "Really? I never thought I'd see the day, but you're kinda softening my black heart up. I could explain what you've told me. I could probably even get Izzy on side. You and Iz never really got along, obviously," I chuckle. "But if you could get to know her, she's actually kind of amazing. She could be a good friend for you."

"But that's just it, isn't it?" Stepping back, she grabs one of the missed travel packs out of my cart and sets it on the shelf. "If I thought Jimmy might one day soften toward me, I'd probably wait for him. I'd continue hitting pause and wonder when he would chase me down and declare his feelings. I know he won't. You know he won't. But I'd still end up hitting that pause, and we'd end up back in the same place we are now, but twenty *more* years will have passed. And as for Iz..." She tucks blonde hair behind her ear and blows out a smiling breath. "I'm sure she's lovely somewhere behind the threats to beat me up, but I don't want to be her friend. I don't want to hear about her perfect life with her perfect man and perfect little family. It's petty, but it's how I'm going to be able to go on with my life. Let him hate me; it's actually the kindest thing you could do for me."

In silence, I watch *two-bucks-a-blowy* Belle walk away from my cart in aisle three and let herself into the storeroom at the back. Her heels clip the floors, and her salon hair brushes her slender back as she moves. Stopping inside the room, she slowly closes the door and sends a small smile my way.

For the first time, *ever*, a Kincaid is in Jonah's store and not walking out again with a scowl for the woman we collectively hate.

"Finally!" I look up as Jimmy swings around the aisle and tosses a dozen bags of M&Ms on top of the tampons. "I thought she'd never leave. I told you not to talk to her, B! Where's your brain?"

Let him hate me; it's actually the kindest thing you could do for me.

"Sorry." I accept the stack of apple pies when Aiden walks up. Setting them in the cart, I throw another glance back to the door that potentially hides a version of me without Kit. That reality hurts me, and shames me for how we treated Belle. I mean, bringing her story to me twenty years too late doesn't excuse her shitty behavior, but it kind of puts her in a new light, and letting Jimmy hate her or not, I'm not sure I'll ever be able to laugh at a Belle joke again.

She's paid her dues. She's still paying them.

"We got everything?"

"Apple pies, candy, ice-cream." Aiden adds a jumbo tub on top of the pile. "And girl stuff. We're set."

"Okay." On autopilot, I lead my brothers to Belle's register, but it's not she who steps up to serve us. "Hi, Janie. How's it going?"

"Good here." The younger-than-us Janie accepts our metric ton of tampons and snacks and says nothing about how weird we are. She doesn't mention Belle's disappearance, or Jimmy's scowl. She just does her job, bags our shit, and smiles as we leave and head outside to the car.

I thought a run in with Belle would either leave me satisfied that I slammed her for her shitty behavior, or pleasantly happy with her apology. But I'm neither, because I can't live without Kit. It always comes back to Kit, and now Belle's Kit is willingly, *happily* walking away and going home to someone else.

I love Izzy like I love so few, so I wouldn't trade her for anything, but I hope Belle finds a little peace in her new town. A new home, a new job, a new adventure. I hope she gets a taste of what she's been so desperate for all these years.

"Bobby!" Finding myself sitting in the driver's seat of our family van, Jim leans forward far enough his nose almost touches mine. "You in there? Let's go already."

"Yeah." Pushing the key into the ignition, I switch the engine on and catch one final glimpse of Belle walking along the street, away from her family store, with her head down and her purse dangling from her shoulder. "Yeah, I'm ready."

"Don't worry so much, B." Aiden's gray eyes catch mine in the mirror. "Brookey will be fine. This isn't as big a deal as you think it is."

CHAPTER 26

KIT

My daughter's falsified period lasts weeks. *Weeks!* Just to keep Bobby off my back and focused on anyone except me. Brookey and I spoke the night I threw her under the bus; she's willing to play along for as long as it needs to go, in exchange for no chores. For the entire time. *Plus*, an additional month of no chores once it's done. But seeing as Bobby can't know I'm scheming, I have to do those chores on the downlow.

'You make your bed, princess?'

Brooke would glance my way with a wicked grin and twinkling eyes. *'Yes, Daddy. Of course I did.'*

'Can you unload the dishwasher, sweetheart?'

Brooke would lift her brows and rub her belly. *'Sure, Daddy. I'll do it right now.'*

I've created a monster. A mini-me! And she's both terrifying and brilliant. But it works, so I sneak through my house, do my daughter's chores, then I rush out again as soon as Brooke cries of exhaustion and cramps and Bobby would start fussing.

"Finally!" As soon as I walk through Tina's studio doors, she grabs my shoulder and rushes me along the hall that looks almost the same today as it did the first time I was here. Her wall of shoes has been updated, her props upgraded, but the iron-scroll bed remains the same, and the lamps are in almost the exact same position as always. "You gotta get changed. I have a *real* client coming in an hour, so shake your ass, so we can photograph your ass."

"Why are you so mean to me?" Unlike last time, I don't hide away in the small change room to strip down. The woman formerly known as Tina Cooper has been my sister-in-law for more than a decade, and I'm not sure there's a single nook of my cranny that she hasn't seen. Stopping in the middle of the studio room, I tug my tank top off to reveal my lacy black bra and grin when Tina nods her approval.

"Good choice. That'll photograph really well. Got your poses figured out?"

"Yeah." Kicking my handbag across the floor, I watch her tug the printed pages out and unfold them. Instantly, her face burns red right up to the tips of her ears. "Lord help us. Are we doing stylish boudoir, or straight up porn?"

"Sorry, but we're going for the centerfold this time."

"Kit! How'm I supposed to eat dinner with you tonight after this? He'll know something's up, because you'll make me blush."

"He won't know." Sliding my denim shorts down my legs, I kick them away and stand in front of my sister in a matching thong and bra. "We've got the home base all sorted. I think Brooke might have a career in Hollywood or something, because she's got him hosed. If you blush, add a giggle, then bat Aiden's hands away. That'll convince everyone he's diddling you under the table."

"You're disgusting." Little Miss Southern Charm walks across her studio and collects her fancy camera that is much shinier and bigger than the one she owned for my first shoot. Back then, she was broke and abused, living off scraps and hiding away from bad men who wanted to hurt her. Now she's a married mom, rolling in her ex's black money and donating most of her income to help women in need and get them and their babies out of situations that she was in.

Tina's scarred face bears the marks of the man that came before Aiden Kincaid, but her left hand shows a beautiful diamond ring, and her belly carried his daughters not long after that.

Tina lives the good life now, which is why she's comfortable tossing sass out like it's confetti. "Get on the damn bed and shut up!" Racing around the room, she flips lamps on so the sound of electricity powers through the studio and almost makes my teeth ache. "Start with your legs together. At least let me warm up to this shit."

"I'm a real client, by the way." Huffing, and trying my damnedest not to blush when she comes around with her camera up, I push my hair back and breathe through my near panic. "I'm paying for this session."

"You are not," she clicks and scoffs in one. She didn't say we were starting, but alrighty. *Don't look like a pig. Don't look like a pig. Don't look like a pig.* "Your ink looks epic, by the way. You've added onto your back?"

"Yeah–"

"Turn your head to the right. Give me the 'I'm a seventy-year-old cougar and I'm coming to get your man' eyes."

I was sucking in my stomach, but let it out again and laugh at this idiot. "I went in to see Ian a month or so ago. He touched up the fading stuff and added more detail to the leaves."

"Ian's kinda hot, right?"

"Right!" I turn to her and scrunch my nose when she clicks again. "He's kinda hot. I'm surprised Bobby lets him work on me."

"Quality is quality." She walks around the bed and shields most of her face with the monster camera. "He can see past the jealousy, since Ian's the best at what he does. But the second Ian slips a glance to your ass, it's game over." Her camera shakes when she laughs. "I don't know how you girls put up with their Neanderthal ways. Bobby is insane with his need to be up in your business all the time."

"I kinda love it," I admit. "The day he doesn't ask what I ate for breakfast or what I'm thinking, is the day I might freak out that our relationship is in trouble. I pretend he's overbearing, but he's really not. He just cares so deeply."

"Kinda like you, huh? You're the female Bobby." I see her wide grin behind the camera. "Is it weird being married to a dude version of you?"

"Nope. I happen to think I'm awesome, so..."

"Lie on your back, you arrogant toad." Turning, I flop down and laugh at the way her covers cloud up and settle around me. Dropping her camera so it hangs around her neck, Tina walks closer and physically moves my legs for me. "Lie your head on the pillow. I want your legs so one is straight down, the other bent at the knee."

"Of course it's bent at the knee. You want me to bend at the shin?"

She swings a fast hand out and smacks my bare stomach until I fold up and grunt. "Ouch!"

"Don't be a smart ass. It ages a lady. Legs, like this." She fixes them how she wants them, then arranges my hands so they're exactly where they're supposed to be. Coming in close enough I could almost wonder if she was going to kiss me, she tucks my hair back and tidies the loose strands with a kind smile. "You're so pretty, Kit. I know why he obsesses about you."

"You're just trying to sweet talk me."

"Nah." Stepping back when she's happy, she picks up her camera and starts clicking again. "You're so beautiful. You're kind. You're scary." We both snicker. "You're the queen bee, and Bobby's your king."

"You're being all sweet and weird," I sniffle. "Are you dying or something?"

"Not today," she laughs. "I guess I'm just feeling a little nostalgic. The first time we met was in this studio." *Click. Click. Click.* "You were terrified of stripping down in front of me, but you were so kind.

Evie blew my cover and wandered down the stairs, so I had to go fire my sitter and pray to God you wouldn't fire me."

"And I was so insanely jealous of how pretty you are." I love that her cheeks color. "You were the blonde bombshell we all wish we could grow up to be. You were tall, like Tink wanted to be. You were blonde and curvy like Iz wanted to be. And you were just straight up stunning and seriously messing with my self-esteem. We wanted to hate you."

"But instead, you hugged me and adopted us into your family." *Click. Click. Click.* "Bobby's going to go bananas for these shots. They're even better than last time."

"Really?" Sitting up when she signals she's done, I angle closer to get a look at her screen. "I was fifteen years younger and pre babies then. I have stretch marks now."

"They look badass on you." She flips through the images and proves her point. "They look as badass as your ink and the black eye from that fight that time. Isn't it funny how we always see beauty in everyone else, but we tear ourselves down? Also, I'm gonna need you to open your legs."

My face flames, but I do as I'm told and scrunch my eyes closed. "You saw me and freaked out because you thought I was beautiful." *Click. Click. Click.* "I saw you, and wanted to be you for the same reason."

CHAPTER 27

BOBBY

"Come around, Knox. Hands up, bud."

My freshest contender swings around, fast on his feet and dripping sweat onto the canvas beneath us. His hair dangles in his eyes, sweat runs along his sharp jawline, and his shoulders bunch and flex as he brings the sixteen-ounce gloves around for a rip.

"Watch your feet!" I spin around and make him chase me. "Watch your feet, or get knocked onto your ass. Come on, hands up." I lift the pads between us and flex when he comes up for a fast round-house. "Good." I grunt when his shin makes contact with the pad and pushes me back a step. "Good, move around, hands up. Do it again."

"Peacock?" Jon stands outside the ring and rests his arms on the ropes. "Benny's here. He wants a run with you."

"Tell him to wait his turn." I swing my arm out and make Knox duck fast. "Go around, bud. Fuck. You're standing in one place too long, they're gonna knock you the fuck out."

"Peacock!" Jon snaps. "It *is* Benny's turn. He's on the roster. He worked for this slot."

"He's gonna have to wait," Knox grumbles. Panting, and a little pissed I took a shot at him, he pivots fast to the left, then slides in under my guard and skims a jab along my ribs.

"That would've hurt if I had cement feet like you." I skip away and thank my daddy for the billion hours he spent in the yard teaching me how to move my feet. *Fists are worthless if your feet are stuck in the mud, Bobby. Your feet are what carry you through life, they're what get you out of dangerous situations, or run you toward what's important. You might think we gotta practice hitting, but I'm telling you we gotta work on your feet.* "Good slip, Knox, but you got shitty feet. Once more, then you're out and Ben's in."

Satisfied, Jon walks away to summon the teen, but Knox turns angrier each time I parry his jabs away. He's eighteen and has a lot of promise, but just like my wife way back when she fought, instead of using his failures as fuel to do better, he gets angry. Angry means sloppy. Sloppy means you get knocked the fuck out.

I want this kid to succeed, but if he wants to fight angry, then he can do it on his own time. I'm not nearly as inclined to care about his head as I was about Kit's.

Everyone used to tease me after Kit's early fights. I got somewhat protective after the first time, and they all teased it was because I was being a Neanderthal. But in reality, I remembered Kit's poor footwork, I remembered how she'd get angry and whale on her competitor – which, in the moment, worked just fine – but all the while, I remembered those evenings in the yard with my dad. *You fight angry, you lose. You fight without moving around, you get knocked the fuck out.*

I was willing to accept the overprotective label if it meant keeping my girl safe.

I was doing the right thing. I was doing what my daddy would have wanted me to do.

"Alright. Slow it down." When Knox comes in with a roaring one, two, rip, but misses two of the three, I drop my guard and slip out of his reach. "We're done."

"Not yet, Coach." Bouncing on his feet the way I've been asking him to do for an hour, he lifts his guard and ignores Benny when he steps up to the ropes. "Give me another hour. I'm not done."

"Bitch, get out of the ring!" Ben steps up and parts the ropes to climb through. He's sixteen, to Knox's eighteen. He's closing in on six feet in height with a vengeance, whereas Knox has already topped that by an inch. But Benny is the thug that was taking swings at cops... and just so happens to be a cop's son. "You had your hour. It's my turn."

"No." Knox turns his back to the teen and comes back to me. "One more hour. Please. I don't feel done. You said my feet suck; I can't fix them if you send me home."

Jon stands on the outside of the ring and watches our exchange. Benny doesn't give a fuck, pushes into the ring and slams his counterpart aside to take his place. "Ready, Coach."

"I wasn't done yet!" Knox roars. "I said I wasn't done!"

"Alright." Jumping between them, I look the kid up and down and consider my next move. Knox is sweaty and done for the day. Benny is fresh as spring and ready to roll. "Knox, I want you outside the ring where I can see you. I want a thousand skips." I meet his eyes. "One thousand. And every second, I want a crisscross and a side swing. A thousand! That'll keep you warm. By the time you're done, Benny'll be warm, then you can spar each other."

"Suits me." Using his teeth, Benny tightens the Velcro on his gloves and starts bouncing on the balls of his feet. "Don't wear yourself out too much, kid. I got energy for days and a deep-seated hate for pricks who think they're above the law. Get your ass off my canvas."

Chuckling, Jon drops his forehead against the ropes and shakes his head. "I think we've found our new peacock, Peacock. Never thought I'd see the day we had someone more arrogant in here than you."

"Shut up." Assuming my fight stance, I nod when Ben does the same without prompting; I needed to tell Kit every single time we stopped and started. *Left foot forward, baby, right foot back. Feet, shoulder width apart. Don't let your stance get too narrow, or you'll just fall over.*

Holding my pads up, I secretly smile at Ben's sharp, snapped jab. "Attaboy." We circle as Knox climbs out of the ring and wipes a towel over his sweaty face. "Ropes, Knox. Give me a thousand. Jon's counting."

"Yes, Coach."

I catch Ben's next jab with a laugh, because I know the fucker slipped it in hoping I wasn't paying attention. "Eyes front and center, Coach. This is *my* hour."

"You jealous, Benny? Don't wanna share my attention?"

"Nope." He snaps a fist out again and produces a perfect thud against the pads. "I ain't ashamed to admit it. Not many fighters get a chance to train with the Kincaids, and I'm not signing myself up to clean your machines to buy class time, only for you to spy your other fighters when I'm standing right in front of you."

"You're still a baby, Conner. You still have a couple years of high school, then college. *Then* you worry about fighting."

"I can do both." He snaps another jab into my pads with a grin and skips out of reach. He's too fucking fresh, he makes me look bad. "I'm worthy, Kincaid. Don't overlook me because I'm young. He's not worried about college."

We both turn and watch Knox spinning his rope at lightning speed.

"Right, that's true. But he ain't my kid, nor is he my friend's kid. Oz is my friend, and seeing as you belong to him, I'm gonna worry about your college. Show me perfect grades at school, and I'll increase your sessions. Grades slip, sessions are replaced with washing the locker room."

"Harsh." Setting it up – and telegraphing his intentions – Benny brings his leg up for a snappy roundhouse that I block with my pads or risk getting knocked out. "You didn't go to college."

"Nope, and I'm a dumb shit, too. If I didn't have fighting, we'd have to rely on my wife's income to support us. That's kinda lame, right?" I swing my pad out and nod when he ducks. "Decent round-house, but you gotta follow through." I lift my pads again to signal what I want. "Follow through, otherwise you're just putting your toes on my face, and that's just weird."

Chuckling, and fucking up his footing because of it, his leg slices through the air again, but pulls back with barely a tap. "You made me laugh."

"You think you're so badass. What're you gonna do in the octagon if the other guy presents a feather and tickles you. You gonna tell them in the press conference he made you laugh?"

"You're a tool." And yet, he laughs. Giving up on his feet, he slides beneath my guard and slams his jabs into my ribs until I cough them out of my lungs. "What are you gonna tell them in the press conference, Kincaid? The kid beat you?"

"I love his smack talk," Jon laughs. "I swear, I never met someone this arrogant before. Aiden." Waving my brother and niece into the main room, Jon nods toward us and turns back to study Ben's feet. "I found someone more arrogant than the peacock. Can ya believe it?"

"I can." Evie is my teenaged niece who's been training in this gym since she was three. It started out rocky, with a broken arm straight off the bat, but she wouldn't be Evie 'Smalls' Kincaid if she let a broken bone slow her down. She learned fast that a cast on a skull feels like a brick, and she didn't stop there. Now she's fifteen, she has a bedroom full of trophies, wild, curly hair that takes up fifty percent of her body weight, a mean right hook, and a meaner tongue that spews sass like there's just no off switch. "Everybody knows Benny is arrogant, but we also know he can't fight for shit."

"Shut up, Kincaid!" Ben steps around me, as though to give her his back. The one thing every loudmouth craves is an audience, and

Benny knows how to piss Evie off the most. "Let's go, Bobby. My hour is being wasted by everyone. What happened to shutting these sessions down for privacy?"

I lift my pads and accept his one, two, jab. "We are shut down, Conner." I shrug. "I don't see any public in here."

"I see a fighter that can't fight or skip. I see a loudmouth with big hair who wants to heckle."

"Shut your face, Conner!"

"And I see Aiden and Jon."

"You got a problem with me, Benny?" Aiden's deep voice booms through the gym and bounces off the walls for a second assault. We all know Benny and Evie have *something* going on; it's not a romance, seeing as she's our baby and Ben would be murdered in his sleep, but it's something, a love/hate friendship they both deny. And seeing as she's Aiden's baby girl, Ben better watch his attitude or be banished from this gym – and Evie – for life. "Because I didn't realize you wanted to step up to the big boys yet. We can talk if you wanna."

"No." Ben lifts his hands as though to cover up from me, but in reality, he's ducking my younger brother. "I have no problem. I just want my training session."

Scoffing, Evie turns away from the ring in her teeny tiny shorts with the Roller logo on her butt, and heads toward Knox. Timing her jumps, she slides on in and starts skipping in his rope so they're face to face and his angry scowl turns to a crooked grin.

Which in turn produces an angry scowl on Benny and Aiden's faces.

Swinging my pad out while he's distracted, I smack Ben on the side of the face and knock him six feet to the left until he slams into the ropes, but his eyes remain on the skipping duo. Hands down by his sides, shoulders drooping pathetically, Ben watches Evie giggle with my eighteen-year-old fighter. But strangely, he says nothing.

Unlike Aiden. "Nope!" He moves forward and physically removes his daughter from that rope. Angrily, he points at Knox, and then the front door with a snarl. "Go, tractor tire, now. Don't come back in here again till Bobby summons you."

"I was skipping!"

"And now I'm gonna strangle you with your own rope. Don't test me, boy!"

"Biggie!" Evie, the Smalls to the Biggie Smalls combo turns and slams her hands to her hips. "What the focaccia are you doing? What's your problem?"

"I'm saving you from your own bad choices and ridiculous rebellious streak. Gloves on now, you can spar with me."

"Biggie!"

"Now. And you." His feral eyes go to Knox. "Are you deaf or straight up stupid? Get outside now and give yourself heat stroke."

Nostrils flaring, Knox looks my way for protection, but he won't get it from me. I've known Smalls since she was tiny and learning her first swears. No way in hell am I taking his side and letting my niece spiral into bad choices. Not a fucking chance. "We're done for today."

"You said I could spar!"

"And now I changed my mind. You got your hour. Come back tomorrow and we'll keep going."

"I didn't invite her into my skipping. She did it! She's trying to be all rebellious and shit, and used me as her pawn."

"And next time, you'll know not to smile when she feels like being cute. Go home, Knox."

Balling his rope and snarling at our group, my fighter snags his bag, overflowing with towels, wraps, and leaking water bottles, and storms away until the doors slam at his back.

"It's not cute to play with our fighters, Smalls." I wait for her electric blue eyes to meet mine. "I love you, honey. But you're in the wrong. Flirting ain't cute when you know you're doing it to get people in trouble."

"I was skipping! I get you guys can be overprotective sometimes, but I was only skipping with the dude!"

"In short shorts," Ben snaps. "With a big ol' flirty smile and a *fuck you* for the rest of us in the room. You did that on purpose!"

"Did what?" She steps toward the ring and broadens her chest as though stepping up to fight. "What did I do wrong? I skipped rope. I've been doing that since I was five. Hung out with a boy? Same! My first four boyfriends were fighters. They're now my uncles. Or is the problem that I hung out with someone that isn't you? It must really sting when I hang out with a male friend whose name isn't Ben."

"You don't know what you're talking about."

"That makes two of us, then, because you're pretty damn clueless yourself, dumbass." Lifting a hand, my cherubic niece points straight between his eyes. "Mind your own damn business. Shit or get off the pot. Make a choice and live with it. Do whatever the fuck you gotta do, but stop being a little pussy about it."

"Evelyn!" Aiden grabs her arms and pulls her back. "Stop swearing!"

"Why not? Everyone else can!"

"Because you're a child! Because you're my baby! Because I fuckin' said so!"

"Oh, please." Snatching her arm out of his hold, she turns away with a huff and stalks off on strong legs. "I've been living with potty mouths my whole damn life. Now's not the time to start implementing rules about swears."

"It's not as simple as you think, Evie." Finally, Benny speaks without attitude. His words crackle, and his shoulders droop. "It's not that easy."

"Sure it is. You *choose* to make it this way."

The door slams against the wall as she tears it open, then slams again when it closes.

"What the fuck is going on with you and my daughter, Conner?" Aiden steps up and ducks between the ropes. "Why is my daughter lashing out and pointing it at you?"

"No clue." Turning, he lifts his hands and steps into fight stance. "Can we keep going?"

"No!" Aiden grabs his collar and spins him. "My daughter is a smartass, we all know that. She's mean, sassy, and too witty for her own good. But she's not a flirt, and she doesn't lash out like that. If she has a problem, she comes straight out with it, smacks whoever pissed her off in the face, then she moves on with her life. But she doesn't play games. She doesn't lash out like she just did. So what did you do to her that makes her like this?"

"I didn't do anything! She's my friend. Barely. Mostly we swear at each other. But I didn't do anything to her, I swear."

"What's not so easy?" Jon asks. "She said you choose this, and you said it's not so easy. That tells me you know what her problem is."

"It's nothing. It's nothing!" he repeats when Aiden's eyes flare. "It's bullshit that literally isn't real, but is being blown way out of proportion because she's got a bad attitude. Your daughter's bad attitude isn't my fault, Aiden. It's not my fault, and it's not my responsibility to fix. I'm sorry she's lashing out, but I can't change it." Ben's eyes come back to mine. "Can we please just do this hour? Otherwise I'll go home and do a circuit with Mac or something."

Aiden meets my eyes for a long minute. Ben is a smartass, too. He's got a bad attitude more often than not. And an arrogant streak as wide as Evie's. But he swears her bad mood isn't his fault...

Benny's mom works in this gym, his aunt is our athletic trainer, and his sister is cute as a button. Bad attitude or not, he's never given us reason to doubt him.

"Okay." I drag his attention back around. "We're gonna do the hour. You worked for it, so you get it. Hands up, give me a one, two, rip, rip, then a roundhouse and follow through."

"Yes, Coach."

CHAPTER 28

KIT

"The invitations have gone out?"

"Yup." Sitting in my living room with Tina, Iz, Tink, and my party planner, Meg, we tick each item off our massive to-do list.

Iz turns to a breastfeeding Meg. "Catering?"

"Organized. I have a brother-sister duo coming in. They catered Oz's wedding, too, so they're good."

"That food was delicious." Sitting back on my couch, my best friend and partner in crime, Tink, digs her hand into a bag of chips and crunches noisily. "The chicken was amazing. Can you ask them to do the dessert thing again? That pudding was delicious. It tasted a bit like red velvet, a bit like chocolate mud, and maybe some sex thrown in there, too. It was amazing. And don't even get me started on the appetizers."

"Hey, T. What song did Lindsi and Oz dance to?"

She turns to me with her pixie face and frowns. "I have no clue. Why should I remember that?"

"What color were the tablecloths?"

"I see your sass, Catherine. You wanna back up."

"What color was Jon's shirt?"

"Shut up!"

I turn to Meg and laugh. "She doesn't know what color her husband wore, but she remembers the red velvet and the chicken mains. Why isn't she fat? It's not fair that she can eat the way she does and not be fat."

"Anywho. Yes, same caterers." Meg expertly nurses and writes at the same time. "And they usually do massive parties. Like, thousands of guests. So this'll be like a vacation for them. We're not doing a sit-down dinner though, right?"

"Right." I reach into Tink's bag and smile when she growls. "Finger food. Walking waiters. And we can't forget the pizza truck. Bobby will have a conniption if we surprise them with this party and there's no pizza."

Meg shakes her head, but she writes it down. "You do realize the parties I plan are usually black tie and formal, right? No pizza, no brawling, and no beer kegs."

"Lower your standards," Izzy says. "This is a Kincaid party, not a Montgomery affair. We're still doing black tie, but I guarantee Kit will be wearing Chucks beneath her gown."

Meg's narrowed eyes burn a hole into the side of my head.

"It's true." I shrug and tickle her baby's toes. "I'm not wearing heels. I don't have to, because I'm not short like an Oompa Loompa."

My five-foot-tall best friend smacks my thigh. "I know you're teasing right now, Gigantor. What's your problem with me? Do we have to take it outside? Because I'm not scared of you, woman. I know you have a bad knee *and* shoulder. Two pops with a baseball bat and I'm all set." Meg's shoulders bounce as my chihuahua spits at me. "I shared my chips, you douchebag!"

I push my hands into the foil bag again and crush her chips. "I'm just saying; yes to the pizza truck, yes to the Chucks, no to the five course meal."

"Fine, whatever. You savages," Meg whispers. "Guest of honor?"

"Has no clue this is happening." Smiling, I sit back so Tink and I rest shoulder to shoulder. "I've slogged my guts out for this thing. I've lied, stolen, and cheated just so I could get a moment to make plans without Bobby breathing over my shoulder. If anyone blows this, I'm gonna rampage."

"Whoa up, momma bear." Tina snickers. "Nobody's gonna blow it. But you'll probably have to blow Bobby once he realizes you lied."

"My jaw already aches!" I toss a chip across my living space and laugh when it smacks her face and lands in her lap. "I'm already working triple time, because I can't lie for shit. I have to drop to my knees twenty times a day, because he's asking questions that I can't answer. And when I can't answer, he asks more questions, which means more BJs. I'm exhausted!"

"Twenty?" Izzy's smile turns sour. Bobby is, for all intents and purposes, her big brother. "That's disgusting, Kit. Seriously, I get that the party is important, but we could just do a barbecue in the back yard and get the same results."

"No! This is a big year, so this is what we're doing. Get on board, or run interference with my husband so I can do it in peace."

"Stop bickering," Tina grumbles. "We have catering and venue. Cake?"

"I got that," Meg says. "Triple tier, mud cake, and a topper from your wedding on top. You just gotta get the topper to me."

"Yeah, I'll search for it this week, I promise. I think Em was playing with it, so I bet its under her bed somewhere."

"Fine, whatever." Meg shakes her head and makes more notes. "It's not the end of the world if it's not there. The party will still go ahead."

"It's a big deal," I interject. "I'll find it."

"Music?"

"The band is playing," Meg answers. "Marc's band is doing it for free."

"But they're on the invite list! How are they playing, but also guests?"

"I dunno," she shrugs. "I've been round and round with Marc about this since Oz's wedding. He says they can play and party at the same time. He swears they've been doing it since high school. He *wants* to play, so they're playing."

"Decorations?" Tink asks – with a mouth full.

"That's on us." I snap her jaw closed and laugh when she tries to lick my hand. "We're decorating the place ourselves. Invites say six in the evening. Catering will start setting up at noon. Right?"

Meg nods. "Right."

"So we're there from sunrise getting it ready. We'll be done when catering rolls in, then we can come home and get ready."

"Tina's on makeup?"

"Yup."

"Geez, thanks for volunteering me."

I flash a wide grin. "It's like old times, right? But this time, you get to go to the party too, Cinderella. We dress up, don our gowns, look pretty, then we escort our clueless men in. Sounds fun, right?" When she stares with pursed lips, I laugh. "Oh, and by the way; are my photos done?"

"Uh-huh. They're at the studio drying, but they're not framed or packaged yet. Aiden came in and almost saw your cooch, so I had to walk away and lock up. I'll finish them soon and send them over. When are you giving them to him?"

"On his birthday." I drop my feet on the coffee table and fist more chips. "He's gonna go nuts when he sees them. I swear, if he takes the old pictures out and compares them side by side, I might scalp him."

"Baby?" The front door slams open and startles Meg's dozing baby. As a group, we toss notebooks, pens, and stop short of throwing the baby under the couch, and sit back like we're totally innocent as Bobby and Aiden walk through. Meg fixes her top and stands Baby Chance on her thighs as they stop at the entrance. "Oh, you guys are all here?" Bobby glances around the room, like he knows we're up to no good. "Is Smalls here?"

Tina perks up at her daughter's name. "I thought she was at the gym?"

"She was earlier, but then she flipped her shit at Benny and left. It's not a big deal; she's probably at your place. I just wanted to give her a squeeze, since she seems so *extra* lately."

"Evie's always going off at Benny," Iz murmurs. "She's always been extra. That poor kid has no clue what's coming for him."

"Nothin's coming for him," Aiden grumbles. He walks into the living room and stops on the arm of Tina's chair. "Benny won't come near her if he knows what's good for him. And since he's a guy and guys are stupid, I'll help him remember what's good for him. My baby is still a baby. She sure as shit isn't dating yet."

"Soon," Tink teases. "She'll. Be. Dating. Soon..." She wags a finger between each word. "It's coming, big daddy, so be prepared."

"No." Frowning, he studies the floor for a moment. "No. It's not coming yet. She cares about what I think, so if I say no, she'll listen."

As a group, every woman in the room busts out laughing so loud that Chance jumps in Meg's lap and Aiden's eyes narrow. "What? She will! Smalls is more than my baby. She's my pal. She's my best friend. She'll care what I think."

"Aiden..." Tink lets out a dramatic sigh. "I had a best friend once. Her name was Kit and she was super pretty. But then I met the man I would one day marry. After that day, Kit was dead to me."

"Hey!"

She snickers. "I'm just saying, your baby girl cares what you think... most of the time. But boys make us stupid. They make us rearrange our priorities. Your life is gonna suck for the next few years while she rearranges her list of priorities, and I'm not saying that to hurt you, but you won't be *numero uno* for much longer. Plus, Benny's cute as hell. He challenges her every single time she speaks. Personally, I'm excited for the explosion."

"No." Standing, Aiden pulls Tina up and drags her toward the door. "There will be no explosion, there won't even be party poppers. There's just... No. Are you done here?"

"Yeah." Tina peeks around his broad shoulders and meets my eyes. "I'll go to the studio for a bit this afternoon to finish off some work. But I'm free for now."

They disappear out of my living room, so when Bobby stands at the door and rocks on his heels, the others jump up.

"Yup!" Izzy grabs her bag and sneakily shoves a notebook in before pulling it over her shoulder. "Where's Jimmy?"

"At the gym."

"Alright, I'm out. See you guys at dinner."

"Meg." My husband does the manly, deep voiced thing in way of greeting. Megan Montgomery is a friend, but she's not tight with us the way me, Tina, Izzy, and Tink are. Even my brother's wife, Britt, straddles that line; she's one of us, but she's also one of them. *Them* being the cop family; Alex is the chief, Britt is his sister, and Meg's man is Marc, foster brother to Alex and Britt. So while we're all friendly, there's way too many of us to open our dinner table to *them* every night. So we don't. But we definitely invite them to birthday parties. "You doing okay?"

"Yup." She stuffs her baby stuff in an oversized handbag and juggles like a pro. "We were just hanging out while the guys were practicing, but I've never been a cock block, so I can show my way out."

"I appreciate that." My husband flashes the most handsome smile in the world and rudely shuffles my guest away, then turns back to face Tink.

"Well, I've always prided myself on being a cock block." She plunges her salt covered hand into the bag of chips and comes out with an overflowing handful. "You do you, because Jon isn't home yet and the boys are tearing my place up. Mommy needs time out, so I don't mind sitting here and either ruining this, or watching it. It's your call, big boy."

It's amazing how such a little person can challenge a champion fighter with no fear. But my husband has no manners, and we so rarely have the house to ourselves. So he picks my best friend up and places her on the front porch with a pat on the head, only to slam the door in her smiling face and turn back to the now empty living room. "Kit?"

Giggling, I run to the kitchen and open the cupboard doors. "Anyone in here? Brookey?"

I get no answer. But Bobby catches on and starts searching. "Bry? You here, buddy?"

I open the laundry door and look inside the washer and dryer. "Em? You here, sweetpea?"

"Living room is clear!"

I run into the hall and duck into the guest bathroom. "Laundry and bathroom are clear!"

Bobby's heavy feet thump against the tile. "Kitchen's clear. Holy shit, baby. Nobody is here!"

I dart across the living room and into the front foyer. "We didn't lose them, right?"

"Nope." He walks into sight with a wicked grin and a glint in his eyes. "Brooke's with Bean, Em's with Britt, and Bry's on the skateboards outside." He walks to the front door and flips the locks with a telling snick. "We have twenty minutes of just us." His eyes flash when I turn at the bottom of the stairs and place my left foot on the first step. "Run, baby. I want to fuck you for nineteen of those minutes."

"Bobby..." I lift my hand in a fruitless attempt to slow him down. "They could knock any moment. Bobby. Bobby!" I laugh as he stalks closer. "Bobby!"

"Run."

Squealing like a girl, I pivot and dash up the stairs and giggle when he bounds up behind me and slaps my ass. "Bobby!" I run, I stumble, I laugh, then I scream when he scoops me up and carries me along the hall like a football. Busting into our bedroom at the end, then tossing me on the bed, Bobby's tank top pops threads as he tears it off without care and tosses it to the floor.

"I'm sweaty, baby. I didn't shower since the gym, because I was busting to get home to see you." Climbing onto the bed between my legs, he sets my insides on fire when he picks up my bottom half with rough hands and pops my shorts button open. "But you look all fresh and shit, so I'm gonna eat you up. I'm gonna spend maybe fifteen of my twenty minutes eating you up and counting the times you come on my face." *And I'm done.* No more giggles. No more denials. I slide out of my shorts when he tugs them over my ass, then I lower down and bite my bottom lip as he slides the tip of his finger under the waistband of my cotton underwear. "I wonder how loud I could make you cry before the neighbors hear?"

"Bobby." I don't even pretend to play hard to get. I slept with him on our first date, we declared our love within hours of that, and our train hasn't slowed since, so I'm sure as hell not going to play coy now. "Maybe you gotta hold your hand over my mouth." My throat goes dry when he tugs my panties down with one single finger on the crotch and my legs tangle together. "*Make* me be quiet."

"I can do that, baby. I'll do whatever I have to do to feel my cock being crushed inside your pussy." Sliding his tattooed hand along the inside of my thigh, he uses the other hand to push his shorts down and free his cock. "We're good with the pill, right? All your lady doctor stuff is squared away?"

"Yeah." I clear my throat and pretend my blush is a product of being turned on. "It's all fixed up. We're good to roll."

"My favorite thing ever." Grinning, he slams two thick fingers inside my pussy, then a smothering hand over my mouth when I cry out in surprise. Sliding them in, then out, he grins when I lick his hand and grind my hips in search of more. "I always liked your tongue, baby." Leaning over me, he replaces his hand with his mouth and pulls my tongue against his. "I always thought it was amazing the way it could spew mean comebacks, or loving words, or swirl around the tip of my dick." He changes direction of his fingers and transforms my chuckle to a groan mid-breath. "I always loved your witty comebacks, and the way you promised loyalty to whoever you thought worthy." Skipping the *eating me out* portion of today's plans, Bobby removes his fingers and replaces them with a rock hard cock and slams in hard enough to move me up the bed.

Kissing me, he swallows my cries and makes no apologies when he brings my legs over his shoulders and crushes me beneath his heavy body. "I still love you so much, baby." His voice is strained, his muscles bulging while we slam together and my hands tighten against the bedspread. "You still feel so good."

I can barely keep my eyes open. Barely breathe. Barely do anything except *feel* his assault and let his words coil inside my heart. Nobody has ever felt as loved as I do. It's not possible. It's simply not possible that someone on this planet loves more than my husband.

Bobby's shoulders strain, and his pecs bead with sweat, because even with the house being cooled, the heat between us is undeniable.

"Mom?" The front door slams downstairs and sends my heart into a panicked race. "Hello? Mom?"

"Come on, baby." Letting my legs drop and pulling out, Bobby flips me with ease and pushes my face into the pillows. He knew I'd need the pillows, because then he slams inside me from behind and pulls my hair until I scream. Finally, my walls lock down around his shaft and drag him over the ledge so all two-hundred and forty pounds of fighter muscle crush me against the bed and we both smile as the aftershocks make us groan.

"Mom?"

"In my room, honey." Vibrating from the way Bobby uses my body in the best way, I clear my throat and try to hide the smile in my voice. "I'll be out in a sec, okay? I'm just getting changed, so don't come in here."

"Can we make ice-cream after dinner?" My eleven-year-old son stands in the hall, shielded from what would scar him for life by just a thin door and no lock. "Mom?"

"Yes, honey!" My voice breaks when Bobby teasingly bites the back of my neck and unapologetically crushes me beneath his body. "Later. Hours away."

"I wanna fuck you again," Bobby whispers in my ear. "Reckon we could do it again without you making a single peep?" Slowly, he slides out to the tip, then back in again until my eyes flutter closed.

"Shit..."

"Mom?"

"Go downstairs, honey!"

CHAPTER 29

BOBBY

"Baby?" Another stifling hot week passes us by, another week of working with Knox, but shaking my head at his lack of control, then working with Ben, and shaking my head at his overabundance of control. The first might prove to be a waste of my time, and the second is, as the girls say, an explosion just waiting to happen. Ben's so tightly wound with responsibility, add in my pressure when I mentioned his grades, his sullen face because not only doesn't Evie yell at him anymore, but she acts like he doesn't exist at all, and then my other niece's angry glares at the guy for hurting her cousin, and my gym is a pressure cooker waiting to blow.

But it's not real drama. It's stupid, teen drama.

Somehow, I miss the good old days of murderous exes and drug funded night clubs.

Back then, it was black and white, and we dealt with our problems head on. But now, the only troubles I have in my world are a boiling hot gym that we can't cool no matter how hard we try, a hormonal gaggle of females on my property who all go through PMS at the same time, and a wife who I suspect is lying to me about something.

"Kit?" I head up our stairs and drop my gym bag halfway. "You in here, baby?"

"Yep!" I was turning one way to go to our bedroom, but head the opposite way when Kit's voice comes from my youngest daughter's bedroom. Entering just as Kit jumps up from her crouch on the floor, I narrow my eyes at the bag she has tossed over her shoulder and tilt my head so she *knows* I know she's up to something. "Hey!" Walking forward with a little too much enthusiasm, Kit stops in front of me so her toes touch mine and her eyes glitter with... *lies.* "You're all hot and sweaty, babe. Want something to drink?"

"Nah, I got a Gatorade, but thanks. What are you doing?"

"I'm looking for something. I think Em was playing with it recently, but I can't find it."

"Oh yeah?" I glance down at her seemingly empty bag. "What is it?" I follow Kit when she walks out of the room. "Baby? What is it?"

"What?" She doesn't turn back at my question. She walks away so fast, her long hair sways and tickles an almost naked back but for the ink she's been adding to over the years.

"Baby?" I grab her hand and swing her around. "What's the thing you're looking for?"

"Umm..." She can't look me in the eyes. My wife, my fucking soulmate, can't maintain eye contact.

"Catherine Maree Kincaid? Answer my question now."

"My tampons," she blurts out. "Um, Emmy was playing with the box, but I lost the applicator and knew she had it in her room. But this is like the lady doctor thing; I didn't want to give you all the nasty details." Turning again and not once meeting my eyes, Kit strolls onto the stairs and heads down. "I'm going over to Tink's for a bit, okay?"

"What's over there?"

"Uh..." Kit stops at the bottom of the stairs and meets my eyes. "My best friend. You might remember her; cute as a button, crude as a pirate, swears like a sailor, eats like a pig. About..." She holds a hand up to her belly button. "This tall."

"Mm." My heart pounds, pounds, pounds in my chest, because my wife so rarely lies. Her body rejects the deceit, it makes her voice rise and her eyes twitchy. She can't lie, and therefore, she so rarely tries. So why today? Why the last few weeks? "I was thinking movie night in." Slowly, I make my way down the staircase, prowl toward her and show her I won't be lied to. "I even bought you the good ice cream, since I knew you'd want it."

"Um..." She clears her throat and gets busy pawing through her empty bag. "Raincheck?"

"Um." I grab her jaw and bring her eyes back to me. "No. I wanna watch a movie with my wife. This afternoon. Tonight. Then I want to take her to bed and remind her why we're perfect together." *Don't lie to me, baby. Don't pull away after everything we've survived.* "Or maybe we could go out to dinner? I don't do that often enough. I don't romance you like I promised in our wedding vows."

"Babe." Her eyes flutter closed now, not because of a lie, but because she's as powerless to me as I am to her. Leaning into my hand, she sighs. "I would love to go to dinner with you. But can we do it tomorrow?"

"What's so important at Tink's house?"

"Nothing in particular." And yet, her voice cracks. "I just promised her girl time, and we so rarely get one on one time. I'd feel like a total jerk for telling her no."

"Where's Jon?"

She shrugs, but powerlessly, steps closer and accepts my half-hug. "I don't know. I didn't ask her."

"So how do you know it's one on one time? He might be there. Then you'll feel like a dummy for leaving me at home."

Snickering, she presses a kiss to my chest. "Then I'll come back and get you."

"So I'd be your backup booty call?" I lift her chin until our eyes meet. "Our vows said I was your first call booty, not your backup."

She laughs and steps away. "I love you. You're not my backup anything, okay? You're my number one always, but tonight, I'm hanging with Tink."

Hours after my wife walked away with that empty bag and a whole bunch of lies, I sit in front of my television while my kids sleep and my pizza cools in the box on the coffee table.

Her lies ruined pizza for me.

Checking my cell every three seconds and scowling when I find nothing, I look up with a lifted brow when Jon walks through the front door in pyjama pants, old man slippers, and a baby monitor in his hands. He closes the door with a silent snick, and throws a glance toward the stairs to make sure he didn't wake my kids.

He's been a dad a hell of a lot longer than me, so he knows what's up and the rules about being noisy past eight p.m.

"Hey, Fart. I'm in here."

Chuckling, he moves through my front entrance and into the dark living room. Plopping down in the recliner beside mine, he sets the monitor on the coffee table by my feet and grunts when he releases the foot rest. "I'm spent, Peacock."

"Why? You're lazy all day at the gym. Not sure why you'd be tired."

Jon learned a long time ago not to take my bait. So he only smiles, then tunes into my TV and gets lost in the story for a minute. "What is this?"

"A movie."

He purses his lips. "What's it about?"

"Uh... I think he's military, but he gets caught in some weird time continuum and goes to a new time." I shrug and sip my water. "They went full artistic license with this, because I don't get it. But he goes to a new time and meets this chick."

"You watching a chick flick, Peacock?" Sitting forward, he catches my eyes. "All by yourself?"

"Yup. I'm not ashamed."

The television is the only light that shines over us as Jon becomes absorbed in the same chick flick he mocks me for. "Is that the Australian actor?"

"Yup."

"Ever wonder why he doesn't sound all 'G'Day' when he speaks?"

"Pretty sure that's part of the acting 101 classes they take. Pretty standard, I think."

"Mm." Nodding, he goes back to watching. "Maybe. Don't know. Acting ain't really my thing."

"I know." Pushing back into my chair, I glance at Jon's monitor when one of his boys rolls over. "Why are you here?"

"Lonely." He shrugs. "Went to see Sissy, but she's not home either."

"Where is she?"

Again, he shrugs. "Out with the girls."

Instantly, my brows pull close and my heart slams. "Which girls?"

"All of them, the same pack of crazies as usual. Duh."

"You mean Kit, right? Kit and Tink?" When he nods, I ask, "They're not at your place?"

"Nope. They went out a while ago."

"Where the fuck did they go?" I slam my foot rest back and turn toward my best friend. "Kit told me it was a Kit and Tink one on one girls night in."

"You better get quiet, B, or you'll be dealing with awake babies."

"Dude!"

"I don't know where they are. They were getting dressed a couple hours ago, then they went out. They said they'd be back later. Unlike you, I can just say *cool beans* and not need every detail."

"She lied to me, Fart. She fuckin' lied, again!" Pushing up from my chair, I dart upstairs and drag on a pair of jeans and a fresh shirt. Racing past my kids' rooms, I make sure they're out, then I sprint back down again and slam my cell against my ear.

"What's your problem? Bobby?" Jon stops in front of me and clicks his fingers. "What's the problem?"

"She lied to me." I listen to Kit's dial tone. It rings, and rings, and rings, then I get voicemail and hang up. "What the fuck..." I dial again, and will my heart to slow. I don't expect her to answer, so when she does and music blasts, I have to push my cell away from my ear or risk damage.

"Bobby?"

"Kit! What the hell is going on?"

"Are you guys okay? Are the kids okay?"

"Everyone is fine... except you! What the fuck is going on?"

"What?"

"You said girls night in!"

"No." Her voice cracks as she shouts and lies. "I said girls night, right? I just said girls night."

"Where are you?"

"We're at the club, but we're leaving in a second anyway. It's boring here, so we're going to head out."

"Our club? 188?"

"Of course! Listen, is everyone okay? Are the kid's fine?"

"Yes! Everyone's fine, but I thought my wife was across the street watching Pride and Prejudice, not clubbing in the middle of the damn week! Is this like a mommy midlife crisis? You're tired of being a wife and mom, so you're lashing out and partying?"

"No! Of course not. I'm just with my best friend while we listen to some music. Why are you so mad?"

"Because you lied to me! You've been lying to me!"

"I'm not lying to you. I'm just... Ugh! Want a BJ when I get home?"

My dick thickens in my pants. Instantly, she paints a vision of her on her knees, her eyes gazing through long lashes, her dimple popping so much more because of her hollowed cheeks, and the way she'd touch her own pussy while she works me, because she doesn't want to miss out. I'm supposed to be mad, but all I see now are her breasts falling out of a tight bra, her ass framed by the sexiest lace thong, and her eyes sparkling with lust and hunger while she laps me up and brings me undone.

"Babe?" she whispers huskily. "Do you wanna come in my mouth?"

"Yes." I turn away from Jon and stride toward the kitchen. "Yes, I really want that."

"I'd swallow it all up. I won't let any go to waste, I swear."

Groaning, I rub a hand over my hardened crotch and lean with my forehead against the fridge. "I want you so bad, baby." Snapping my jeans open, I slide my spare hand in and fist my cock. "Please?"

"As soon as I get home, I promise. I'm going to sneak in, I'll put my panties in your hand, then I'll sit on you and wake you up. Does that sound nice?"

Loud club music beats through my phone, but I still hear her as if she were standing right in front of me and whispering into my ear.

"Bobby? Is that what you want?"

"Yes."

"Okay." Her voice is breathy, like maybe she's touching herself, too. "Soon, okay? I'll be home soon, then I'll show you what I can feel right now."

"You're touching yourself, baby? Right now?"

"Mmhmm. I'll see you soon, okay?"

"Okay."

"Go to sleep, that way I can wake you up again."

"Okay."

"I love you. You're my number one. For the rest of my life."

Smiling, I let out a contented sigh and let the anxiety leech from my bones. "I love you too, baby. See you soon."

Remaining against the fridge, I let my phone drop away from my ear and my hand to play with cock. Alone, I remain in the dark and think of how it'll feel when she slides into our warm bed. When she swallows me up and forces me to hold my breath or come too soon.

But in the next breath, the motor on my fridge kicks on, the double doored contraption rattles against my skull, and reality washes away my lust and my brain registers what the fuck just happened.

"That little sneak!" Charging back into the living room, I find Jon eating my pizza and watching my Mel Gibson movie without a care in the world. "Get up, Fart. We're going out."

"Hm?" Glancing over, he looks me up and down and lifts a brow. "Need a minute alone, brother? Or bigger jeans? Because I don't wanna see the shape of your dick through your denim."

"She tricked me!" Lifting my cell again, I dial Aiden. He only lives across the street, but it's easier to call than it is to march over there.

"Yeah?"

"Is Tina with you?"

"Nope." Ridiculously, I hear Mel Gibson's voice twice; in my living room, then again through my cell. "She went out with the girls. Said they'll be back later."

"Is Evie there?"

"Yup. She's watching a movie with me."

"Would you mind sending her over? Just so she can sit with my kids?"

He lets the silence hang for a minute. Two minutes. And then a third. "What are you gonna do, Bobby?"

"My wife has been lying to me. Obviously they're not lying to you guys, since Jon said he knew Tink was out, too. So it's me. I'm the sucker they're lying to."

"Okay..."

"Well, I'm going to find out what they're doing. She tricked me just now! I called her up and found out she's at 188, but when I demanded answers, she distracted me."

"Distracted you with what?" Jon sniggers. "What was her bait?"

"None of your business! Go put pants on, Fart. You're coming. Aiden, please send Smalls. I won't be gone long, I promise. You can come with us too, if you want."

"I'm absolutely not coming with you," he scoffs. "I'll send Smalls, but it's getting late, so don't be gone long. My baby needs her sleep."

"An hour tops, I promise."

Just three minutes after hanging up, my niece lets herself in my front door in gym booty shorts and an oversized sweatshirt. She's a Roller through and through. She was baptized in the sweat of fighters, and broken in running drills like she's a guy. She's fifteen and moody, but she's my baby, even if she's technically Aiden's baby. "Thank you, Evie. I'll owe you for this."

"Mmhm." Stepping onto her tiptoes and pressing a kiss to my cheek, Evie makes her way to my recliner, grabs my remote and turns that movie up again, then eats my leftover pizza like it's not rude to walk into someone else's house and make yourself at home.

It's not. On our estate, in our family, it's not rude.

"We'll be back soon, okay?"

Lifting a hand only, Evie flashes a peace sign and begins sipping my water.

Alrighty. Turning to Jon, who now wears *his* jeans and *his* shirt, both of which came from *my* clean laundry pile, I smack his shoulder and walk away. "You're the reason my wife is having a midlife crisis. Not only is she doing our laundry, but she's doing yours, too."

"Stop bitching." He follows me out the front and slides into the passenger seat of my SUV. "I saw Jimmy's fight trunks in there, too. So I'm not the only one. But don't worry, I saw *your* tank in *my* washing yesterday. So now you got *my* wife cleaning up after you? Asshole. Don't throw rocks if your head is made of glass."

He rolls the window down and lets the summer air come into the car as the estate gates swing open and I move out to the public access street. "It's so hot, B. Maybe Kit's just going weird because of the heat."

"No." I slide the car into gear and start cruising toward town. "We've had a lot of summers together, Fart. She's never been a straight up liar like this." I press a hand to my chest and grimace. "It hurts me to call her a liar. That's my wife, and the last time she lied, Izzy was pregnant with Bean and our whole world exploded."

Just as expected, Jon grabs his own chest, because despite that being more than a decade ago, his baby sister being a pregnant teen near killed him. "It's probably not what you think it is. In fact, it's probably not even close to whatever you're thinking. And when you finally figure it out, you'll feel bad for being a dick about it."

"You think so?" I glance across in the dark and study my best friend's profile. "Do you really think I should back up? She's never given me reason to doubt before, so... I dunno." I sigh. "I don't know what to do, but lying scares me. Why are they at 188 listening to that band?"

His brows furrow. "Which band?"

"Marc's band. Luc's. Scotch's. All of them."

"They're watching them?"

"Well. Yeah. They're at 188." Turning left, I enter Main Street and keep moving. "Kit said they're at the club, and I heard Scotch singing, so..."

"I mean, it's okay that we're going to check," he concedes. "I trust my wife. But a club is a club, and those girls have been arrested before."

"That's what I'm saying!" Finally, he's on board. "We're just checking."

"I reckon we don't go through the front." Strong jaw ticking, dark eyes twinkling against the street lights, my best friend transforms from humored to *ride or die*. "Let's maybe go through the fire escape or something. They'll see us coming in the other way, and since we're only checking in, we don't want them to see us, right?"

"Right." Downshifting, I swallow my nerves and turn into the club parking lot.

"We're not snooping. It's more like, if they see us, they'll be hurt we came out to check. So it's probably best if we don't let them see us. Right?"

"Yep." If I keep nodding, I might just convince myself. "Definitely right."

"Alright." As soon as I cut the lights and unclip my belt, Jon flings his door open and heads straight toward the back of the club and the sketchy alleyway that spans the back. It's dark out here, stinky from the trash, and noisy because of the club speakers booming so close. We own this club – or more specifically, Smalls owns this club. Her biological father was a piece of shit. A *rich* piece of shit, who, when imprisoned for being a piece of shit, meant Evie inherited a fuck ton of cash and assets. Tina's been managing the club ever since, while Tink's a floor manager of sorts. As in, Tina does the admin, and Tink slings the alcohol. But when it all boils down to it, our family owns this club, which makes it important to us that the alley out back remains clean, safe, and junkie free at all times.

The bass thumps in my chest, and the adrenaline helps me jump onto the fire ladder with ease. I can accept that the music here is decent, but all it does for Jon is reminds him of the time he threw Scotch Turner across the dance floor to get him away from Tink. It's kinda messy, seeing as Scotch is now – and always was – happily married to his own soulmate, but that doesn't erase from Jon's mind what he *thought* was happening, or the pain those thoughts inflicted on his bruised heart.

A grudge is hard to let go of sometimes, even if the grudge was unwarranted in the first place.

"Why didn't we get rid of these guys yet, B?" He grunts as he jumps to the ladder and climbs up. "They can't play music for shit, anyway."

CHAPTER 30

KIT

Sitting around a tall table inside Club 188 with a glass of juice – no vodka – I listen to Scotch's band and nod at the song they're playing just for us. A rehearsal of sorts, for the party I'm trying to organize, and the dance I'd like to witness.

"They're good, right?" Meg shouts across the table and sends a flirty wink toward her man. "They're nailing this song."

"They totally are." Izzy sits with a straw between her lips and her chin in her hands. "This song is so perfect. It's like..." She sighs. "It's like magic."

"Shush." Meg leans forward and does the hearts in her eyes thing when Scotch steps back and Marc does the guitar solo. "He's so perfect."

"The song, right?" I tap her shoulder and laugh. "We're still talking about the song, yeah?"

"Hell no. We're talking about my man. Do you think they need four men on the stage at all times? I wanna dance at your pretty party, Kit. Let me dance with my sexy farmer while he wears a suit."

"You can dance." Sighing, I imagine this song a week from tonight, at the party none of the men know about, and the outcome I hope to achieve. "I promise to cut you free from coordinator duties as soon as Bobby's on the dance floor and this song is playing. This one is all that matters. Even if the cake flops and the caterers get sick, I just need *this* song."

"It's happening." She lets out a final sigh and stands. Grabbing her purse and pushing her long hair back, Meg flashes a beautiful smile and reminds us all why she was the popular cheer captain and had the boys salivating for her. "Alright. The baby's with my daddy, so I have to scram. But I'm so glad this is what you want. It's so perfect, and your night is going to be amazing. I promise."

"I trust you." I accept her kiss on my cheek and the squishy hug as she passes, then I go back to watching the band as Scotch Turner sings with his amazingly gritty voice and the passion he throws behind every word. He sings of love, because he knows the purest kind. He sings of heaven with purpose, because Scotch and Sammy Turner have been in love since they were fourteen years old, and not for a single day since then have they stopped. "I'm so in love with this song, guys. I'm in love with my husband, with this party, with what it represents."

Iz leans her shoulder against mine and smiles. "Bobby will love this. He'll understand how special it is, then he'll forgive you for lying."

I'm not worried about my marriage. It'd take a lot for Bobby Kincaid to fall out of love. In fact, I'm not sure he knows how. His mom and dad taught him how to do it right, how to do it fully, and how to never let go.

I'm the luckiest woman on this planet.

My cell rings in my lap again. It drags my gaze down on a laugh, since I assume it's Bobby checking in, but when it's someone else, another name I have programmed in, but not a name I would expect to call late at night, I hit accept and bring it to my ear. "Alex?"

"Hey, Kit. Are you at the club? It's loud as hell there."

"Yeah, but we were just about to leave. What's up?"

"Ah..." Chuckling, it's like I can hear the chief brush a hand over his hair. "So, after all these years, I dreamed of this day. Ever since Jon hit my kid brother over a girl, and then years later, your brother and my sister... No." He blows out a frustrated breath. "I always wanted to put a Kincaid in my cages, ya know? I dreamt of it, wished for it, considered planting pot in your bathroom cabinets when I was over for dinner just so I could arrest one of them. But now I got the head Kincaid. I got Bobby *and* Jon. It's a twofer, Kit, and all my dreams have come true, but... well, it doesn't feel as good as I expected it would."

"Wait." I smack a hand over Tink's yammering mouth. "What did you just say?"

"I have Bobby Kincaid and Jon Hart in my cage, because they were doing some shifty shit in the alley behind the club. I was patrolling, seeing as, loyalties aside, I actually kinda like you gals, so I do a routine lap every night if I'm on shift, but what do I find tonight? But a couple delinquents trying to climb the fire exit and break in."

"You're lying!"

"I'm actually not," he laughs. "At the time, I thought it might be a couple troublemakers or whatever. So I was coming in hot to save the day, but by the time I figured it was Bobby and Jon, they were already tossing insults at me, so I had to bring 'em in."

"Wait. You're telling me you arrested Bobby and Jon? *My* Bobby and Jon?"

Finally, Tink's laughter stops. "What?"

"This way." Cackling, Oz Franks – Benny's step-daddy, and Alex's deputy – shakes his head and stuffs Girl Scout cookies into his mouth as we move along the hall. "Swear to you, ladies. It was like winning the lottery." Cookie crumbs hit his shirt when he snorts. "I wasn't supposed to be on shift tonight, but I threw my name in the hat, since

X was on and I didn't want him to be lonely. So we go out to patrol, think we're riding in on our ponies to save you ladies from criminals, only to find out the criminals are our most wanted. It was so sweet." Winking, he tosses the last of his cookie in and turns as he reaches the front of the very cage I sat in once upon a time. I sat on the silver bench that the guys sit on now, beside a super drunk and super contrite Tink, Izzy, and Tina. The guys stood where we stand now, and they teased mercilessly.

"Bobby?" He doesn't lift his head. It's like I can *feel* his disappointment, but beyond that, I see my handsome husband. "I like your jeans, babe. You look sexy on the wrong side of the law."

Jon sits beside his best friend with a crooked grin and a shake of his head. "Can we go now, deputy?"

"Wait, don't let them out." Tink grabs Oz's hand before he unlocks the cage. Leaning against the iron bars and resting her face close, my girl whispers and taunts. "Jon... My sweet, handsome, and strong Leo. Do we need to talk about your birth control options?"

Chest bouncing, he stands and walks toward the bars. "You think you're so clever, Sunshine?" Pressing a kiss between the bars, he leans back and smiles. "I've done hard time. I've seen bad things. And I was with the Peacock the whole time. I *need* you to soothe the nightmares away."

"Bet you do," she snickers. "You can sleep with me, Leo. You can rest." Stopping, then frowning, she asks, "who's with the boys?"

"Aiden. Sorta. He's sitting on his porch watching his house, our house, and Bobby's, since Smalls is with those kids."

On a curse, Tink slides her arm between the bars and slaps her man on the forehead. "We ask to go out *one* time, and you can't keep your shit under control? What the hell is the matter with you?"

"It was him!" Rubbing his forehead, Jon points back toward a still contrite Bobby. "He made me come out, Sunshine! He said I had to."

"If he told you to jump off a cliff, would you do it?" All five feet of my sassy best friend mercilessly puts her heavyweight fighter husband down. "You are a grown ass man, Jon Hart! It's not third grade anymore. You don't *have* to do what he says just because he double dog dared you!"

"But he made me, Sunshine! I was in my jammies, watching a movie, and chowing on pizza. I didn't wanna come out."

"Yeah, and now you've been arrested, dummy. I should leave you here all night. Let you get a little taste of what happened when I was arrested."

"You wouldn't leave me here, would you? That seat ain't comfortable."

"I should," she grumbles. "I really should teach you a lesson for blindly following that dummy into an alleyway."

"What were you doing trying to break into the club, anyway?" Izzy asks. "Everyone here knows you got your own keys. What's your game?"

"Bobby?" I say his name gently, and still, his shoulders hunch. "Baby, look at me." When he does, the sadness I see there kind of breaks my heart. "What were you doing climbing the side of the club?"

"We wanted to–" When Jon's fiery glare swings around, Bobby blows out an explosive breath. "*I* wanted to know what you were doing. I don't like lies, and you said it was a girls night in." Finally, he stands and walks forward so we mirror Jon and Tink through the bars. "I can take just about anything, but lying guts me, baby. I was worried about you, but I was also jealous."

"You got mad about me lying, so to get answers, you got sneaky?"

"Yes."

"Even though on our wedding anniversary every single year, I re-promise everything I promised the first time, I swear you're my number one, and promise a billion years of never letting go, you still panicked?"

"You make me irrational," he answers quietly. "I can't help myself when it comes to you, Kit. My daddy was younger than I am now when he died, so now it's like we're living on borrowed time. I don't wanna miss a thing, not a single minute with you or the babies, so it makes me crazy to think you're not being completely truthful with me."

"I won't ever do anything to hurt you, you know? Everything I do, well, everything except that *one* time I pushed you off the side of the bed for snoring, I do to make you happy. I do it to make you feel safe, secure in what we have."

"I know."

"Do you?" I reach through the bars and cup the sides of his face. "You're stuck with me, Bobby. For the rest of our long, *long*, much longer than this, lives. So maybe if I'm telling a small fib here and there, it's because I want to surprise you with something kinda special. But you're such a control freak, you make it really hard for me to do that."

"You're organizing something?" My husband's chocolate eyes study mine and help me take just another step into love. It's not that I wasn't this in love with him three seconds ago, but he makes the pool that much deeper every day of his existence. He makes it possible to love *more*, and *more*, and *more*, more, more. "You're organizing something for me, baby?"

"Yes, but you're intent on ruining it, huh? You can't just sit back and relax for a minute? You can't trust me to do it myself?"

"I'm sorry." Pushing against the bars and puckering his lips, he waits for me to oblige. "I just want you to be safe, so when I think you're sneaking out to get away from me, it hurts my soul."

"You can relax, okay?" I kiss him again, then a third time. "Trust me to do this without you spoiling it."

"So what are you organizing?" His chocolate eyes sparkle with fun. "It's still a couple months till my birthday, but it's a big one, huh? A whole new decade will begin."

"You're just intent on spoiling it, huh? You just *have* to know."

"I'm sorry. I won't ask about it again, I promise."

CHAPTER 31

KIT

MONDAY

"Hey, baby?"

Glancing up from my planner at the kitchen table, I lift a brow in response. "Mm?"

"What day is the party?"

"Saturday."

"This Saturday?"

"Yup, now stop asking. It's supposed to be a surprise."

CHAPTER 32

KIT

TUESDAY

"Hey, baby?"

Biting off a curse as I try to count guests, but my needs-to-know-it-all husband screws up my count, I look up from my planner and lift a brow. "Yeah?"

"What should I wear to the party?"

"You're not supposed to know this party exists, Robert."

"Baby," he whines. "I just need to know, am I wearing gym shorts or a suit? Jeans, or a swimsuit? Give me something to work on."

"Suit. It's already in your closet, dry cleaned and ready to go. Don't get it out, because if you ruin it, I'm gonna cancel the whole shindig."

"I won't touch it, promise."

CHAPTER 33

KIT

WEDNESDAY

"Hey, baby?"

I drag a frustrated breath through my nose until I resemble a bull ready to charge. Glancing up from my planner, I find my husband standing at the doorway in the very suit I told him not to touch. "Bobby!"

"I just wanted to try it on to make sure it still fits." He turns and pops his ass. "Looks good, right?"

"Looks great. Put it away!"

CHAPTER 34

KIT

THURSDAY

"Hey, baby? Don't panic, okay? I got juice on the suit, but I ran it to the dry cleaners yesterday, and now it's back." He holds a garment bag up and gives it an enthusiastic shake. "See? Good as new."

"Put. It. Back. In. The. Freaking Closet!"

CHAPTER 35

KIT

FRIDAY

"Hey, baby?"

One day to go. One more freakin' day of being married to an overeager toddler puppy, then I get my regular, sexy, mature, fighting machine husband back. *One day. One day. One day.* "Yes, Bobby?"

"So, I know I've been a pest this week." He walks across our kitchen, around the island counter I sit behind, and drops a gentle kiss on my cheek. "I got a little irrational with excitement, but I see the error of my ways now."

"You do?" Dropping my pen and ignoring my bickering children upstairs, I turn and part my legs so he can stand between. "Have you decided to cool your shit yet? Because apart from wanting to surprise you, this week is a massive reason why I didn't tell you. You're like a child when it comes to parties."

"I know, baby, and I'm sorry. I'm on my best behavior now, okay? Pinky promise." Cupping my face, he leans in and presses a kiss to my lips. Then another, then a third with a little tongue, and drags a giggle from my chest. "I promise. You know I love parties, especially with my family, so I let my imagination run away with me. But I see your planner, and the fact I'm supposed to wear a suit and shit. So that says fancy, formal, and no jumping castles, piñatas, or ice cream." He pauses hopefully. "Right?"

"Right! No jumping castles."

He bites off a *damn* and pulls himself together. "Right. So I'm on your team. What do you need me to do? I mean, I know it's a party in my honor, so I won't spoil too much, but I can help decorate or shuttle the kids or whatever."

"You already spoiled it," I tease. "You weren't even supposed to know there's a party. Now everyone knows, *and* you have a court date that you have to keep next month."

"Do not," he chuckles. "Alex is an asshole, but he didn't even fingerprint us. I'm free for another day on the streets. You know me, baby; thug in the sheets, thug in the streets."

"Stop!" I smack his arm and laugh. "Thug doesn't mean what it used to mean, so stop."

"Are *they* invited?" Bobby's eyes turn wider. "Like, Kane and them? Are they on the list? I'm not judging the guy, because I actually kinda like him, but the dude carries weapons everywhere he goes. Everywhere, baby! He carries a whole arsenal everywhere, so it's kinda weird, ya know? If we need help, he's a great guy to know, but look at his girl for three seconds, and you're dead."

"So don't look at his girl!"

Chuckling, he leans over and tries to catch a glimpse of my notes. "I only have eyes for you, baby, I swear I do. But I still *have* eyes, and when I'm searching for the piñata, I might pass Jess and get myself shot. He's a live wire, and I'm impressed and terrified at the same time."

"They're coming to the party, Bobby." Reaching up, I fix the hair dangling in his eyes and make a note to organize a haircut between now and tomorrow. "Britt's one of us, and Jess is Britt's best friend. If

Jess is coming, that means Kane is coming. That means you don't look at his girl, don't ask to see his weapons, and you should be good."

"Did I tell you today that I love you?" Bobby leans forward and presses a smiling kiss to my lips. "I'm so humbled that you tried to be sneaky to surprise me with this."

"So humbled you almost got yourself arrested?"

He chuckles. "I gotta take care of business, baby. My girl was being weird, so I had to be sure."

"You're such a brat."

"You didn't tell me you love me back."

Smiling, I lean forward and return his kiss. "I love you, Bobby. With my whole heart."

"Can we fuck in the fire closet at the party? Ya know, tradition and all that."

"Yes." Leaning back, I nibble on my bottom lip and study the man I married. So many years together could make a girl complacent. I could stop appreciating what I have and just consider it *expected*, but although I get frustrated with his eagerness, I've never taken it for granted, and I never want it to stop. "I love your overbearing ways, Bobby. I just wanted you to know that."

"You do?"

"Uh-huh. I pretend to get mad about it, but the day you stop wanting to be up my ass is the day you break my heart. Don't stop being you."

"I won't." His tongue slides along my bottom lip. "I couldn't even if I tried. I made promises on our wedding day; something about loving you more than all those other douchebags. I can't keep up my side of the deal if I stopped being who I am. Overbearing and all."

"Exactly. And no, there's nothing you can do to help. I have it under control, so all you have to do it not ruin your suit, then be at venue at six on the dot. Can you do that?"

"Yes."

"Are you sure?" I pull back and stare into his eyes. "It's important you're not late. You can't screw it up."

He smiles and shows off perfect teeth. "Promise. I won't screw it up."

"Great, then I'll take care of everything else."

CHAPTER 36

KIT

SATURDAY

The first time I considered planning this party was during a rare quiet moment in my bedroom. It was a Saturday, and though we were supposed to be at the gym running the kiddie classes, Bobby and I took advantage of the fact everyone else was there doing their job, so we stayed home and revisited Kit and Bobby from back in the days we could sleep in and laze around. My husband romanced me with his words and reminded me of our wedding day when we snuck away and laid in his childhood bed for an hour. It was as hot that day as it is now, but Bobby took care of me. He led me upstairs despite the fact it would be rude to leave your own wedding reception, let me lie down, and brought bottles of water to help me cool down beneath the ton of wedding gown that was smothering me.

I was injured, exhausted, and overwhelmed, but he did what he always does; he took care of me.

I was twenty-five, he was two years older, and now we've added more than a decade to that. A decade of happiness, of memories, of family and love and all the good things couples wish for when they're saying their vows in a church or in someone's backyard.

Months ago, I sat on my bed with no clothes but my husband's oversized tank dwarfing my shoulders, and I watched Bobby move around the room, straightening the pictures on the walls, and picking up discarded clothes, since we were too hungry for each other to be tidy when we tossed our things aside.

He moved around in boxer shorts and nothing else, which gave me the perfect view of the beautiful ink that decorates his body. He was already well covered when we met, but now there's more. More of us; special dates, special names. My husband incorporated our three babies into his art, added two more warrior princesses to his back to symbolize his daughters, and a sword for his son. He took a scared woman and created a fighter. Then together, we created a new generation of Kincaids who would grow up to be fighters, too.

It all started somewhere, it all began when a man met a woman, he declared her his, and when she was too scared to jump in, he pursued with every fiber in his being until she was convinced he was it for her.

All these years later, and she still knows.

Now I sit in that very same spot, staring at the wall of framed photographs, and smile at all of the memories we've made. It's good to be a Kincaid. It's magical, even, but more than that, it's an honor that those men share their name with us.

"Mom?" Glancing to the door when Brooke steps in wearing a gown of dark purple and her hair tied half up, half down, she grins when our eyes meet, then does a slow circle with lifted hands. "Does this look good?"

"Yes, honey." Standing in my own gown, wearing heels on Meg's orders, and tucking my professionally styled hair back, I meet my daughter at the doorway and pull her in for a gentle hug. "You look amazing. Daddy's going to swallow his tongue when he sees you."

"Do you think he'll dance with me? Do we have any daddy-daughter songs on the playlist for tonight?"

Bending lower, I press a kiss to the center of her forehead and smile. "All of the songs can be daddy-daughter, honey. You never have to wait for him. Just step on up, push his bimbo aside, and demand your dance."

Giggling, she steps back on kitten heels and smooths the fabric over her narrow hips. "What if you're the bimbo? Can I shove you aside?"

"I mean, I might fight you for him." Our single dimples pop in unison, and matching blue eyes twinkle with laughter. My daughters look like me. And I look like my dad. "You have my permission to push me aside, baby, because when Grandpa Charlie was alive, I would have knocked any bimbo aside, too. That's *your* right as his baby girl. That's your throne, honey, and the only person you have to share it with is your sister."

"But Daddy's got broad shoulders, right? He could dance with us both."

"Exactly. Come on." Turning her around and snatching up my clutch on the way past my dressing table, I head into the hall and lead Brookey downstairs. I've been with Tink, Iz, and Tina at the venue all morning, setting up the decorations, inspecting every last item on the to-do list, and guarding Bobby's suit, lest he spill more juice on it.

The guys stayed at the gym all day, because to the rest of the world, today's a regular business day, nothing special here, so there were still classes to teach and clients to train. But the women took our leave, and we've been going all day.

Meg was with us the whole time, and like a drill sergeant – that breastfeeds and carries her baby in an Ergo – she snapped orders and had the catering and servers hopping to the same beat as my heart.

For some reason, today is more nerve wracking than our wedding day was, and most of that was done in my planner, too, *without* Meg's help.

Reaching the bottom of the stairs, I smile at my troops and accept Tink's side hug when she steps forward. "You look amazing, Kitkat."

"Thank you." I look her up and down when she steps back and swallow the pang of jealousy that my best friend has always been so effortlessly stunning. She's demure, curvy in exactly the right way, but with boobs that the rest of the world would kill for. She wears a two piece tonight; floor length skirt, bare midriff, and a bejeweled top that lifts those puppies and will kill Jon when he sees. Izzy stands beside her in a slimming gown of dark brown and crystal accents, then Tina beside her, in silver. Because she's always been the classiest of us all. Tina's world, before moving here, was crystal and chandeliers. Money and fame.

Sounds peachy, if you ignore the abusive ex.

But now she's thrust in a world of fighters, pizza, beer, and lazy Sundays. So when we get a chance to dress up, she outshines us all. Every damn time, because you can take the princess out of the castle, but you can't dull her sparkle no matter how many keg stands she does.

"You guys look so amazing. And you two." I stop on the end and cup my oldest nieces' cheeks. Evie Kincaid; curly, blonde, sassy, and beautiful. And Bean, our mahogany haired spitfire fighter. They're their mom's clones in looks, but twins in personality. They're both smartasses, loud, lack filters, and don't know how to walk away from a fight. And tragically, they're getting *way* too old, *way* too fast. "You girls look so beautiful. Are you trying to show us up or something?"

Snickering, Bean picks at her dress and pulls the black fabric away from her chest. "I don't know how I feel about this, Aunt Kit. Something keeps poking me. It's annoying as hell."

"It's the cost of looking amazing," I laugh. Turning to Evie, I look her up and down from her silver heeled feet, over the fire engine red gown made for royalty, up to wild, curly hair and sigh. "You look stunning, Smalls. You don't think those heels might break your ankles?"

Lifting her foot, Smalls inspects her grown ass heels and shrugs. "I got it under control. I didn't fall yet."

"All this fighting has got you nimble and shit," Bean smarts. She's too young to cuss, but that never stopped her before. "If you start to fall, just brace and roll and pretend you meant it. You got this."

"Alright." I push them away when they bump fists like tucking and rolling is a solid plan. "We have to move if we're going to pick Grandma up on the way."

"Can I drive?" Evie jumps forward to grab the keys before I do. Nimble as hell and not a single wobble on her heels. "Please, Aunt Kit?" She turns to her mom. "Please? I got my permit, and Uncle Jack has been taking me out to drive. He says I'm an old pro already."

"Honey." I stop at the door and hold it open. "I taught your Uncle Jack how to drive, and he sucked real bad at it." Waving my group through, I don't snatch my keys back, despite the fact I really should. She's fifteen and *super* fresh with that learner's permit, but cussing aside, she's responsible, and *super* smart. "You really shouldn't accept driving praise from him, hon, because he's lame at best, and straight up incompetent at worst."

"He is not," she laughs. "He's really good at it. He teaches me how to drive stick, because he said everyone should know how. He also said if I ever meet a man who can't drive stick, I should dump his stupid ass and push him off a cliff, because only P-U-S-S-I-E-S drive auto."

Frowning, Tina stops on the front porch with her purse in her hands while she digs her own keys out. "Baby, did Uncle Jack spell that word out, or did he say it?"

"He said it," Bean and Evie say as one. "Uncle Jack swears a lot," Evie continues. "Then he says not to snitch."

Tina lifts a scarred brow and looks at me like its my fault. "What?" I throw my hands up. "I got him when he was fifteen! The formative years had already passed. He was who he was going to be by that point. I just kept him outta prison." I close the door when Brooke steps out. "I did the best I could, alright? Stop bitching."

It's only five in the afternoon, the sun is still high, and it'll stay that way for hours yet, but in our heavy gowns and melting makeup, we make our way to the cars and load up. I don't force my niece out of the front. Evie has driven me to the store a few times, and the van is an auto anyway, so as long as she steers right and doesn't mix up the gas and brakes, I trust her to get us where we have to go.

"I'll take the littles," Tina says. "Brooke, Em, boys." She herds the twin boys, my girls, and her own smaller girls toward her car, while I end up with Tink, Bean, Iz, and Evie in ours.

"Let's head over to Grandma's," I instruct and pull my seatbelt on. "You wanna take your heels off first, Smalls?"

"Nah, I got it." Reaching up, she fixes the rearview mirror and flashes a grin at Bean – her cousin, but in reality, they're best friends, and more like sisters – in the back. "Let's rock and roll."

CHAPTER 37

BOBBY

My watch says six fifteen, but apart from Tina and the littles, we're missing way too many important guests.

"Where the fuck is my wife?" I turn with anger slicing through my gut as the band sit on their stage, while Luc taps the drumkit like it doesn't bother him my wife said this shindig starts at six sharp, but here we are, fifteen minutes late, and my bride, two of my sisters, and two nieces are nowhere to be found.

"Cool it, B." Aiden steps forward and pushes my hand down to shield me from my ticking watch. "You know what chicks are like. They're dressing up formal, which means they're gonna be late."

"That's your wife, but not mine." I walk across the semi-packed room and ignore the people we know from the gym, the people we know from around town. "Your wife might need time to dress up, but you know Kit. You know that ten minutes early is already too late." I storm across the hotel function room, which is the same room my prom was hosted in, and head toward the double front doors. "Something's wrong."

"Bobby!" Meg jumps in front of me with her clipboard and eyes filled with anger. "Get back in place, Kincaid. We've busted our asses to make tonight happen exactly how it's supposed to happen, but if you ruin my shit, I'll kneecap you."

"Where is my wife, Megan?" I step around her and slip past Benny, who thinks it's his business to follow me around. "I need to see my wife."

"She's on the way. Damn!" Skidding along the floor when she grabs my arm and I pull her along, I stop again and feel no remorse when the petite party planner crashes against my side. "Kit's on the way. But you gotta get back in place."

"Why are we here, Megan?" I fix my suit jacket and re-tuck the hanky that she messed up. "Why is my wife late? Why couldn't we just do a barbecue for my birthday?" I thrust an arm toward the chandelier. "Why crystal, when I just need a beer and a steak?" I point toward the stage. "Why a whole fucking band, when all we need is an iPod? Why the pretense?"

"Because this is the party she wanted! Why are you questioning it? What's your problem?" Standing behind me, she pushes with both hands and maneuvers me back to my place at the bottom of the staircase. "It's the wedding reception she deserved, so just roll with it, dammit!"

Wedding reception... "Huh?"

CHAPTER 38

NELLY

When you're my age and you've lived the life I have, if the women you consider your daughters – even though you only had sons – turn up at your door with a gown that fits exactly right, and shoes that make me three inches taller, if they lay out a plan to pretty you up and fluff your hair while your granddaughters bustle around the room amid squealy giggles and silly laughs, you just roll with it.

Whatever they're doing, for whatever reason, you roll with it.

Because when you lose the love of your life at such a young age, you realize nothing in this world matters more than family.

Money, houses, cars... gowns and makeup... it's all empty nothingness, unless it's your family forcing you into that dress.

Now I stand at the top of an ornate staircase in a fancy hotel ballroom, wearing a princess gown and so much mascara, I'm not sure my eyes will be able to stand up under the weight. But I stand surrounded by the beautiful women in my life, I feel my heart race in my chest, and I cast a glance over the ballroom filled with familiar faces.

Tables and tables are filled with framed photographs. Some were stolen from my home, some from each of my sons. Some from the little house Bry bought for us so many years ago.

My boys stand at the bottom of the staircase, but none of them see me up here. They bicker between themselves, while my oldest demands to see his wife and looks awfully handsome in his suit.

"Are you ready, Nelly?" Kit stands to my right and clutches to my shaking hand. "You ready for your grand entrance? As soon as you say so, we signal the band, and it all begins."

"Why are you doing this?" Emotion fills my eyes, but it's a happy emotion. A warmth that spreads in my belly and makes me so truly fortunate to be surrounded by love. "What is this party for?"

"For you, of course." Without waiting for my okay, Kit does something that alerts the band, because then the guitars begin. The sweet sound of a well-played piano slides through the large room, and finally, the crowd downstairs silence, they focus, and as one, they cast a glance to the top of the stairs and stop on us.

The young man I know as Sam Turner sings a slower version of Bryan Adams' *Heaven* with such reverence, I feel it in my heart. I understand what this is, I finally understand the gowns, the tears, and the significance of today. Making my way downstairs with Kit's hand in my right, and Izzy's in my left, we time our steps to the beautiful beat of the music and head for the handsome men at the bottom.

I know the girls forced my boys into today with blindfolds on, but the very second my sparkling heel touches the floor, my firstborn son steps forward and pulls me close until we're slow dancing.

"This party was never about me," Bobby chuckles as my other children step back. They line the dance floor, they wait their turn, and nervously fix their ties.

This boy, this man, was once a tiny baby in my arms, a terror toddler, and a sweet kindergartener that looked up to me to fix his hurts and stroke his hair at night. But now he's bigger than me, stronger, possibly even wiser. "My wife is a sneak," he continues.

"Because she never actually said this party was for me. She let me assume."

"Because she knew you'd run with it."

Chuckling, he pulls me close enough that my cheek rests on his chest. "Happy wedding anniversary, Momma. I wish Daddy was here to dance with you."

"I think that's where you come in," I whisper and clutch his strong hand in mine. "You look just like him. You sound like him." A hot tear slides through my lashes and over my cheek. "You're just like him, baby. Big, strong, handsome, and so certain about who your soulmate is. If I just close my eyes, I could pretend I'm dancing with Bry."

"So close your eyes," he whispers. Burying his nose in my hair and leading me in a slow sway, my son allows me a moment to pretend, to go back in time and be with my soulmate again. "I'll keep mine open, I'll keep you safe, and you can dance with Daddy again for a minute."

ACKNOWLEDGMENTS

Sometimes, those who love us the most have to lie to us, if only to protect us. It's not malice. It's not deceitful in the true sense of the word.

It's protection, because that's the promise they made long ago at Piper's Lane amid dirt flurries and crazy teens looking for a little fun.

Bry wasn't looking for fun. He was there for *her*, and he refused to walk away until he'd secured her heart and made her believe he'd protect her for life.

But the thing is, he secured her heart and forgot to give it back. He took her with him, but in exchange left her with two new Harts. Two deserving, loving, but immeasurably hurt children that *needed* Nelly to be their mother.

There *must* have been a grander plan. A mission to make them safe.

Bry said it long go; there are only so many angels roaming this earth at one time. For him to make Jon and Iz safe, he had to barter his own life.

He had to go home again.

He didn't know that's what he was doing that day he drove out, but it's what happened anyway. And if forced to replay that day and choose left rather than right, he'd still leave Nelly with those baby Harts.

He was their angel, and the plan was so much more than him and Nelly.

Though of course, that doesn't ease the way our hearts hurt right now.

Rest In Peace, Bry. You can rest now, because she's back in your arms.

ALSO BY EMILIA FINN

(in reading order)

The Rollin On Series

Finding Home

Finding Victory

Finding Forever

Finding Peace

Finding Redemption

Finding Hope

The Survivor Series

Because of You

Surviving You

Without You

Rewriting You

Always You

Take A Chance On Me

The Checkmate Series

Pawns In The Bishop's Game

Till The Sun Dies

Castling The Rook

Playing For Keeps

Rise Of The King

Sacrifice The Knight

Winner Takes All

Checkmate

<u>Stacked Deck - Rollin On Next Gen</u>

Wildcard

Reshuffle

Game of Hearts

Full House

No Limits

Bluff

Seven Card Stud

Crazy Eights

Eleusis

Dynamite

Busted

<u>Gilded Knights (Rosa Brothers)</u>

Redeeming The Rose

Chasing Fire

Animal Instincts

<u>Inamorata</u>

The Fiera Princess

The Fiera Ruins

The Fiera Reign

<u>Rollin On Novellas</u>

(Do not read before finishing the Rollin On Series)

Begin Again – A Short Story

Written in the Stars – A Short Story

Full Circle – A Short Story

Worth Fighting For – A Bobby & Kit Novella

LOOKING TO CONNECT?

Website
Facebook
Newsletter
Email
The Crew